AUNT BESSIE TRIES

AN ISLE OF MAN COZY MYSTERY

DIANA XARISSA

❀ Created with Vellum

For Bessie's biggest fans. I truly appreciate your continued support.

AUTHOR'S NOTE

I can't believe this is book twenty in the series. I'm still enjoying writing about Bessie and her friends, but I'm starting to think about taking things in a different direction once I finally get to Z. I can't imagine not writing about Bessie, so I'm going to find a way to change things up but keep Bessie front and center. I always recommend that you read the books from the beginning in order (alphabetically by the last word in the title), but each story should be enjoyable on its own if you'd prefer not to do so.

Aunt Bessie made her first appearance in my romance novel *Island Inheritance*. As she'd just passed away when that novel began, this series started about fifteen years before the romance.

This is a work of fiction. All characters are creations from the author's imagination. Any resemblance they may bear to real people, either living or dead, is entirely coincidental. The mysteries are set on the Isle of Man, which is an amazing country in the Irish Sea. The historical sites mentioned in the story are all real, but the events that take place at those sites within the story are fictional. All of the businesses mentioned in the book are also fictional creations that have been located where convenient for the story, rather than where any real businesses exist on the island. Any resemblance these businesses may bear to any real businesses, on the island or elsewhere, is coincidental.

Because of the setting, I primarily use British English (with a bit of Manx here and there). There is a short glossary of terms at the back of the book for readers outside of the UK. I've also included a few other notes that might help readers with some things that might be unfamiliar. The longer I live in the US, the more likely it is that Americanisms and other errors will creep into my books. I try to correct these when they are pointed out to me.

I'd love to hear from you. All of my contact details are available in the back of the book. Please take a minute to say hello.

CHAPTER 1

"Where do you want this?" Carol Jenkins asked.

Elizabeth Cubbon, known as Bessie to just about everyone, looked over at Carol and laughed. "This" was a huge cake, and Bessie could only just see the top of Carol's head over it. "I thought it was meant to go on that little table in the corner," Bessie replied. "Isn't that what Elizabeth said?"

Carol shrugged. "Dan has been dealing with Elizabeth. I just came in to help today. I'm sure he has notes on where everything is meant to go, but I didn't want to ask him. He's in the middle of a dozen different things and he's, well, grumpy."

"Dan is grumpy?" Bessie repeated. "I've never seen him grumpy."

Carol set the cake down on the nearest table and then shrugged. "We're having problems," she said in a low voice. "Not us, as a couple, but with the baby. My doctor thought that I needed to relax more, so I quit working and did nothing for months, but I still haven't fallen pregnant. We're both going for a bunch of tests in the new year, but for now we're both, well, I'm not sure what we are, but catering a baby shower isn't helping."

Bessie pulled the other woman into a hug. "I'm sorry," she said. "If I'd known, we could have held this somewhere else."

"No, no, we're happy to have the business. We're actively looking for a larger building, hopefully in a better location, where we'll be able to do events like this without having to shut the restaurant while we're doing them."

"I hope you find something soon, but I'll be sorry to see you move further from Laxey. I'll happily visit often, wherever you go on the island, though. Dan is a genius in the kitchen."

"As soon as we know anything, we'll be telling everyone," Carol replied. "We've already found someone who wants to take over this place, anyway."

"Really? That's good news."

"You may know the woman, actually. Her name is Jasmina. She's currently running a café out of a tiny shed of a building near the Laxey Wheel."

Bessie nodded. "She does wonderful food and she definitely needs a larger place. I hope it all works out for all of you."

"Me, too," Carol said. She picked up the cake and carried it to the table in the back of the room. "I think that's everything," she told Bessie as she walked back towards the kitchen. "Unless I've missed something, we're just waiting for the guests now."

Bessie turned slowly in place, studying the small café. "It looks perfect," she told Carol. "The first guests should be here in twenty minutes or so. Grace should arrive in forty minutes if everything goes to plan."

Carol nodded. "I may slip out before she arrives," she said softly. "I'm not sure that I can, that is, I'm sure Dan can handle things without me."

Bessie wanted to hug the woman again, but Carol quickly rushed back into the kitchen, one hand swiping at her eyes as she went. Sighing, Bessie walked slowly around the room, checking and rechecking every detail.

The small café in Lonan didn't usually do special events, but as they grew their business they were starting to try new things. Baby showers were an American tradition, one that Bessie had been happy to import on this occasion. Hugh and Grace Watterson were expecting their first child, and Bessie was determined to celebrate the happy event. Hugh was a police constable and Grace was a primary schoolteacher. They'd only been married for a short while when she'd fallen pregnant, and Bessie knew that money was tight for the happy couple. This shower would allow Grace's friends and family to "shower" the pair with gifts for the new baby.

The party had been planned by Elizabeth Quayle, who was currently the island's only party and special event planner. After dropping out of numerous universities and failing to find a job she liked, Elizabeth had decided that party planning was the perfect career for her. While there had been a few missteps along the way, as far as Bessie could tell, the girl's business was already becoming a success. It probably helped that Elizabeth's parents, George and Mary, were wealthy and well connected on the island. In any case, Bessie was pleased to see that the girl was willing to work hard and that she seemed to have a real talent for what she was doing.

It was Elizabeth who was meant to be at the café now, fussing over the final details, but a last-minute change of plans had resulted in Bessie rushing over to take her place. Elizabeth would be arriving with Mary, and they were going to bring Grace with them. Grace's mother, who was originally going to be bringing Grace, was going to be late, if she was going to be able to be there at all. Grace's younger sister, Prudence, had managed to fall down a flight of stairs and was currently sitting at Noble's Hospital waiting for X-rays on her ankle.

Bessie paced back and forth, wishing she had been more involved in the planning for the day. While the shower had been her idea, she'd been more than happy to let Elizabeth and Mary handle all of the details. She and Mary were meant to be splitting the cost of the day equally, but Bessie was certain, as she looked at the elaborate cake and the sophisticated decorations, that Mary was paying for more than her share. That was something to discuss with the woman when the event itself was over, though. For now, Bessie just had to act as temporary hostess as the guests arrived.

Fifteen minutes later, she was already starting to feel overwhelmed. A huge group of Grace's friends had all arrived together and they were chatting loudly in one corner. Several of Grace's family members had trickled in, and Bessie found herself struggling to remember everyone's names as another small group of women came through the door.

Bessie had lived in Laxey from the age of eighteen. Now somewhere between sixty and a hundred, she felt as if she knew just about everyone who lived in her small village. Grace, on the other hand, had grown up in Douglas. Although still a small town, Douglas was much larger than Laxey. While Bessie knew many people who lived there, the majority of the shower guests were strangers to her. She was just trying to remember who the pretty blonde who'd arrived first was when her mobile phone rang.

"Yes?" she said, trying to find a quiet corner so that she could hear the caller.

"It's Elizabeth. We're on our way. We should be there in five minutes," came the reply.

"Can't Grace hear you?" Bessie asked.

Elizabeth laughed. "She and Mum are in another car. Mum thought it would be nice for Grace to arrive in a limousine, so I'm driving myself in my car. I'm right in front of them."

"We'll see you in five minutes, then," Bessie said, feeling butterflies in her stomach.

"Probably only four now," Elizabeth replied before the call ended.

"Grace is about four minutes away," Bessie announced.

A shriek of excitement went up from one corner, and then everyone laughed.

"Should we hide?" someone asked.

"Maybe we could turn off the lights," Bessie suggested. "I'm not sure how we could hide, really."

"I can pull the blinds," Dan suggested from the kitchen doorway.

The front of the café had several huge windows. It only took Dan a few seconds to shut the blinds on them, though, leaving the room considerably darker.

"The light switch is right behind you," Dan told an elderly woman who Bessie remembered was one of Grace's aunts. The woman

4

flipped the switch and a few people gasped. It took a moment for Bessie's eyes to adjust to the sudden darkness. She moved closer to the door, trying to stay out of the line of sight through it. From there, she could see the car park across the road. It was empty, as the party guests had all been asked to park on the street behind the café. No one wanted Grace to suspect anything before she arrived at the party.

"They're here," Bessie said as Elizabeth's sports car turned into the car park. Mary's limousine was right behind it. Bessie watched as Mary and Elizabeth quickly climbed out of their cars. It took Grace a little bit longer to struggle her way out of the back of Mary's car. She looked tired and a bit miserable as she joined the other two women walking towards the café. Her blonde hair was pulled into a simple ponytail and she was wearing a pretty maternity dress with flat shoes that almost looked like slippers.

"It doesn't look open." Grace's voice carried into the café.

"I'm sure it is," Mary said firmly. As she and George were investors in the business, she should know, Bessie thought, struggling to resist the urge to giggle from nerves.

They reached the door and Mary pulled it open. The trio stepped inside as Grace's aunt switched the lights back on.

"Surprise!" everyone shouted.

Grace looked around, her gaze moving from person to person. When she saw the large sign that read "Welcome, Baby Watterson," she burst into tears.

Mary was quick to pull Grace into a hug. "Your mother will be so sorry she missed this," she told the girl.

"Leave it to my sister to break her ankle today," Grace sniffed.

Bessie handed her a tissue and then found herself being hugged tightly. "You were behind this, weren't you?" Grace demanded.

"The whole thing was Bessie's idea," Elizabeth said loudly. "When she mentioned it to me and Mum, well, we couldn't help but want to get involved."

Grace wiped her eyes again and then shook her head. "I can't believe you're having a party for the baby," she said.

"It's a traditional American baby shower," Elizabeth told her. "I've spent ages researching how they're meant to work. We're going to have games and prizes and lovely food, and, of course there are lots of gifts for the baby."

"Gifts? You shouldn't have brought gifts," Grace protested.

"Of course we should," Mary told her. "We all wanted to do something special for the baby because we're all incredibly pleased for you and Hugh."

Grace smiled and wiped her eyes again. "I'd argue more, but I'm not sure I can say no to presents for the baby."

"Of course you can't," Mary agreed.

"Let's let the woman sit down," one of Grace's friends called out. "I've been eight months pregnant. She needs a chair."

After much laughter, Grace was led to a large table along the back wall. "You must sit at the head of the table," Elizabeth told her.

Grace flushed and then dropped heavily into the chair. She rubbed her tummy. "They're having a party for you," she told her bump. "So many people already love you and you aren't even here yet."

Someone cheered and then everyone began to clap. Grace laughed. "That's woken the baby," she said. "He or she is having a good kick now." She sat back and took a few deep breaths.

"Let's have a party game," Elizabeth suggested loudly. The guests all found seats around the various tables. Bessie found herself sitting between Mary and one of Grace's cousins. When everyone was seated, Elizabeth passed around folded sheets of paper and pens to everyone. "When I say 'go,' you may open your paper and begin. Each scrambled word has something to do with babies. And go."

Bessie unfolded her sheet and worked her way down the list. Word games were one of her hobbies, so it didn't take her long to unscramble all of the words. When she was done, she looked around. Everyone else was still hard at work.

"When you're finished, raise your hand," Elizabeth said.

After a moment's thought, Bessie decided not to comply. No doubt the first to finish would win a prize and Bessie wanted the other guests to win, not herself. She watched Grace, who was working on the word list, too.

There had been a time when Bessie had assumed that one day she would marry and have children, but that had been so long ago that Bessie could barely remember it. When she'd been eighteen, she'd lost the only man that she'd seriously considered marrying. Her life had turned out very differently from what she'd expected when she'd been a child, but she had no regrets over any of the choices that she'd made over the years.

"I'm done," a woman shouted, raising her hand. Elizabeth took her sheet and glanced at it. "Number three isn't right," she told her, handing it back. "Keep working, everyone, you can still win."

A second later, three hands shot up. Elizabeth checked them all and then declared them joint winners. They all received small wrapped parcels from a large box that had been tucked into a corner.

While the women were opening their prizes and exclaiming over the expensive candles inside, Elizabeth disappeared into the kitchen.

"We have time for one more game before lunch," she announced when she reappeared.

Bessie read through the list of children's songs and rhymes and found herself unable to fill in the blanks with the lyrics for most of them. While she'd been happy to act as an honourary aunt to many of Laxey's children over the years, most of the visitors to her cottage had been unhappy teenagers. At her age, she was unable to remember any of the nursery rhymes from her own childhood, which may well have been different anyway. She'd been born on the island, but she and her family had moved to the US when she had been only two. If she'd sung children's songs, no doubt she'd sung American ones, rather than the traditional British ones she was now being asked to recall.

While everyone was hard at work, the café door swung open and Grace's mother rushed inside. "I'm sorry I'm late," she said loudly.

"Pru isn't coming?" Grace asked.

Grace's mother rolled her eyes. "Prudence has a broken ankle. Your father is staying with her while they put the cast on it. If we're still here when they're done at Noble's, your father may bring her here, otherwise she'll have to miss the fun."

"She'd probably be bored, anyway," one of Grace's friends

suggested. "Although I'm sure she'd do better than I am on these stupid songs."

That seemed to remind everyone about the game. People got back to work. "I have it," a woman shouted a short while later. Elizabeth checked her answers and then gave her a prize.

"Keep going," she told everyone. "The person who comes second gets a prize, too."

Once that had been awarded, Elizabeth turned to Grace. "I asked Dan to make us a meal that celebrates babies," she told her. "I think he did an amazing job."

Dan laughed from where he was standing in the kitchen doorway. "You all know that the café here is known for its sample plates. Today we've done a four-course meal instead. Your starter is a salad made from baby lettuce leaves. That will be followed by a selection of roasted baby vegetables. The main course is alphabet pasta with baby meatballs. Of course, for pudding, we have the cake." He gestured towards the back of the room, earning a few "oohs" from the guests.

Grace sighed. "It all sounds wonderful," she said.

Dan nodded and then turned and shouted something into the kitchen. A moment later a handful of servers appeared with plates full of salad. Dan moved between the tables, refilling drinks and chatting with the guests.

"Everything is wonderful," Bessie told him as he walked past her.

"Thank you," he replied with a smile.

The smile didn't quite reach the man's eyes. Bessie reached over and squeezed his hand. "I hope everything is okay," she told him quietly.

"It's fine, really, we're just struggling to adjust our expectations to our reality," he sighed. "Business is good, anyway."

"That's good news."

The man nodded and then walked away, leaving Bessie feeling sad for a moment. She liked Carol and Dan and she thought they'd be excellent parents. Across the room, Grace was laughing, and Bessie forced herself to focus on Grace and her happiness. She could worry about Dan and Carol another time. Today was for Grace and Baby Watterson.

An hour later, Bessie was stuffed. "Delicious," she said to Mary. "I wish I could afford to hire Dan to cook for me every day."

"He's not interested in being a private chef," Mary sighed. "If he were, I'd have already hired him for Thie yn Traie."

Bessie knew that Mary was having trouble keeping staff at the mansion home she and George owned on the cliff above Laxey Beach. While some people simply didn't want to live and work in Laxey, seeing the village as too small to offer much excitement, Bessie knew that others were starting to believe that Thie yn Traie was cursed. A number of tragedies had occurred at the mansion in the past eighteen months or so, but Bessie also knew that Mary loved the house in spite of everything.

"I keep hoping we might persuade Andy to work for us when he finishes culinary school, but that might be awkward in many ways," Mary continued.

Andy Caine was a brilliant young chef who was currently finishing his last few months of study at culinary school in the UK. As far as Bessie knew, he was still planning to open his own restaurant when he returned to the island. That had been a lifelong dream of his, one that had seemed impossible when he was younger. An unexpected but very welcome inheritance had made culinary school a reality and meant that he didn't really need to work at all. In spite of his money, the last time Bessie had spoken to him Andy had been adamant that he wasn't simply going to sit around and fritter away his new wealth.

In recent months, Andy had been spending quite a bit of time with Elizabeth Quayle, and Bessie often wondered if the girl's recent enthusiasm for hard work and her determination to begin supporting herself weren't down to Andy's influence. While Bessie would have been happy to see Andy working at Thie yn Traie, not least because she was often a guest there, she could see a number of potential pitfalls in the arrangement.

"I think he'd rather have his own restaurant," she told Mary.

"Maybe we'll fire our current chef and just eat at Andy's restaurant every day, then," Mary sighed.

"Maybe being poor has its advantages," Bessie said with a laugh.

Mary shrugged. "I'd be quite happy to get rid of the chef, actually. I can cook. I did when George and I were first married and he never complained. He loves having staff, though, and I think he believes that he would have failed me in some way if I had to start doing the cooking again."

"Have you talked about this with George?"

"Endlessly," Mary smiled. "He simply doesn't truly believe me when I say I'd be happy to cook again. He's right that I used to complain about doing the cooking years ago. What he doesn't seem to understand is that in those days I also had three small children to look after. Now I feel as if my days are long and empty. Cooking meals for George and Elizabeth wouldn't be much work, and it would give me something to do with my time, as well."

Bessie nodded. She knew that Mary was painfully shy, in contrast to her salesman husband, who was gregarious and loud. Her shyness made it difficult for Mary to do much volunteer work around the island, although she did as much as she could force herself to do. "Perhaps the next time your chef quits, you could simply not get around to replacing him or her for a while," Bessie suggested. "If you find once you've tried it that you really don't like doing the cooking, you can start hunting for a replacement, but if you do enjoy it, you can just keep telling George for months on end that you haven't found anyone yet."

Mary laughed. "He might not ever notice," she said. "He's often so distracted by work that he fails to notice anything at all."

Once again Bessie wondered how the pair had made their marriage work for so many years. It was difficult for her to imagine, as she'd never been married herself. Maybe if Matthew had survived the Atlantic crossing and they had married, she would understand the dynamics of marriage a bit better.

"Cake," Elizabeth said as the waiters cleared away plates. "As it's an American baby shower, I went with American-style flavours for the cake. Half is what they call devil's food, a sort of extra-rich chocolate, with chocolate buttercream filling, and the other half is a vanilla cake with custard in the centre. It's all iced in buttercream icing."

"I want to try both flavours," someone shouted.

"Me, too," came another voice.

"We can do that," Dan laughed. "Give us a minute to slice it."

"It's gorgeous," Grace said. "It seems a shame to cut into it."

"Stay out of the man's way," one of Grace's friends shouted. "Don't get between me and that cake."

As everyone laughed again, Dan and his staff cut into the cake. Within minutes, everyone was given a plate with slices of both types of cake on it. Bessie took a small bite of each and sighed.

"I was hoping I might not like them both," she told Mary.

"They're both wonderful," Mary agreed. "I think I like the chocolate better, but only just."

"I prefer the vanilla, but again, only just," Bessie replied.

After the cake plates were cleared, it was time for a few more games. Bessie and Mary sat and sipped coffee and chatted while the others battled to win prizes. After a few minutes, Grace's mother joined them.

"Thank you for doing this for Grace," she said.

"We did it for the baby," Bessie told her. "We're all incredibly excited about the baby."

"We are as well," Grace's mum replied.

After the games, it was time for Grace to open her presents. Mary and Elizabeth had taken her to a few shops about a month earlier, to get an idea of what she and Hugh wanted for the baby. The pair had just bought their first house together, and money was tight. Grace had made a short and very modest list of things she thought they needed before the baby arrived. After that, Mary had taken her back through the shop, urging her to imagine what she would buy if money were no object. It was items from that second list that Mary and Bessie had focussed on purchasing.

Grace was in floods of tears as she unwrapped the beautiful but expensive cot that Mary had purchased. "It's the one I really wanted, the gorgeous expensive one," she gasped as she looked at the box. "You shouldn't have."

Mary shrugged. "It wasn't much more than the least expensive one in the shop, and I think the quality is much better. You and Hugh might decide to have more children. If you do, this cot should last you through half a dozen."

Grace's eyes went wide and then she shook her head. "We won't be having half a dozen, anyway. I would like more than one, though, even if my sister is a pain."

"Hey, I didn't mean to fall down the stairs," a young girl said loudly from the doorway.

Grace laughed and then struggled to her feet. "Pru, come and give me a hug," she said.

The girl slowly made her way across the room on crutches. The sisters hugged and then Grace laughed again.

"I think you might be slower than me now," she said.

Pru rolled her eyes. "I'll be off the crutches in a fortnight. You still have six weeks to go."

Grace sighed and sat back down. "Every day I wake up and think that I can't possibly get any bigger, and every night I feel at least ten pounds heavier."

"Babies gain a lot of weight in the last few weeks," Mary told her. "It isn't quite ten pounds a day, but I remember feeling the same way with all three of mine. The last month is the hardest."

"And I'm not even there yet," Grace sighed.

Bessie had bought the couple the fancy pushchair that Grace had coveted during her shopping trip. Grace was in tears again when she unwrapped it.

"Baby Watterson is going to travel in style," she said through her tears.

As the pair didn't know if they were having a boy or a girl, Grace was given lots of gender-neutral clothing. She also received dozens of packages of nappies, baby wipes, and other practical items that she and Hugh were going to need.

When all of the gifts were opened, the party began to break up.

Everyone who hadn't won a prize in any of the games was given a wrapped parcel on the way out. Mary insisted on sending Pru home in her car, making the teenager blush as the chauffeur escorted her out of the café. Hugh arrived as the guests were saying their goodbyes.

"What are you doing here?" Grace asked the man as he walked into the café.

Hugh flushed and chuckled. "It's nice to see you, too," he replied.

Bessie grinned. Hugh still looked not much more than fifteen to her, with his brown hair that always seemed to need a cut and just the faintest hint of a moustache on his upper lip. He was over six feet tall, which meant he towered over Bessie as he gave her a hug. Hugh had had a difficult childhood and had spent a lot of time at Bessie's during his teen years. His parents hadn't been happy with his decision to join the police, but they'd come to accept it. Now they never complained about Hugh's choices, because they loved Grace and were delighted about the baby.

"In answer to your question, I was told that I needed to come and collect all of the presents, as there were going to be tons of them," Hugh told Grace.

"There are, too," Grace replied, waving a hand at the stack of gifts in the corner.

"There's some cake left, too," Dan said. "I'll box that up for you while you load up the gifts."

Hugh's eyes lit up at the idea of cake. A few of Grace's friends who hadn't left yet began to help him fill his car while Dan carried away the remains of the cake.

"I hope you enjoyed your shower," Bessie said to Grace, smiling to herself as the girl's eyes filled with tears again.

"It was wonderful," she replied. "I never imagined anything like this. I can't believe how much we have for the baby now. Hugh and I won't have to buy anything, really, which is a huge help as we've been buying things for the house rather more than we should have."

Bessie watched happily as Grace and Hugh left together. Grace was still excitedly telling Hugh about everything that had happened at the shower as they went. Bessie looked at Elizabeth and Mary and smiled.

"I think that went well," she said.

"It was splendid," Mary replied. "I'm so glad that we did this."

"What could we have done better?" Dan asked.

Bessie laughed. "Nothing at all. The food was amazing, the decorations were fabulous, everything was perfect."

"I can't take credit for the decorations. That was all Elizabeth," he protested. "I'm glad you enjoyed the food, anyway."

"I've a number of meetings coming up with other people who are planning events," Elizabeth told him. "I'll be ringing you to check dates and see if you can do a few of them."

"Great. Maybe not another baby shower, though," Dan replied.

Elizabeth looked confused and opened her mouth, but Bessie patted her arm. When Elizabeth looked at her, she shook her head. Dan was busy clearing tables and didn't notice the exchange.

"We'd better get out of your way, then," Mary said. "Thank you so much for everything." She handed Dan an envelope. "That should cover the costs," she told him.

He tucked the envelope into his pocket without opening it. Bessie was sure that Mary would have included generous tips for all of the hard-working staff who had been helping that day.

"How much do I owe you?" Bessie asked Mary as they walked out of the café together.

"We'll work it out one day," Mary replied with a wave of her hand. "Elizabeth still has to add up the cost of the decorations and then work out which can be reused. You shouldn't have to pay for decorations that she'll be using in her business in the future, after all."

Bessie was going to argue, but she was interrupted.

"I'm sorry, but Miss Cubbon? Could I have a word, please?" a woman said. Bessie recognised her from the shower. She'd sat with some of Grace's more distant relations.

"Of course," Bessie replied.

"I have my car here. Maybe we could take a short drive along the coast together," the other woman suggested.

Bessie hadn't been looking forward to squeezing herself into the tiny backseat of Elizabeth's sports car for the ride home, which was probably why she agreed so easily with the stranger's plan. After giving both Mary and Elizabeth hugs, she followed the woman to an older car that had a few rust patches here and there.

"I've had this car for twenty-three years," she said as she opened Bessie's door for her. "I don't expect I'll get another one now before I go."

Bessie fastened her seatbelt and waited while the other woman climbed into the driver's seat. She glanced at Bessie and shrugged. "I definitely won't if someone has their way, anyway."

"What do you mean?" Bessie asked.

"Someone is trying to kill me," she replied as she turned the key in the ignition.

CHAPTER 2

"*A*re you certain of that?" Bessie asked.

The woman shrugged. "As certain as I can be. Odd things have been happening, you see. I tried to ignore the first few, but as they kept happening I started to worry. When I saw you at the party today, I knew I needed to talk to you."

"You should talk to the police."

"I can't do that."

Bessie waited for her to add to the statement, but she was silent as she maneuvered the car through Lonan and onto the coast road towards Ramsey.

"Why not?" Bessie finally asked.

"That would be like accusing my family or friends of attempted murder."

"But someone is trying to kill you."

"Maybe I'm just imagining it all. That's why I wanted to talk to you. You know all about murder. I keep reading in the local paper about how you help Inspector John Rockwell solve murders all the time. I saw you when I first arrived at the shower and I thought, that's who I need, Aunt Bessie."

"I'm happy to hear your story," Bessie said, trying not to sound as eager as she actually was, "but once we've spoken, if I believe someone truly is trying to kill you, I'm going to insist that you go to the police."

"As I said, I may be imagining everything. I don't always sleep well and I often have quite vivid dreams. Maybe everything that's happened has only happened in my dreams."

"Do you think that's the case?"

"No, not really," the woman admitted. "I'm sorry. I'm probably not making much sense. I can't really talk and drive at the same time, for a start. Maybe we could get tea somewhere in Ramsey."

"We could."

"You'll have to tell me where to go, though. I don't get to Ramsey very often, really."

Bessie gave her directions to a quiet café outside the town centre. It was far enough away from the high street to discourage foot traffic, but they had wonderful cakes and biscuits.

"Right across the road from the police station?" the driver asked as she pulled into the car park. "Are you planning on dragging me over there as soon as we've finished our tea?"

"Not at all," Bessie assured her. "I just know they do the best cakes and biscuits in Ramsey."

"After all that cake we had at the party, I shouldn't want cake, but now that you've mentioned it, I might be able to manage a slice. I'll have it in place of my dinner, I think."

They made their way into the café and found a table in the back. About half the tables were full, and a waitress Bessie didn't recognise was rushing around taking orders and delivering everything.

"I'll be over as soon as I can," she called to Bessie on her way past with a full tray.

"Take your time," Bessie told her. She took a seat across from the other woman and gave her an encouraging smile. "I'm afraid I don't even know your name," she said apologetically.

The woman nodded. "I came in a bit late to the party, after everyone had been chatting for a while, and I suppose I missed the introductions. I'm Lora White."

"It's nice to meet you. Are you one of Grace's relations?"

17

"No, no, I'm just a neighbour. Young Grace's family lives in the house across the road from mine. Grace's mother was kind enough to include me today because I've known them all for such a long time."

"What can I get you?" the waitress asked.

"Tea for two, and I'll have the Victoria sponge," Bessie told her.

"Oh, that does sound good. Victoria sponge for me as well, please," Lora added.

"I'll be as quick as I can, but we're rather busy and short-handed today," the girl replied before she dashed away.

"I'll take you home when we're done here," Lora said. "I hope you aren't in any hurry to get there."

"Not at all," Bessie assured her. Bessie had never learned to drive, so she often found herself relying on the kindness of her friends to get her to and from her home on Laxey Beach. If needed, she could always ring the car service that she'd been using for more years than she wanted to remember. They were always reliable and they gave Bessie a generous discount to thank her for her years of patronage.

"I'm not sure where to begin," Lora sighed. "What would you like to hear about first? Me? My life? My family? The happenings that have me worried? What?"

Bessie frowned and tried to think. What would John Rockwell do, she wondered. He was a police inspector with the Criminal Investigation Division of the island's police force. Currently in charge of the police station in Laxey, he'd been the lead investigator into many of the murders in which Bessie had found herself involved over the past two years.

"Why not tell me all about you first," she said eventually. "The more I know about you, the better my chances of working out what's happening." She silently added 'I hope' to her words and then sat back to listen.

"As I said, I'm Lora White. My maiden name was Meadows, but I got married at nineteen and I'm seventy-three now, so I barely remember using it," she laughed. "My husband, Cecil, passed away, oh, twenty or so years ago. The first year on my own was difficult, but over time I've almost forgotten what being married was like, too. I suppose the brain just adjusts to its new reality after a while, but now that I've been on my own for twenty years, I can't imagine living with someone else again."

"You said you live across the road from Grace's family. Was that your home when you were married, too?"

"Oh, aye. Cecil and I bought the house when I was expecting our first child, over fifty years ago. It's a tiny little bungalow, really, but it was bigger than the cottage I grew up in, anyway. We had four bedrooms, which felt like a lot when it was just Cecil and me. Again, the brain adjusts, doesn't it? Now that I'm alone in the house, it doesn't feel that big to me at all. I use one bedroom as an office, not that I need one, really, but Cecil made it an office after the children left home. Another bedroom is my sewing room. I've always loved to sew, although now I mostly sit in there and think about sewing rather than actually doing anything. That leaves one bedroom for the grand-children when they stay over for a night or two, besides my room. It isn't much room at all, really."

"It sounds just about right."

"Yes, that's what it is, just right," Lora agreed.

"Tea for two," the waitress said. "The cake will be out shortly," she added after she'd given them both their tea.

Bessie took a sip and then smiled at Lora. "If you have grandchil-dren, then you and Cecil must have had children?" She made the statement a question.

Lora nodded. "I don't often talk about myself, I suppose. Other-wise, I'd be better at it, really. I'm just wandering all over the place, where I should be giving you facts and dates and whatnot."

"If you talk to the police, you can worry about facts and dates. I'm happy to just chat."

"I knew talking to you would help. I feel better already," Lora replied. She sat back and took a sip of tea. "And yes, we had children. Women did in those days. There weren't many ways to prevent it."

Bessie nodded. "My sister had ten children."

Lora gasped. "After my third, I made Cecil sleep in one of the other bedrooms," she told Bessie. "That took care of that problem. Oh, he complained, but he got over it. My oldest girl wasn't happy, either, because it meant she had to share a room with her sister, but I always told them that they'd have to share with more than just one sister if I'd kept having babies."

"Things have improved for women today," Bessie suggested.

"Oh, yes, things are much better, really, in that area, anyway. Let me tell you about my children, then, as they might be relevant. I have three, which I already said, didn't I? Charles is the oldest. He's going to be fifty soon. Then comes Doreen, she's forty-seven, and then Baby Martha, who is forty-one."

"There's quite a large gap between the girls, then," Bessie said.

Lora laughed again. "I made Cecil sleep in the spare room for several years after I had Doreen. She was hard work, that one. She didn't sleep through the night until she was nearly six. Once she was finally sleeping, I made the mistake of letting Cecil back into our bedroom. Nine months later Baby Martha arrived."

"And you still refer to her as Baby Martha."

"Not to her face, at least not often. Actually, that child was a huge blessing. She slept well, ate whatever she was given, and went along wherever she was dragged from the day she was born. I never heard a single complaint out of her, either. Her brother and sister used to treat her like their own personal servant, too, and she never complained about that, either."

"My goodness, the poor girl."

"When I look back now, I probably should have given her more of my time and attention, but I didn't realise it then." Lora sighed. "If she's the one trying to kill me, I suppose I wouldn't blame her."

"Do you not get along well with Martha, then?"

"Oh, we're very close, actually. I don't truly think she's the one who's trying to kill me. I can't imagine that any of my children are behind what's been happening, but I'm less certain about my grand-children." Lora frowned, and Bessie could see a shadow of sadness pass over her.

"Before you tell me about the grandchildren, maybe you should tell me about your children's spouses," Bessie suggested.

"Oh, yes, of course." Lora sighed. "It's a very good thing I haven't gone to the police. They'd probably lock me up for wasting their time. I can't seem to work out what I'm meant to tell you or in what order I should be telling it. I'm sure on telly the police inspectors only ask witnesses two or three questions each before solving the crime in a sudden flash of brilliance."

"I'm afraid I'm not prone to sudden flashes of brilliance," Bessie told her. "Any help I'm able to give the police is mostly down to my knowing the people of Laxey so very well. I don't have that advantage with you, as you live in Douglas and I don't know your family at all."

"Which is why I should be telling you all about them in a clear and logical fashion," Lora said smartly. "Here we go. Charles is married to Ann. She's a few years younger than he is, but not a significant amount, at least in my opinion. They never had any children and they've never expressed any regrets about that to me. What Ann used to tell her own mother, I don't know."

"You aren't close to Ann?"

"She's a bit, well, distant," Lora said. "She's very nice, really, but she's a very private person. When she and Charles first married, I used to try to get her to meet me for lunch now and again or to go out for a day of shopping with me. She nearly always made excuses not to join me for things. Once in a while, if one of my daughters was coming along as well, she might join us, but she never seemed truly comfortable with us."

"Cake," the waitress interrupted. "Sorry it took so long. The café has become busier lately for some reason and we don't always have enough staff scheduled on any given day."

"The last time I was here, Tammy was the only one working," Bessie told her.

The girl grinned. "The regulars love her, but she's something of an acquired taste for those who don't know her. She's only working three days a week now, and only during the very quietest times. She's not as young as she used to be."

"None of us are," Bessie replied.

"That's very true," the girl laughed. As she walked away, Lora sighed.

"I'm probably giving you the wrong impression of Ann," she said as she picked up her fork. "She's lovely, and she and Charles seem very happy together. I suspect she's quite shy. She was an only child, too, so suddenly having two sisters-in-law probably came as something of a shock to her. I may have tried too hard to befriend her in the first years of their marriage, and I suspect I haven't tried hard enough in the years since." She stopped and took a bite.

"You don't think that Ann dislikes you?" Bessie asked between bites.

"I certainly hope not. I can't see her being behind the murder attempts, anyway. It simply isn't in her nature."

"You'd be surprised," Bessie murmured.

"I know, I know. You've been involved in a lot of murders and probably very few of them were committed by the most likely suspect."

"I'm not sure that any of them were," Bessie told her.

"What else can I tell you about Charles and Ann?"

"What do they each do for a living?" Bessie asked, not because she thought it was relevant so much as because she wanted to seem to be asking questions.

"Charles works for one of the high street banks. He has done for pretty much his whole career. That's where he met Ann, actually. She worked in customer service when they first met, but she quit when they got married. After a few years, she went back to work for an insurance company. She's been there ever since."

"They have enough money coming in to meet their needs?"

Lora nodded. "And then some. They live very well in a large flat in Ramsey. They both have fairly new cars and they seem to trade them in for even newer ones on a regular basis. Last year they went to Hawaii for a fortnight in the spring and then spent another fortnight in Iceland later in the year. Money doesn't seem to be a problem for them at all."

Bessie wondered if she ought to be taking notes. She was learning a lot about Lora's family and there was a chance she was going to want to share everything she was hearing with John Rockwell. Taking notes over tea and cake seemed rude, though.

"Tell me about Doreen and her family, then," she suggested after she'd washed down the last of her cake with a sip of tea.

"Doreen is married to Carl Sanders. He's the same age as Doreen. In fact, their birthdays are only three days apart. They met in primary school and have known one another for almost their entire lives."

"Were they childhood sweethearts, then?"

"Not at all. They weren't even really friends until they were doing their A levels. At that point, Carl became involved with Doreen's closest friend, but that didn't last long. He dumped the friend for Doreen and they've been together ever since."

"How angry was the friend?" Bessie wondered.

"She hasn't spoken to Doreen since," Lora sighed. "It's quite sad, really, as they'd been friends forever up to that point. She and Carl weren't even serious. They'd only been out together a few times before he decided he preferred Doreen and ended things with Susan. That hasn't stopped Susan from blaming Doreen for the whole thing, either. She still talks to Carl. They work together actually, but she completely and pointedly ignores Doreen whenever she sees her."

"How unfortunate."

"Doreen blames herself, too, which is sad. I keep telling her to ring Susan and try to resolve things, but she still feels guilty about taking Carl away from Susan."

"This all happened a long time ago, right?"

"About thirty years ago," Lora told her.

Bessie shook her head. "It's high time Susan forgave Doreen for what happened."

"It's further complicated by the fact that Susan has never found anyone else. She's still single, and quite bitter about it, really. I think it would be better for all of them if Carl found another job so that he wouldn't have to see Susan anymore, but he loves what he does and he doesn't see the problem."

"What does he do?"

"He's the manager of the ShopFast in Port Erin. Susan manages the frozen food department at the same location."

"I'm surprised Doreen isn't jealous, really."

Lora shrugged. "I'm sure she trusts Carl. Whether that trust is misplaced or not, I can't say for certain."

"What does Doreen do?"

"She used to work for ShopFast, too, but she quit when she fell pregnant. She's never gone back to work, even though their only child is twenty-two now."

"Tell me about their child, then."

Another cloud seemed to cast a shadow over Lora's face. "Linda is, well, I'm not even sure how to describe her. She quit school at sixteen to work for ShopFast. I believe she thought that her father could help her move up into management fairly quickly, but the company insists on its managers having some qualifications. Linda didn't agree."

"More tea?" the waitress asked. Both women nodded.

"So Linda quit school without any qualifications?" Bessie asked, after Lora remained quiet once the waitress had left.

"Yes, sorry, I don't like talking about Linda. She was a difficult baby and an almost impossible teenager, and she isn't any better as an adult. I love her dearly, but I don't much like her."

"And you think she's behind whatever has happened to you lately."

Lora flushed. "I never said that."

"But you do, don't you?"

"As much as I hate to admit it, the more I think about it, the more I wonder. I can't honestly imagine anyone wanting to kill me, but I do believe someone has been trying. Linda seems to have more of a motive than anyone else, I suppose."

"What motive?"

"Money, of course. Charles and Ann don't need money, and I believe Carl and Doreen are doing okay. They don't live quite as luxuriously as Charles and Ann, but they have a comfortable home and Carl has a company car. They take a holiday every year, usually spending a fortnight in Spain, and I've never heard of them complain about being short of funds."

"But Linda needs money?"

"Linda always needs money. Once she realised that she wasn't going to be made manager of a ShopFast within a few weeks of starting behind the tills, she quit that job and decided to become a hairdresser. That meant going back to school, which wasn't inexpensive, but Carl and Doreen agreed to pay for her training. She lasted less than six months before she decided it was too difficult."

"Oh, dear."

"Yes, indeed. Of course, Carl and Doreen couldn't get their money back, but Linda didn't care. She went across after that. Doreen was always sending money over to her and paying off her credit card bills since Linda didn't have any income. She finally came back to the island after a year or so. As I understand it, she's been working odd jobs and talking about going back to school ever since. She brought a boyfriend back from Liverpool with her and the pair live with Doreen and Carl, which is difficult. Zack is anti-establishment, anti-work, anti-government, and anti just about everything else. He's more than happy to live off of the hard work that Carl and Doreen do, of course. He simply isn't willing to find a job and do any work himself."

"He sounds charming," Bessie said dryly.

Lora laughed. "Actually, he is charming, in a way. He can be sweet when he wants something, and he's absolutely gorgeous, as well. He's just incredibly lazy and more than happy to take advantage of Linda and her parents."

"Do you think he might be behind the murder attempts?"

"I'm not sure he's smart enough to manage them. He's handsome but dumb, although I suppose that could be an act. I don't really know him well. Linda rarely comes to family events these days and when she and Zack do attend, they never stay long."

"Why don't Doreen and Carl tell them to get jobs and their own place?" Bessie asked.

"That's a question I ask Doreen every time I talk to her. It's complicated, of course. She loves her daughter and doesn't want to see her living in a tiny flat somewhere with barely any money coming in, but I can't see Linda ever being motivated to do anything with her life without a big push from Carl and Doreen." Lora sighed. "Let's move on. We can talk more about Linda later, if we need to, but talking about her is giving me a headache."

"Is Martha married?"

"Yes, she's married to Tony Page. Technically it's Anthony, but everyone calls him Tony. They've been married for nearly twenty years. They met in a pub, actually, which isn't meant to be a good idea, but it's worked for them. Tony actually runs a pub now, although that wasn't what he was doing when he and Martha met. He was working for one of the hotels in those days, if it matters."

"And does Martha work?"

"She does a few hours at the pub now and then, but mostly she looks after their children. They have two, Christy, who is sixteen and Daniel, who is fourteen. Martha spends most days running one or the other of them to things all over the island, although Christy is learning to drive now, heaven help us all."

Bessie laughed. "You don't think she'll be a good driver?"

"The girl gets lost in her own house. I can't imagine what she'll do when she's driving on her own around the island. I told Martha to expect to get lots of phone calls that start 'Mum, I'm lost,' once Christy has her license."

"You sound very fond of Christy."

Lora chuckled. "I'm very fond of her, actually. Martha had some serious complications when she had Christy and I ended up taking care of the baby for several months while Martha recovered. She had similar problems with Daniel, actually. That time she kept the baby at home, but I kept Christy at my house for over a month. Christy was two and we had a wonderful time together. I found that I enjoyed my grandchildren in a way that I couldn't enjoy my children."

"I've heard that from many people."

"You never had children, did you?"

"I never married," Bessie told her.

"I'd say you missed out, but at the moment I'm not sure having a family was such a good idea."

"You know you love them all dearly."

"I do, really, which is why it's so upsetting to think that someone might be trying to kill me."

"Let's finish discussing Martha and Tony," Bessie suggested. "They don't need money?"

"Not really. Tony gets paid well at the pub and Martha works enough to give herself some spending money. Their cars are older, but they don't seem to mind. Their focus is on their children. They want them both to go to university across, and both children are plenty smart enough to do that, though I say so as their proud grandmother."

"So you have three children, each with a spouse, and you have three grandchildren. You suspect one of them of trying to kill you?"

"There are others who could be suspects," Lora said, seemingly reluctantly. "As I said, I can't really imagine that anyone wants to kill me, not really, but I can't ignore what's been happening, either."

"Tell me about the others, then."

"I have a sister. Ethel is seventy-one. She's been a widow for the last ten years. Her husband, Henry Hayes, died of a massive heart attack."

"How sad."

"Ethel didn't seem all that bothered," Lora said wryly. "I don't think they were unhappy together, but I don't think it was all champagne and roses, either. Not that any marriage is, but Cecil and I were fairly happy, and I don't believe that Ethel and Henry were."

"Did they have children?"

"Yes, two. That was one of the sources of their troubles, of course. Their son, Milton, he's in his mid-forties now. He's only ever been interested in other men. Henry wanted to disown him when he found out, but Ethel refused. There were a lot of tense family parties until Henry died, especially when Milton began seeing Bob. They've been together for fifteen years now and they seem happier than most married couples I know, but Henry didn't approve and always refused to acknowledge Bob."

"What a shame."

"They also have a daughter, Marie. She's Marie Becker now. Her husband, Nathan, isn't my favourite person, but he's easy enough to avoid. He rarely comes to family parties and when he does come, he always brings work or a book to read so that he can sit in a corner and ignore everyone."

Bessie swallowed a dozen questions about Nathan. "Do Marie and Nathan have children?" she asked instead.

"They have a daughter called April, who's eighteen. She's a lot like her father in that social situations make her uncomfortable. She's back and forth to university across. I'm not sure if she's here or there at the moment, actually, but I can't see her being behind what's been happening regardless."

"Do you think that Ethel or either of her children might be behind everything?"

"Do you have siblings?"

"I had a sister, although I never saw her again after my parents and I moved back to the island from the US."

"If you had a sister, you'll know that sisters fight. Ethel and I fought a lot when we were children. We were less than two years apart and there was a lot of sibling rivalry. She always insisted that I was our mother's favourite, and I always felt as if our father preferred her." Lora shook her head. "We're in our seventies now. I think she might have cheerfully killed me when I was ten and accidentally spilled water on the picture she'd spent a whole day drawing for our father, but now? After all these years? I just can't see why she'd bother."

"What about Milton and Bob?"

"For what possible reason? They won't inherit anything from me and I believe they're both fond of me, as well."

"And Marie and Nathan?"

"Again, I can't imagine a motive. They aren't in line to inherit anything from me and they know that. Milton and Marie will both get plenty from Ethel, anyway. Henry left her very comfortable."

"What did he do?"

"He was an advocate. Nathan is too. He was an associate in Henry's office. That's where he and Marie met."

"It seems to me that you suspect Linda is the one behind the things that have been happening," Bessie suggested.

"I'll bet you thought I forgot all about you," the waitress said as she dropped off more tea for them both. "Again, I'm sorry about the wait. Mary in the kitchen told me to bring you a plate of shortbread as an apology." She set the plate in the centre of the table. It was all Bessie could do to not snatch up a piece immediately. While Bessie was well known for making wonderful shortbread, the café's was better, something that annoyed Bessie even as she reached for a slice.

"I suppose Linda would top my list," Lora admitted as the waitress walked away. "The others are all still on the list, though, and I'd probably include a few other people as well."

"What other people?"

"Maybe a few of my neighbours," Lora sighed. "I've known the couple on one side of me for forty-odd years. We've never liked one another, though. A young couple just bought the house on the other side. We've already had a bit of an argument about where they leave their cars, and I know they're going to be trying to get planning permission to add a large addition to their home. I'm sure they're worried that I might object, and I probably will if the addition is anything like what I think they're planning."

"Names?" Bessie asked.

"Percy and Elaine Quinn are the older couple, and Brian and Jill Cobb are the younger pair."

Bessie nodded, adding them to her mental list of suspects. "Right, I think it's high time you told me what's been happening, then," she told Lora.

Lora sighed. "I've been dreading this."

CHAPTER 3

"Why?" Bessie asked.

"I'm almost certain that you're going to think I'm imagining things," Lora told her. "I've nearly convinced myself that I'm imagining things. Each incident, taken on its own, doesn't seem like anything, really, but things keep happening and it's starting to scare me."

"Tell me what happened first," Bessie suggested.

"First, I slipped in the bath."

"Getting in?"

"Yes. I take a bath every night. I have done since I was a child, really. Showers just make me feel chilled. Recently, I was climbing into my bath and my foot slipped. I nearly fell head first into the water."

"You managed to catch yourself?"

"Only just, but yes, I grabbed the edge of the tub and then held on tight while I climbed in."

"And what makes you think that was a murder attempt?" Bessie tried to keep her voice as neutral as possible, but she could hear the skepticism in it as she spoke.

"At the time, I didn't think anything of it, really, not until I climbed back out of the tub. I don't have many indulgences, but I do use a rather expensive oil every night when I get out of the bath to moisturise my skin. Cecil bought me the first bottle of it when I was pregnant with Charles, back when we really couldn't afford such luxuries. Still, it kept me from getting stretch marks, not just with Charles, but with any of my children. I've used it ever since."

Bessie understood the sentimentality. She used the same rose-scented dusting powder every single morning, as it reminded her of Matthew Saunders, the man she had loved and lost. When they'd first met, he'd given her roses, and the smell brought back a flood of memories every day.

"Anyway, after my bath that night, I picked up my bottle of oil and it was half empty. It was a fairly new bottle, one that I'd only used two or three times previously. When I'd drained the tub, I could feel oil on the bottom of it, as well."

"Who could have spilled oil in your tub that day?"

"Anyone and everyone," Lora sighed. "We have monthly family gatherings at my house and we'd had one that day. All the children come with their children and they even sometimes bring friends. My sister is always there with her children and their families. I always invite the neighbours on either side of us, too, since my guests will be parking in front of their houses. It stops some complaints, anyway. My house only has one loo, so anyone who needed to use the loo had access to the bathtub. The bottle of oil was on the shelf above the tub."

"There wasn't any way it could have simply leaked into the tub?"

"It wasn't leaking when I picked it up that night, but I suppose anything might have happened during the party. At the time, I assumed that someone had picked it up to try it out and accidentally spilled it in the tub. They may have even tried to wash it down the drain but failed. At the time, I didn't really give the matter that much thought, if I'm honest."

"And that was when?"

"About a month ago. I cleaned up the tub as best I could and made sure to be extra careful for a few days, but I really didn't give it much more thought than that. A few days later, though, something else happened."

"What happened?" Bessie asked, starting to wish that the woman would hurry up and tell her everything. It was getting late and she needed to have dinner, although the shortbread was taking the edge off her hunger.

"I needed to get something out of the top cupboard in my kitchen. I don't keep much in there, but Ethel wanted to borrow a casserole dish and the one she needed was in that cupboard. When I opened the cupboard, a knife fell out and nearly landed on my head."

"My goodness," Bessie exclaimed. "You could have been badly hurt."

"Yes, but probably not killed. If it was a murder attempt, it was a pretty clumsy one."

"I suppose so, but it still must have been scary. How could it have happened? Was it one of your knives?"

"It was, from a set that was kept in that cupboard with the casserole and a handful of spare tea towels and not much else. They're very fancy knives, ones that Cecil bought for me when he was travelling for work a long time ago now. They're meant to be extra sharp and able to slice through anything." She shook her head. "I've forgotten the details now, but the man who sold them to Cecil had a very impressive sales pitch. The actual knives, though, were less impressive."

"That's often the case."

"Yes, exactly. I used them for a few weeks and then tucked them into that cupboard and more or less forgot all about them."

"Where is the cupboard?"

"It's a small one that we had added over our tall refrigerator. It's awkward for me to reach. Cecil didn't have a problem, but I have to stand on my tiptoes to reach the handle and then struggle to get things out."

"Any idea how the knife managed to fall out?"

"The knife block had somehow tipped over, and as far as I could work out, it was leaning against the cupboard door. When I pulled open the cupboard, the heaviest of the knives fell out of the block. I suppose I was lucky that they didn't all come crashing down on me."

"I assume that had never happened before?"

"No, never, although I have had tea towels fall out of that cupboard when I've opened it on other occasions."

"Really?"

Lora shrugged. "It's always been just after I've had guests. The children know that I keep spare tea towels in that cupboard and we nearly always seem to need one or two when the whole family comes around. If you reach into the cupboard and pull out one towel, it's easy enough to drag another part of the way out, too. Then the next person who opens the cupboard often gets a tea towel on his or her head."

"Which is a good deal less dangerous than a knife."

"Yes. I've now relocated the knives to a different cupboard."

"Sensible. It seems odd that knives suddenly became a danger after all these years, though."

"It is odd, although when I got out my step and looked into the cupboard, one of the towels had somehow become caught around the handle for the sharpening steel. If someone pulled on that towel, he or she may have accidentally pulled the knives to the front of the cupboard."

Bessie nodded. "Was that everything?"

"Unfortunately, no," Lorna sighed. "Again, at the time, I didn't worry too much about anything. I just assumed it was an accident. A few nights later, I was woken up by my carbon monoxide alarm."

"You have a carbon monoxide alarm?"

"Martha saw something on the telly about the dangers of carbon monoxide. She's become a little obsessed with the idea that we're all going to end up poisoned by a faulty gas boiler or something. I didn't pay much attention when she was lecturing me about it all, but I did put batteries in the detector that she got for me."

"It sounds as if you were lucky you did."

"Yes, indeed. She's ever so pleased with herself now," Lora chuckled. "It was one of those days that wasn't truly cold but where there was a chill in the air. I put the gas fire in my lounge on while I was watching telly. I drifted off, which I'm inclined to do these days, and only woke up when something started beeping constantly."

"The alarm?"

"Exactly. It's very annoying, but I shouldn't say that because it saved my life. I'm not sure where Martha found it. She may even have had it shipped over from America. I understand they're more common over there. Whatever, she put one in her house and got one for me, too, and according to the man who came out to investigate, it saved my life."

"What did he find?"

"My gas fire wasn't properly ventilated. The vent on the side of my house was full of bits of grass and leaves and all sorts of things. The man suggested that a bird might have been trying to build a nest in the vent. He said it happens more than you'd think."

"So again it might not have been anything serious."

"Exactly. The more I talk, the less I believe myself."

Bessie shook her head. "You mustn't feel that way. As you said earlier, one or two incidents can be written off as accidents, but as things continue to happen, it begins to seem suspicious. Was that the first time you'd had the fire on since the last family gathering at your house?"

"It was. And before you ask, anyone and everyone could have walked around the house and tampered with the vent. People were constantly going in and out, and several people spent time sitting outside in the back garden, as the day was fairly mild for October."

"What happened next?"

"There are five steps from my front door to the ground. About a week ago, the railing on those steps snapped in two."

"That doesn't sound as if it were an accident."

"It was a wooden railing and it was original to the house. When Charles looked at it, he said it was a miracle it hadn't broken years ago. He said it was weak in several places and I was just lucky that it had broken when I was climbing up the stairs and not down them."

"And you didn't get hurt?"

"Not at all, aside from a bit of shock, really. I'd been relying on that railing to get me up and down those stairs for fifty-one years. I suppose I should have realised it was getting older. I'm certainly well aware that I am."

"But you think someone may have tampered with the railing?"

"I simply don't know. It's just odd, that's all. Again, on its own, it seems insignificant, but taken all together, well, I'm worried."

"Has anything else happened?" Bessie was almost afraid to ask.

"Just one other thing. My car got a hole in its petrol tank."

"That sounds more dangerous."

"The garage said that it could have caused a fire if I hadn't noticed it before I drove the car. Luckily, I spotted the puddle under the car and called the garage rather than trying to drive the car to them."

"Is it a common problem with cars?" Bessie asked, feeling a bit foolish. Since she didn't drive, she had no idea if petrol tanks often sprang leaks or if it could only be caused by deliberate damage.

"Not at all, although it is an older car and the garage felt that the puncture was consistent with me hitting a large rock or a pothole, both of which I may well have done," Lora sighed. "I'm wasting your time, aren't I?"

"I don't know," Bessie said thoughtfully. "While everything you've told me could be explained away, I find it difficult to believe that you've suddenly begun having so much bad luck. I really think I need to talk to John Rockwell."

"Oh, goodness, don't do that," Lora exclaimed.

"He's the expert," Bessie argued. "I'd really like to get his opinion on everything that's happened to you."

"I'm not ready to involve the police, not yet. Not when all of the most likely suspects are family members."

"Or neighbours. You didn't sound as if you suspected them, though."

"I don't know. I'm sure Brian and Jill would be delighted if I'd move away. I suspect they'd buy my little bungalow and tear it down to make room for a massive extension on their property."

"That would be expensive, though."

"They can afford it. They could have bought a much larger house, but they really wanted to be on my street. Jill grew up nearby and she'd always wanted to live there for some reason. As I said, they're already planning an addition onto the house they've purchased."

"So they'd be happy if something happened to you."

"I'm sure they wouldn't be sad, but that's still a long way from murdering me just to get a bigger house."

"Maybe they aren't trying to kill you. Maybe they're just trying to make your life miserable so you go away."

Lora looked thoughtful for a moment. "That's an idea, and one that I quite like, actually. The problem is, I'm not even sure that they came into the house during that last gathering. They may have stayed outside. Regardless, if either of them needed the loo, they probably would have simply gone back to their own home rather than use mine. They had theirs redone recently. It's very nice."

"What about Percy and Elaine Quinn?"

"I can't imagine why they'd decide to kill me after all these years. We aren't friends, but we pretend to be friendly whenever we see one another. They always come to my gatherings and sit together in a corner making rude comments about my children and grandchildren under their breaths."

"My goodness."

"I do the same when they have parties," Lora told her. "Although their parties have always been infrequent, and I don't believe they've had one in the last few years."

"I'm not sure what I can do, if you won't let me talk to John," Bessie said. She caught the waitress's eye and gestured for the bill.

"I was hoping you'd be able to convince me that I'm imagining things."

"It's entirely possible that you genuinely have just had a run of bad luck," Bessie replied. "If any or all of the things you've told me about truly were murder attempts, they were half-hearted ones at best, really. Blocking up the gas fire vent was probably the most likely to actually harm you. Do you use it often?"

"I wouldn't say often, but I do use it when the weather is chilly but before I'm ready to turn on the central heating. I suppose the vent could have been blocked since last spring, which was probably when I used it last before the night of the alarm."

"So maybe someone has been trying to kill you for many months," Bessie said.

"Pardon?" the waitress gasped. She had Bessie's bill in her hand, but her eyes were wide and she looked shocked.

"Nothing," Lora said. "Bessie was just talking about the plot from a movie we both saw."

"Really? Which movie?" the girl asked.

Bessie glanced at Lora and shrugged. It had been years since she'd been to a movie theatre.

"Something from the fifties that we both enjoyed," Lora said, naming an old film that Bessie only dimly remembered. "It's all about this woman who keeps trying to kill her boyfriend, but he keeps escaping."

"Sounds interesting. Maybe I'll have to try to rent that one day," the waitress said. She handed Bessie the bill and then walked away, shaking her head.

"I should get that," Lora said. "I've taken up your entire afternoon for nothing."

"I don't think it was for nothing," Bessie replied. "We can split the bill in half. That seems fair."

Bessie left a generous tip for the overworked waitress and then followed Lora out of the building.

"You're going to have to give me directions to your house," she told Bessie as she started the car.

"Just take the coast road back to Laxey. Once you're in the village, I can give you directions from there."

The drive didn't take long. As Lora drove down the steep road to Laxey Beach, she glanced at Bessie. "I thought you might laugh at me."

"Even if I thought you were imagining things, I wouldn't have laughed. As it is, I'm worried about you."

"I'm sure I'll be fine," Lora said. She opened her mouth to add something and then gasped. "What an amazing view," she said as they turned the corner and Laxey Beach appeared in front of the car.

"This is my cottage," Bessie told her, waving towards the small cottage at the bottom of the road.

"It's adorable," Lora told her. "I can't believe that I've never been to Laxey Beach before today. I think we're spoiled, really, with so many miles of coastline. There are beaches everywhere, so we don't appreciate them."

She parked the car in the small parking area next to Bessie's cottage. "Do you mind if I get out and walk on the beach for bit?" she asked.

"It's a public beach. You can do whatever you'd like."

They climbed out of the car and Lora followed Bessie to her cottage door.

"What's the cottage called?"

"Treoghe Bwaane," Bessie told her. "It's Manx for widow's cottage."

"Even though you never married?"

"The cottage had its name before I bought it. I must admit that I felt it was an appropriate name when I did purchase the cottage. The man I'd loved and left behind in the US attempted to follow me here. He didn't survive the ocean journey. Before he'd left home, he'd made a will, leaving me everything he owned. It wasn't much, but it was enough to allow me to buy Treoghe Bwaane, anyway."

"Would it be too nosy if I asked to peek inside?"

Bessie couldn't object. She was fascinated by other people's homes too. She'd been considering asking if she could visit Lora's to look at the gas fire and the kitchen cupboard herself.

"Come in," she said now. "It's tiny, but it's home."

She unlocked the door that opened right into the small kitchen. Lora glanced around and then sighed. "It's perfect just for the views."

Bessie glanced out the window and nodded. She never grew tired of looking out at the beach and the sea.

Lora peeked into the sitting room and dining room before rejoining Bessie in the kitchen. "Cecil and I bought our house together. It was exactly what we needed at the time, but I often wonder what I might have chosen if the decision had been mine alone to make. Of course, if I didn't have Cecil, I wouldn't have had the children, either, which means I could have lived in a much smaller home."

"I never expected to be in this cottage for this long," Bessie confided. "I was only eighteen when Matthew died. I assumed that one day I would fall in love again, but I'm not sorry now that that never happened."

"I met Cecil when I was still in school. He was the only man I've ever kissed. Sometimes I wonder if I missed out on things, but it's a bit too late now to worry about it, really."

"Ready for a walk on the beach?" Bessie asked.

Lora nodded. "I think that's just what I need."

Bessie pulled on a heavier jacket for the November weather and then she and Lora began a slow stroll towards the water. Before they reached the wet sand, they turned to walk parallel with the sea.

"These are all holiday cottages, aren't they?" Lora asked after a short while.

"Yes, Thomas and Maggie Shimmin own them."

"I know Maggie," Lora said. "I think everyone in the island knows Maggie, though. She's very, um, social."

Bessie laughed. "That's one way of putting it." A very diplomatic way, she added to herself. Maggie was nosy and she loved nothing more than gossip, although Bessie knew that the woman was also kind and a very hard worker, even if she did complain constantly about nearly everything.

"Do you think I'm crazy?" Lora asked after several minutes.

"Crazy?" Bessie echoed.

"My mother suffered from dementia as she got older. I worry all the time that I'm going to have the same issues. Maybe all of the things that have been happening to me aren't really things. Maybe I'm just slowly losing my mind."

"You've definitely had a run of bad luck lately," Bessie replied, choosing her words carefully. "Whether the various incidents add up to something more serious or not is really a question for the police, not me."

"They'll laugh at me."

"They won't laugh at me. John Rockwell won't laugh at you, either. He's a professional and he's very good at his job. He'll listen and take careful notes and then, at the very least, he'll offer you some advice. If he thinks there might actually be someone trying to harm you, he'll investigate as well."

"I can't imagine having the police question my family and friends."

"He may not have to do any questioning, at least not at this stage. He would probably start by talking to the garage that repaired your car and to the man who came out to look at your gas fire."

"I suppose it wouldn't hurt to have him talk to those people, as long as my family didn't know he was doing so."

"It probably won't be John doing it, actually. He works out of the Laxey station. One of the inspectors from Douglas would probably be put in charge of any investigating that needed doing."

"Do you know any inspectors in Douglas?"

"I know Pete Corkill. He's very good and very nice, although he can seem a bit grumpy when you first meet him."

"I don't want to talk to the police," Lora sighed. "I can't quite get my head around any of this. No one has any reason for wanting to kill me, none at all."

"Except your granddaughter, for your money," Bessie said softly.

"She isn't getting much in my will. Most of the money is going to my children, with smaller amounts for the grandchildren. I assume they'll inherit from their own parents eventually, but I didn't want to leave them out entirely."

"Does she know that?"

"I've never discussed my will with anyone aside from my advocate. I've half a mind to tell everyone that I'm leaving every penny to charity, though. That might stop things, mightn't it?"

"If someone truly is after your money, it might. If you do tell people that you're leaving everything to charity and the incidents stop happening, at least you'll know what was behind them."

"But I still won't know who was behind them. I know Linda always needs money, but maybe someone else is looking for a windfall."

"If you truly don't want to go to the police, let me talk to John Rockwell," Bessie said.

"That must be Thie yn Traie," Lora changed the subject. She gestured towards the large mansion that was perched on the cliff above the beach. "It seems to be in the papers all the time at the moment."

Bessie nodded. "Mary loves Thie yn Traie," she told Lora. Mary and George still had a larger home in Douglas, but they'd recently put that house on the market, and as far as Bessie knew they were living at Thie yn Traie now.

"I'd love a better look, but it would be rude to climb up the stairs, wouldn't it?"

"I suspect you'd have their security team chasing you away before you could see much," Bessie told her.

Lora sighed. "Of course they have security. I suppose I don't blame them. I wonder if I could hire someone to protect me."

"You could, of course. I've no idea what it would cost, though."

"If I spend all of my money on security guards, then no one would have any reason to kill me," Lora laughed.

"I'm going to ring John Rockwell after dinner," Bessie said. "I won't sleep tonight if I don't talk to him. You may be in real danger."

"I felt that way after the problem with the gas fire, and then again when my petrol tank began to leak, but once the issues are repaired and a few days go by, I start to think that I'm imagining things again."

"I hate to say it, but if something does happen to you, it will be important that the police know about everything else."

Lora nodded. "I know you're right, I just feel as if I'll be wasting their time."

"I'm happy to waste a bit of John's time for this. I'll have him over for tea and a chat. He won't mind, not if I give him biscuits."

"Men are like children," Lora laughed.

They turned around and began the walk back to Bessie's cottage.

"If you aren't doing anything tomorrow, I'm having another gathering at my house," Lora said after a short silence. "I expect everyone will be there."

"I don't want to intrude on a family occasion."

"It isn't a family occasion, really. Percy and Elaine always come to everything, mostly to complain about how expensive the island is and to eat as much of my food as they can. Brian and Jill will probably pop over at some point, too, so they can look down their noses at me and find things to laugh about when they talk about me later."

"My goodness, why do you keep inviting these people?" Bessie asked.

"If I didn't invite them, they'd complain about the cars in front of their houses. This way, they tolerate them for three or four hours. I usually invite Grace's parents, too, but they rarely come. People park in front of their house, too, of course."

"Your children will all be there?"

"They always are. As I said, I have everyone over once a month. The children and the grandchildren all come. No doubt Linda will drag Zack along and then use him as an excuse to leave early. April has a boyfriend, but I've never met him. I don't think Christy is seeing anyone, but if she is, he may come along."

"What time tomorrow?" Bessie asked, trying to remember what plans she'd made for the day.

"People will start arriving around four. I'll have food out from four until seven or eight, really until everyone leaves."

"And you think that the last one of these gathering was when someone tampered with your gas fire, the knives in the kitchen cupboard, and the bath?"

"You'd think I would have noticed something, but you'll see tomorrow, if you come, that the gatherings are slightly chaotic. People are moving around all the time, getting food or drinks or moving into a different room to talk to different people. The weather was still nice enough for some people to sit outside last time. I don't expect that to happen tomorrow."

Bessie nodded. The wind was picking up and the air was cold. She couldn't imagine wanting to sit outside at the moment.

"So you'll come?" Lora asked when they reached the door to Treoghe Bwaane.

"I'll come if you'll agree that I can ring John," Bessie told her.

Lora sighed. "I suppose that's a fair trade." She dug around in her handbag and found a pen and some paper. After writing her address and telephone number on a sheet, she gave it to Bessie.

"I could come and collect you, if you'd like," Lora offered. "It would have to be quite early, though, maybe around one. I have a lot of cooking and baking to do after that."

"I'll get a taxi," Bessie told her. "I'll aim to get there around half three so I can tell you what John said before the other guests arrive."

"That sounds perfect." Lora took a step towards her car and then stopped and looked back at Bessie. "I really do hope it's all in my head," she said sadly. "I'd rather be losing my mind than find out that someone I love is trying to kill me."

"Maybe it's one of your neighbours," Bessie suggested.

Lora smiled, but it looked forced. "I suppose that would be better, although still quite sad."

Bessie watched as the woman climbed into her car and drove away. When the car disappeared from view, she let herself back into her cottage. It was time for some dinner, she thought as she glanced at the clock. After cake and shortbread at the café, she wasn't very hungry. A bowl of soup was all she needed to fill her stomach. After washing up, she sat down at the kitchen table and picked up the telephone, hoping John would be home from work and able to chat.

CHAPTER 4

"Hello?" the voice that came down the line was definitely not John's.

"Amy? It's Elizabeth Cubbon. I was hoping to speak to your father."

"Dad's not home from work yet, but he should be here soon. Do you want me to have him ring you back?"

"Yes, please. If you have dinner ready, he can ring me after he's eaten. It isn't urgent."

"That's good news. I've made a beef roast and I have everything ready to do the Yorkshire pudding the second he gets home. I don't want the pan to get too hot and I'm sure it would if he rings you right away."

"You enjoy your dinner. I can wait," Bessie assured her.

She put the phone down and frowned. Now that Amy had mentioned roast beef and Yorkshire pudding, she was feeling hungry again. Perhaps it might have been nice to have had children, if they could have been relied on to make delicious meals every evening. With John Rockwell on her mind, she made herself some tea, adding a few biscuits to a plate to enjoy with her drink.

Bessie had originally met John when she'd discovered her first dead body nearly two years earlier. He'd only been on the island for a

44

short time, but he'd already fallen under its spell. His wife, Sue, however, was less enamoured of the island, and she did everything in her power to convince their children, Thomas and Amy, that they weren't happy there, either.

After several difficult months, Sue and John agreed to divorce. Sue had never stopped loving a previous boyfriend, Harvey, and they'd recently been reunited. Once she and John separated, Sue had taken the children back to Manchester and she and Harvey were engaged before the divorce was final.

They'd married in the summer and then left the UK for a lengthy honeymoon in Africa. Harvey was an oncologist who wanted to spend some time making a difference in a developing country. While Bessie thought that was the least romantic honeymoon plan she'd ever heard of, apparently Sue had been happy to agree.

When they'd left, they were expected back in September. The children were to spend the summer with John on the island and then go back to Manchester to stay with Sue's mother for the first few weeks of the new school term, just until Sue and Harvey returned. Once Sue and Harvey arrived in Africa, however, they kept changing their plans. Their return date kept getting pushed back and contact was sporadic. In the end, John had enrolled the children in school on the island, and he was ready to fight Sue for custody when she finally made her way back to the UK, whenever that might end up being.

As far as Bessie could tell, Amy and Thomas were happy staying with their father on the island. As John worked long hours that were often unpredictable, both children had become increasingly independent, not only learning to be responsible for their schoolwork themselves, but also learning to cook and look after the house that they shared. Thomas was only a few years away from leaving for university, and Amy wouldn't be far behind. Bessie knew that John was grateful to be able to have the children with him, at least for the moment.

When the tea and biscuits were gone, Bessie curled up with one of her favourite cosy mysteries and let herself get lost in a fictional world. She jumped when the phone rang.

"Amy said you rang," John told her.

"I did. How was dinner?"

John chuckled. "Fine," he said loudly. Bessie heard a door shut and then John spoke again in a much lower voice. "The Yorkshire pudding didn't rise, but it still tasted reasonably good. The beef was, well, rather tough, let's say. Thomas was less complimentary, but I managed to eat my share."

"She'll get better with practice."

"Yes, well, tomorrow night it's Thomas's turn to cook. I'm sure Amy is hoping that he'll make some terrible mistake somewhere, but I really hope whatever he comes up with is edible."

"I should have you all here for dinner one night," Bessie said.

"Doona is making dinner for us later in the week," John replied. "I know no one will go hungry that night. That's assuming she's feeling better, of course."

Bessie smiled. Doona Moore was Bessie's closest friend, even though Doona was much younger. They'd met in a Manx language class several years ago and Bessie had given Doona a shoulder to cry on while her second marriage had been falling apart. Doona had returned the favour by helping Bessie through the various murder investigations that she'd found herself caught up in recently.

Doona was a receptionist at the police station where John worked, and Bessie was certain that the pair were developing feelings for one another, but there were a number of complications. John's children were one issue. Doona's money was another. When Doona's second husband had died, she'd been shocked to discover that he'd named her as the main beneficiary in his will. They'd been in the middle of a divorce when he'd met his untimely death.

Although most of his estate was still tangled up in legal proceedings due to the illegal business practices of the man's former business partner, Doona had already received the proceeds of several life insurance policies. She was still working and living modestly while she tried to decide what to do next. Bessie knew that the money made both Doona and John uncomfortable. She was happy to hear that the pair were spending time together, though. Perhaps John and Doona were going to get a happy ending one day.

Doona was suffering from a bad cold at the moment, which was why she'd missed Grace's baby shower. If she was planning on cooking a meal for John and the children soon, then she must be feeling a bit better.

"Any word on when Sue and Harvey will be back?" Bessie asked.

John sighed deeply. "I spoke to her a few days ago, after she'd talked to the children. She said something along the lines of knowing that the children don't truly need her any longer, as they're nearly grown, but that the men, women, and children that she's working with in Africa, they need her."

Bessie swallowed a dozen different replies. "I think she's mistaken," was the one she finally gave.

"Yes, so do I, and I told her that, as well, in no uncertain terms. The problem is, if she decides that I'm right and comes back to the UK, she's going to want the children back in Manchester with her. I find myself arguing that the children need their mother and then wanting to fight her over custody of them."

"What do the children want?"

"Ideally, they'd like Sue and me to reunite. I don't think they care if we do that here or in Manchester. Of course, you and I both know that isn't going to happen, but I'm not sure that Thomas and Amy understand."

"I'm sorry," Bessie said. "That seems inadequate, but I don't know what else to say."

"I appreciate that, anyway. It's difficult, but I'm doing my best to keep the children happy while they're here. We'll work out what happens next once Sue actually decides to come back."

"I'm sure the children miss her."

"They do, but they're both incredibly frustrated with the situation, too. I know they feel as if Sue has abandoned them." He sighed. "You didn't ring to hear about my problems, though. What's on your mind?"

"We had the baby shower for Grace today," Bessie told him. "After the shower, one of the guests wanted to speak to me."

"That sounds ominous."

"The woman's name is Lora White," Bessie said, spelling the woman's Christian name, as the spelling was unusual. "She's afraid that someone is trying to kill her."

"Maybe I should come over and get all of the details from you," John suggested.

"If you aren't busy and the children won't miss you, you know you're more than welcome."

John laughed. "If I'm honest, I'm using you," he said. "I have to drop Thomas off at a friend's house. He's going to spend the night there. Amy has a dance class and then she's going to one of her friend's houses to watch a movie. I can drop them both where they need to be and spend an hour or so with you before I have to go back and get Amy. The last time something like this happened, I went home in between and fell asleep in front of the telly. Amy wasn't best pleased when she had to ring me to come and get her."

Bessie laughed. "I'll start a pot of coffee to be ready for when you arrive."

"It won't be long after half seven," John told her. "I can't get Amy to her class late, not again."

That left Bessie with enough time to read a few more chapters. She was just piling chocolate biscuits onto a plate when John knocked on the door.

"Coffee?" she asked.

"Yes, please," he sighed. "Amy won't be ready to be collected until midnight."

Bessie poured them each a cup of coffee and put the biscuits in the centre of the table. When she sat down across from John, she studied him.

He was still just as handsome as the first time she'd seen him, she decided. His brown hair had a bit more grey scattered through it, but his green eyes were still bright. He'd lost some weight during the divorce, but now he was back to looking fit and healthy. Tonight, he didn't even look as tired as he normally did.

"You look well," she said after he'd taken a sip of his drink.

"Thank you. Things are finally settling into a routine at home. I'm getting seven or eight hours of sleep each night and eating better than ever now that I have to feed two hungry teenagers. Doona has been taking the kids grocery shopping twice a week, and they're keeping the cupboards and refrigerator full. Aside from the uncertainty with Sue, things are going well. It helps that the crime rate in Laxey seems to have fallen a bit in the last few months."

"Let's hope that lasts," Bessie said ardently.

"Things are going well between me and Doona, too," John said, blushing. He looked down at the table and then up at Bessie. "Does she tell you anything? Do you have any idea how she feels about me? We're friends, of course, good friends, but I was thinking that maybe, given some time, she might come to see me as more than just a friend."

"I think this is a conversation you should be having with Doona," Bessie told him.

John sighed. "Maybe I'm too old to be chasing after love again. Sue broke my heart, but things were difficult between us for years before we actually separated. I know Doona's been through two divorces, or nearly. Maybe we should just stay friends."

Bessie swallowed a sip of her coffee and thought carefully about her reply. "Doona has been through a lot, and as her closest friend, I want to protect her. If you aren't sure about your feelings for her, please don't rush into anything. Give yourself and Doona time to adjust to life with the children on the island. If you truly do care for her, that shouldn't change if you wait to tell her for a week or a month or a year."

"I know you're right," John told her. "It probably isn't fair asking her to take on becoming a stepmother, anyway."

"She seems to enjoy spending time with Thomas and Amy, but that's very different to taking on responsibility for them. It might be better to wait until Sue is back before you make any big decisions."

John nibbled his way through a biscuit, his eyes focussed on the wall behind Bessie. "Right, tell me why Lora White thinks someone is trying to kill her," he said briskly after he'd washed the biscuit down.

Bessie told him everything that Lora had told her. As John took notes, Bessie began to feel that it was all much ado about nothing.

"I think the smart thing to do at this point is to share everything you've told me with Pete," John said when Bessie was finished. "I'm going to suggest to him that he have a word with the garage and with whoever repaired the gas fire. If we're lucky, one or both of them might have photographs of what they found, but I'd be very surprised if that were the case."

"Maybe I should tell Lora to start taking pictures whenever anything like this happens."

"If anything happens again, pictures would be smart," John said.

Bessie wondered if she were imagining that he'd emphasised the first word in his reply. "I'm going to see her again tomorrow."

"Why?"

"She's having another gathering at her house."

John frowned. "I'm not sure I want you getting involved in this. It's just possible that someone is trying to kill the woman."

"There are going to be a dozen people there, maybe more. If I keep an eye on everyone, perhaps I'll be able to interfere with any plans anyone might have made."

"If she's really worried, there are outside security firms that can help," John told her. "Cameras can be set up in various locations around the house, for example. They might capture someone tampering with something, if it happens."

"I don't know that she'll want to take things that far," Bessie said. "I suppose a lot will depend on how tomorrow goes."

"If someone from that particular group of people is trying to kill her, then he or she will have lots more opportunities to try tomorrow."

"If someone is trying to kill her, he or she doesn't seem very determined, really. I mean, after nearly half a dozen attempts Lora is still alive and well."

"Even the most incompetent person can get lucky."

John's words made Bessie shiver. "Can you investigate Linda and her boyfriend?" she asked.

"I'll have Pete take a discreet look at them, but unless Lora wants to call Pete in to investigate properly, there isn't much he can do."

"What could she have Pete investigate?"

John frowned. "Probably not much at this stage, not unless he learns anything interesting about the car or the gas fire. The railing from the steps might be worth a look, too. What did Lora do with the broken pieces?"

"I've no idea. Do you want me to ring her and ask?"

"You can ask her tomorrow when you see her. If she still has them, Pete can take a look and even refer them to a specialist if he thinks there's anything suspicious there. What was Zack's surname?" John asked as he flipped back through his notes.

"I'm not sure Lora ever said," Bessie frowned. "I should have asked, but I didn't."

"Ask her tomorrow and let me know. I may be able to get it from other means, anyway, but that will be easiest."

Bessie nodded. "Is there anything else I can ask her that might help?"

"Find out where she took her car and whom she used when the carbon monoxide alarm went off," John said.

"I should have thought of both of those things," Bessie sighed. "I suppose it's just as well I never joined the police."

"If you had, you would have been trained and you would have known what to ask. For what it's worth, I think you would have made an excellent police inspector."

Bessie flushed. "Thank you."

They chatted about Thomas and Amy for a short while. Bessie heard all about the classes they were taking at school and the various sports and other activities they enjoyed.

"It sounds as if they keep you busy," Bessie remarked.

"They do, and I love it. Doona does at least half of the driving for me, though. It's been tough this week, with her sick at home. I've had to leave work early most days to take Thomas to football. It will be easier when he's driving, but I'm not in any hurry for that to happen, really."

"Hopefully Doona will be well again soon."

"She was sounding a bit better when I visited her this afternoon," John said. "I've been taking her lunch every day, and today she actually managed to eat something. She reckons she's turned the corner, anyway."

Bessie hadn't realised that John was visiting Doona during her illness. She'd offered to take the woman some soup, but Doona had insisted that Bessie stay away from her while she was contagious. "She's lucky to have you looking after her," she said.

"Someone has to. She's terrible at looking after herself."

Bessie nodded. "What time do you have to collect Amy?"

John glanced at the clock on the wall. "Not for hours yet, but I'm sure you're tired, so I'll go."

"I'm getting tired, but you don't need to rush away."

John shrugged. "I might go into Ramsey and do some shopping, actually. ShopFast is open until midnight. Doona has been craving those chocolate biscuits that they do, but I haven't had time to stop to get them for her. I know we need a dozen different things at home, too, as the children both seem to eat constantly."

"Do you have a list?"

John frowned. "A list would be a good idea."

Bessie hid a smile as she found paper and a pen for him. He was always incredibly well organised at work, but for some reason that didn't seem to spill over into his home life. She helped him think through a few different meals and then listed the various ingredients that he might need to make them.

"I hadn't realised how much Doona has been doing for me," he said when they were done. "She must make lists with the kids before they try to cook anything. She's probably been giving them recipes, too, as I don't think I own a cookbook."

"Just make sure you appreciate her properly."

"I do, or at least I try to. I'm going to buy her flowers tonight to go with the chocolate biscuits."

Bessie nodded. "Flowers are always nice."

John yawned and then got to his feet. "If I walk slowly enough, I should be able to kill an hour at ShopFast. By the time I take the shopping home and then go back out, it should be time to collect Amy."

As he headed for the door, Bessie followed. "Good night," she said as he opened it.

"Good night," he replied. "Let me know how tomorrow goes."

Bessie nodded and then shut and locked the door behind him. She quickly dealt with the washing-up and then headed up to bed. She fell asleep wondering if Lora was overreacting to a few simple accidents or if a killer truly was targeting her.

It was one minute past six when Bessie's internal alarm woke her. It was nearly always reliable, so much so that Bessie hadn't set an actual alarm for years, unless she truly had to be somewhere quite early in the morning. Today she wasn't planning anything before half three, so she got up slowly, showering and then getting dressed at a leisurely pace.

Having had tea and biscuits quite late in the evening the previous night, she wasn't feeling especially hungry when she reached the kitchen. Instead of making herself breakfast, she went out for her morning walk first.

Bessie had been walking on Laxey Beach every morning for all of her adult life. She credited the exercise and the fresh sea air with her continued good health. While she'd stopped counting birthdays once she'd received her free bus pass, she knew that she'd had the pass for quite a few years now. She was still some years away from a telegram from the Queen, however, which she'd decided some time back would be when she would start to consider herself as reaching the tail end of middle age.

It was cool with a stiff breeze and Bessie walked briskly along the water's edge to Thie yn Traie. While she would have liked to walk further, a light rain began to fall as she passed the stairs to the mansion, so she reluctantly turned around. If the weather improved, she could always have another walk later in the day. The beach was usually crowded in the summer months when guests filled the holiday cottages, but this time of year Bessie nearly always had the entire beach to herself. She hadn't gone far when she heard her name.

"Bessie? Good morning," a loud voice shouted.

Forcing a smile onto her lips, Bessie turned towards the woman who was rapidly crossing the sand towards her. "Good morning, Maggie," she said.

"How are you today?" Maggie asked, narrowing her eyes and studying Bessie closely.

"I'm fine, thank you. How are you?"

"I'm fine. Oh, my back has been bothering me again and one of my toes has gone crooked and might need some sort of treatment. Thomas has had a horrible cold for months, which means he's impossible to live with right now. Men are always dying when they get sick, you understand, even though he only really has the sniffles. I caught it from him, of course, but I never complained once and I recovered very quickly. He's still moping around the house, coughing and sneezing all the time. Anyway, you know I never complain about anything. Doesn't do any good, anyway, does it?"

"I do hope Thomas feels better soon," Bessie said.

"He managed to convince his doctor that he has pneumonia, of all things. He's been taking antibiotics for the last two weeks and I think he's finally feeling better. As I said, I had the same thing, but I managed to get through without any antibiotics. Women are much stronger than men, anyway."

"Pneumonia is quite serious, isn't it?" Bessie was suddenly worried for her friend.

"It can be, but they caught it early and he only spent a few nights in hospital. He'll be fine, I'm sure."

"I certainly hope so."

Maggie nodded and then took a deep breath. "I hope so, too," she said in a low voice.

It wasn't often anyone saw Maggie's softer side, but Bessie could tell that the woman was genuinely concerned about Thomas, however much she tried to pretend that nothing was seriously wrong.

"If you need anything, you know where I am," Bessie told Maggie.

"Thank you," Maggie said. She took another deep breath and then shook her head. "But that's enough about me. I understand you've suddenly become close friends with Lora White."

"I wouldn't say that," Bessie replied, not the least bit surprised that the island's gossip network had already informed everyone that she and Lora had visited the café in Ramsey together yesterday. "We met at Grace's baby shower. She invited me for a cuppa after the shower."

"I was rather hoping for an invitation to the shower," Maggie said, sounding slightly hurt.

"I didn't realise you know Grace."

"I don't know her, exactly, but I've met her husband many times, especially after the unfortunate incident in our holiday cottage."

Bessie wasn't sure she'd call a man's murder an "unfortunate incident," but she wasn't going to quibble with Maggie over that. "The café in Lonan has a limited amount of space. Most of the guests were Grace's friends and family members from Douglas. Only a handful of guests were from Laxey, really."

Maggie shrugged. "I heard it was a nice party, but then I'd expect nothing less from a party arranged by Mary Quayle. She can afford the very best."

"Actually, Elizabeth made all of the arrangements. She's turning out to be an excellent party planner."

"Imagine being able to spend your days planning parties for people. It isn't a real job, is it?"

"From what I've seen, it's incredibly hard work, actually. People can be very demanding, especially brides. The hours are long, too, as most parties happen late at night or on weekends."

"I suppose," Maggie replied, clearly bored with the subject. "But what did you and Lora find to talk about for so many hours in Ramsey yesterday?"

"We talked about everything and nothing, really. We wouldn't have spent hours at the café if we hadn't had to wait so long for our tea and cakes."

"Things have gone downhill now that Tammy is only working part-time," Maggie sighed. "She was horrible to the customers, but she got things out of the kitchen in a timely fashion and kept the customers moving, too."

The rain was still falling and Bessie was growing tired of getting wet. "I really need to get out of this rain," she said. "Was there anything else?"

"If Thomas and I apply for planning permission to tear down the last cottage in the row and rebuild a larger cottage in its place, will you object?" Maggie asked in a rush.

"How much larger?"

"It would sit in the same footprint, but with an extra level. We could add two more bedrooms that way and rent it out to larger parties."

"I can't see why I'd object," Bessie said after a moment's thought. "As it's all the way down on this end, as far as it can be from my cottage, it wouldn't really affect me."

"That's what I thought," Maggie said triumphantly. "Thomas was worried that you would object, but I told him that it isn't you we have to worry about. I'm concerned about George and Mary Quayle. I'm sure they don't like having to share the beach with the guests in the holiday cottages. It isn't as if our guests are the sorts of people with whom George and Mary socialise."

"I don't believe either of them spends much time on the beach, though. I'm not sure they're even aware of how many guests you get in the summer months."

"Elizabeth knows. She was down here several times this past summer, lying around on a large chair that someone brought down for her. She used her phone to ring up to the house to get drinks and food carried down to her, as well. I wonder if she'll object to our changes."

"If I talk to her, I'll ask her," Bessie said.

"Thomas and I were talking about adding a few more cottages, as well," Maggie said tentatively. "Just a few more, maybe two on this end and one on the other end."

"One closer to my cottage?" Bessie asked, frowning.

"Maybe. We have to check exactly where the property lines are, though."

"I don't believe you'll have room to add another cottage next to mine," Bessie told her. "I believe my property line is quite close to the cottage that's already there."

"Maybe you'd like to sell us some of the land around your cottage," Maggie suggested.

"I don't think so," Bessie said firmly. "What I'd really like to do right now is get out of the rain."

"Oh, of course," Maggie blushed. "I'm sorry to have kept you so long."

"You know where I live. If you want to talk to me, you can visit anytime."

Maggie nodded. "I may just pop in one of these days," she said brightly before she turned and began to walk back up the beach.

Bessie continued on her way back to Treoghe Bwaane. Inside the small downstairs loo, she took off as much of her wet clothes as modesty would permit and hung them over the tub. Upstairs, she dried her hair and then changed into dry clothes. It was later than she'd thought, and she still hadn't arranged for a taxi to take her to Lora's that afternoon.

Ringing her favourite taxi firm crossed that job off her mental chore list. She'd been using the same company for a long time. Bessie had been friends with the man who'd started the business in Laxey. He'd given her a generous discount on their services. When he'd sold the company to a Douglas firm, she'd continued to use them, as she was fond of many of their drivers.

Bessie spent a quiet day reading and relaxing. Planning the baby shower had been stressful, even though Elizabeth had done nearly all the work. The strain of keeping the event a secret from Grace had been considerable. They hadn't even told Hugh about the event until a few days ago, so that he couldn't object to everyone's generosity.

When Bessie finished one book and went to look for another, she started to think about how badly she'd been neglecting her research.

As a strictly amateur historian, she'd spent years studying the many wills in the island's archives. The more she'd discovered, the more interested she'd become in the subject. Marjorie Stevens, the Manx Museum librarian and archivist, acted as a mentor, helping Bessie choose new items to study over the years. Bessie had even taken a class in reading old handwriting, to allow her to read some of the older wills in the archives. After giving papers at two consecutive conferences that had been held on the island, this year she was attending as a spectator rather than presenting any of her own research. While she felt as if she ought to be doing more, with everything else that had happened in her life in the past year and a half she was also somewhat relieved that she wasn't trying to write a paper while helping Lora.

After a light lunch, she tidied up the cottage, running the vacuum through the ground floor and wiping down the kitchen counters. That left her feeling less guilty about curling up with another book until it was time to get ready to go into Douglas.

She decided on a simple grey dress for the occasion with no idea of whether it would be appropriate or not. When in doubt, she preferred to be overdressed rather than underdressed. Her favourite driver, Dave, picked her up at three o'clock.

"I haven't taken you into Douglas lately," he remarked as they went. "As far as I can remember, I've never taken you to this address before, either."

"No, I'm visiting a new friend today," Bessie told him. "I met her at Grace Watterson's baby shower yesterday."

"Oh, I heard there was some fancy party at the café in Lonan yesterday. The wife wants to have a party one of these days and have Elizabeth Quayle plan it for her. Apparently all of her friends are doing so."

"That's nice for Elizabeth."

"She doesn't really need the money, though, does she?"

"Her parents have money, of course, but she does need to work and support herself. She can't live off her parents forever."

Dave laughed. "I think if I were her, I'd try."

Bessie shook her head. "I know you better than that. You're a hard worker and so is Elizabeth. I'm sure that you'll be impressed with her if you and your wife do have her plan a party for you."

"We'll see. First we have to come up with some sort of reason to have a party," Dave said. "Here we are." He'd pulled up in front of a small bungalow.

Bessie checked the address with the note Lora had given her and then smiled at Dave. "I'll ring the office when I'm ready to go home."

"I'm off at five today, so you'll get someone else. Do you want me to put this trip on your bill?"

"Yes, and make sure that you do. I'm certain you've left some off recently."

"I forget where I've been and what I've done sometimes," he told her. "I hope you enjoy your afternoon."

Bessie nodded and then climbed out of the car. She had a feeling the afternoon was going to be interesting, if not exactly enjoyable.

CHAPTER 5

"*B*essie, you came," Lora said when she opened her door.

"I told you I would."

"Yes, but, well, I thought maybe, after you'd had time to think about it, you'd decide not to bother. I do hope you didn't talk to your policeman friend yet. I've been thinking about everything and I'm sure I'm just adding two and two and getting six or some such thing."

"I did talk to John," Bessie said. "He wants to know where you took your car and who came out to repair the gas fire."

Lora frowned. "As I said, I'm sure it was all nothing. Let's not worry about such things for now. I must get back to the kitchen before something burns."

Lora turned and walked back into the house, leaving Bessie on the doorstep. Before Bessie followed, she took a moment to look at the railing next to the steps she'd climbed. It was obviously new, with wooden posts that disappeared into the ground and a large handrail. Shrugging, Bessie followed Lora, shutting the front door as she entered the house.

The door opened into a small sitting room. There was a long couch and two comfortable looking chairs arranged in front of the gas fire. A small television sat on a stand next to the fire. Bessie could hear noises coming from somewhere near the back of the house. She followed them into the kitchen, which was right behind the sitting room.

"So much to do," Lora said. "Everyone will be here soon."

"What can I do to help?"

"If you could put the kettle on, I'd appreciate it. I'm dying for a cuppa."

Bessie picked up the kettle and filled it at the sink. "You've had this kettle for a fair few years," she remarked as she plugged it into the wall.

"Yes, I have at that. It still works just fine, though. Martha keeps telling me to replace it, but it still boils water, so why would I?"

From what Bessie could see, the kettle wasn't the only thing in the kitchen that had been around for a while. Most of the appliances looked older than Bessie's, and Bessie hadn't bought anything new in over twenty years. The pots on the hob were battered and Bessie could see a few chips in some of the serving plates that Lora had laid out across the counter.

"The new railing outside seems quite sturdy," Bessie remarked as casually as she could.

"Yes, Charles had it put in for me. They came and did it the same day the old one fell apart."

"What happened to the old one?"

"Charles took it home with him. I rang him as soon as it happened and he came over straight away. He was happy to get the broken pieces, anyway. He's always looking for more wood for his bonfire."

"Bonfire?"

"Cecil always used to do a big bonfire on Bonfire Night when the children were small. Actually, he did it every year, whatever age the children were. After he passed away, Charles has carried on the tradition. It isn't quite the same, but the grandchildren enjoy it and it's another chance to get the family together."

"You seem to get together a great deal."

"I grew up with six aunties, three on each side of the family. We used to go to see the aunties every single Saturday, visiting each for an hour at a time. When I was old enough to question it, I asked my mother why the aunties couldn't all come to see us at the same time so that we could get all of the visits done in an hour. My mother wouldn't even consider the idea, but once I was an adult, I stopped going to visit everyone every week and started having them all here once a month. The aunties all died off eventually, of course, but by that time I'd had children and so had Ethel. The monthly gatherings were a firmly established family tradition."

"When I lived in the US, we used to visit distant relatives all summer long," Bessie recalled. "We'd start just after school ended, driving for hours and hours to see my father's third cousin or my mother's niece's husband's brother. Family used to be a good deal more important to people in those days."

Lora nodded. "I'm doing everything I can to keep the monthly gatherings going. I hope Charles will take them over once I'm gone, although it may be Martha who ends up doing so. She seems to care about them more than the others."

"And eventually it will be up to the next generation. Do you think Linda will take over one day?"

Lora laughed. "I suspect the tradition will die out with my children. I can't see Linda doing anything she doesn't have to do. Christy is better, but she doesn't get along with Linda. I suppose I should be grateful that I'll be gone before things get to that stage."

The kettle boiled and Bessie made them each a cup of tea. As she handed Lora her cup, she smiled apologetically. "I'm afraid I've forgotten Linda's boyfriend's name," Bessie said.

"Zack? He doesn't look like a Zack, though. I'm not even sure if it's his real name. He's probably called Nigel but wants to pretend he's called Zack because he thinks it's cooler."

"What's his surname? Maybe I know the family."

"He's Zack Payne, but I doubt you know the family. Linda brought him back from Liverpool. I'm not sure where he's actually from, but it definitely isn't the island."

Bessie nodded and then sipped her tea. That was two of four questions answered. "Do you mind if I take a look at the gas fire?" she asked after a moment.

"There isn't much to see. It's just a standard gas fire. It's actually the newest thing in the house, as I had to have the old one replaced about two years ago. It was blocked up from the outside, not the inside, though. There's nothing to see from in here."

"I'm just going to take a quick peek," Bessie said. It only took her a moment to find the small sticker that gave the date of the last service. She made a mental note of the name of the company that had performed it and then rejoined Lora in the kitchen.

"Did you want to look at the outside vent?" Lora asked. "You can go out this door," she added, gesturing towards the house's back door.

Bessie hesitated and then nodded. "If you don't mind."

"I don't mind, but I'm sure you're wasting your time. As I said earlier, I'm sure I'm just overreacting to nothing."

The door opened onto a low step. Bessie stepped down and then walked around the corner. The vent was small, and Bessie frowned as she noticed a few twigs sticking out from it. She pulled them out and then bent down to take a closer look.

"She needs to keep that clear," a voice said from behind her. "That gas fire of hers nearly killed her."

Bessie turned around and smiled at the man who was staring at her. He had to be at least seventy. He was bald and he was squinting in the autumn sunshine. "Lora was just telling me about that. It's a good thing she has a carbon monoxide alarm."

"Bah, we didn't have such things before and we all survived," the man scowled. "It's all about looking after your property correctly, that's all. She neglects things terribly and then is surprised when they stop working."

"I'm Bessie Cubbon."

"Oh, aye, I know who you are," he replied.

As Bessie was pretty sure she knew who he was, too, she didn't bother to ask. "I suppose Cecil did most of the work around the house when he was alive," she said instead.

"He wasn't much better than she is," he shot back. "Brings down the whole neighbourhood when one household doesn't keep the standards up."

Bessie glanced around. From what she could see, the houses all looked very similar in terms of upkeep. The only exception, really, was the house on the other side of Lora's, which appeared to have had a great deal of money spent on it recently. The windows all looked new, as did the front door. The exterior of the house had been painted and the railing outside the door looked brand new as well.

"The neighbourhood has changed, of course," the man told her. "New people are moving in and making all sorts of changes. They want to add an extension." He nodded towards the house that Bessie was assuming belonged to Brian and Jill Cobb. "Used to be kids shared bedrooms and houses had one loo for everyone. Now people seem to think that they need fancy bedrooms with en-suites and that every child needs his or her own space. No wonder kids today are the way they are."

Bessie swallowed a few replies, choosing to be diplomatic. Arguing with him wouldn't help anything. "My sister and I shared a bedroom until she got married. I must say, I do prefer having my own space, though."

"Does Lora think someone blocked up her vent, then? Does she think someone wants to kill her?" the man asked.

"Goodness, I hope not," Bessie exclaimed. "Do you think someone wants to kill her?"

"I can't imagine why anyone would bother, but when my wife saw you arriving in a taxi, she wondered why you were here. You've never been to Lora's house before, have you?"

"No, I just met her yesterday. She was kind enough to invite me to her family gathering today and I thought it might be interesting to attend. I don't meet many new people these days."

"Ha. You meet plenty of new people, they just keep getting murdered on you." He began to laugh at his own words, not stopping until he started coughing.

Bessie stood and waited until the coughing stopped. "Lora said she always invites her neighbours to her gatherings. I suppose I shall see you later." She was just annoyed enough with him to turn and walk away before he could reply. That didn't stop him from shouting after her.

"If I don't get murdered first," he called, laughing again as she opened the door into Lora's kitchen.

"Percy thinks he's very funny," Lora told her when Bessie had repeated the encounter to her. "Maybe you can see why I've never really liked him."

"I didn't like him, either, but do you think that other people might suspect that you invited me today because of the incidents that have been happening to you?"

"I don't know what anyone will think. If anyone asks, I invited you because I like to have new friends at these gatherings. Years ago, I always invited a handful of new people every time, but I've fallen out of the habit in the past few years. I shall have to start doing it again, if only to keep people from wondering about you."

Bessie nodded. "It might have been better if you'd have invited a few others today."

"Yes, I suppose I should have thought of that. Never mind. As I said, I don't truly want you investigating anything, so we don't have to worry about what anyone thinks. The idea that someone would want to kill me is a crazy one, really."

Bessie didn't bother to reply. The pair talked about nothing much until the doorbell rang a few minutes later.

"That will be Martha," Lora said. "She's always the first to arrive."

Bessie followed Lora to the front door. A moment later the small sitting room felt crowded. Martha was a pretty brunette who appeared younger than forty. Her husband, Tony, looked like an average man in his mid-forties to Bessie. Christy was pretty, and she greeted Lora with a huge hug. Daniel stood awkwardly to one side of the room, looking as if he was already bored.

"This is my new friend Bessie Cubbon," Lora told them. "We met yesterday at the baby shower I told you all about."

"I read about you in the paper," Daniel said, suddenly excited." You keep finding all those dead bodies, don't you?"

"I have found a few," Bessie admitted, "but I prefer to talk about other things."

"That means no rude questions," Martha said firmly to her son. Daniel looked disappointed and then crossed the room and sank into a chair.

"What can I do to help?" Martha asked her mother.

"Why don't you come into the kitchen with me?" Lora said. " Bessie, you can stay here and chat with Tony and the children."

Bessie nodded and then crossed to the couch. She sat down and waited for the others to join her.

"So you just met Lora yesterday?" Tony asked.

"Yes, we went for a cuppa after the baby shower, and Lora was kind enough to invite me to today's gathering."

"Do you think someone might get murdered today?" Daniel asked.

"Goodness, I certainly hope not," Bessie exclaimed.

"Nothing exciting ever happens at these family gatherings," Daniel complained.

"Murder is not exciting," Bessie said firmly. "It's horrible. Besides, you wouldn't want any of your family to die, I'm sure."

Daniel shrugged. "If the old guy from next door comes, I wouldn't mind if he dropped dead. He's always shouting at us if we try to play outside and accidentally kick a ball into his garden."

"Daniel, that's quite enough," Tony said. He looked at Bessie and gave her a nervous smile. "Daniel is just kidding, really. He would be sad to see anything bad happen to Percy or anyone else."

Another knock on the door saved Bessie from having to reply. Tony got up and opened the door. The couple who walked into the sitting room were expensively dressed. The man had dark hair with hints of grey that gave him a distinguished air. The woman was wearing an attractive suit, with pearls around her neck. Tony was quick to perform the necessary introductions.

"This is Charles, Lora's oldest child, and his wife, Ann." He told the new arrivals Bessie's name, but didn't bother to explain her presence.

"I'll just bring some chairs in from the dining room," Charles said after a quick look around the room.

Before he returned, someone else was at the door. For the next several minutes, it seemed as if people were constantly arriving. Bessie did her best to remember who everyone was as she was quickly introduced to each new arrival in turn.

She found herself sitting between Lora's daughter, Doreen, and Ethel, Lora's sister, when Martha appeared in the kitchen doorway.

"The food is ready," Martha announced.

Bessie stayed in her seat while everyone else seemed to head for the kitchen at the same time. As a queue began to form in the doorway, Ethel dropped back in her seat next to Bessie.

"It isn't as if she's going to run out of food," Ethel said. "Lora always makes enough to feed an army."

"It seemed easier to wait until everyone else had filled their plates," Bessie said.

"It is, yes," Ethel agreed. "I'm surprised we've never met before. It isn't that large of an island."

"I spend nearly all of my time in Laxey. I suspect you would say the same about Douglas."

Ethel nodded. "I was born and raised in Douglas. I've never really been one for exploring the rest of the island."

"Of course I visit Douglas to shop and for the historical sites, but nearly everyone I know lives in Laxey," Bessie told her.

"How did you happen to meet Lora, then?"

"We were both at the baby shower for Grace Watterson yesterday."

Ethel nodded. "Of course, because she grew up over the road from here and now she's married to that police constable in Laxey." She laughed. "It really is a small island, isn't it?"

"Miss Cubbon? My father said I should come and apologise for not letting you get your food first," Daniel said, blushing bright red as he stood in front of Bessie with a very full plate.

"It's not a problem," Bessie assured her. "You go and enjoy your dinner. I'll get something later."

The boy nodded and then disappeared into the dining room.

"He didn't bother to apologise to me," Ethel complained. "Children today have no respect for their elders."

"Granny? I brought you a plate," a low voice said.

Bessie smiled at the girl who'd been introduced as April, Ethel's only grandchild. The girl was almost painfully thin, with long brown hair that hung down her back. She wore thick glasses and had braces. "That was kind of you," Bessie told her.

April blushed. "I tried to put all of your favourites on it," she said as she held the plate out to Ethel.

"I'd really rather get my own," Ethel said sharply.

April nodded quickly. "I was only trying to help," she said. Bessie was sure she could hear repressed tears in the girl's voice.

"Yes, well, next time ask first," Ethel suggested as she got to her feet. She crossed the room and disappeared into the kitchen, leaving April staring after her.

"I think it was very kind of you to try to help," Bessie said as she stood up. "I hope you like everything on the plate, though, as it seems as if you're going to be the one eating from it."

April shrugged. "I like everything Aunt Lora makes. I've been away at university and I've really missed her cooking and these family gatherings. Now that I'm here, though, I'm not sure why I missed them." As soon as the words were out of her mouth, April blushed again. "I didn't mean that the way it sounded," she said quickly.

Bessie patted her arm. "I understand what you meant. Family is both wonderful and terribly trying."

April nodded and then shrugged. "I suppose I should eat, then," she said softly before wandering off to the dining room.

By the time Bessie reached the kitchen, Ethel had finished filling a plate. To Bessie, it looked very similar to the plate that April had made for her, but she didn't comment as Ethel walked past her towards the dining room.

"There isn't room in the dining room for everyone," Martha told Bessie as Bessie picked up a plate. "You're more than welcome to stay in here and eat or take your plate back to the sitting room. Of course, knowing Daniel, he's already finished eating, so maybe you can have his chair."

Bessie chuckled. "No doubt he'll want another helping. I'm happy to sit in here and chat with you and Lora while we eat."

"Did you meet everyone?" Lora asked.

"I was introduced to everyone," Bessie told her. "That isn't exactly the same thing."

Lora nodded. "I hope you'll get a chance to talk to everyone before you leave."

"Yes, me too," Bessie agreed. She filled her plate with several different things, all of which looked delicious. There was a small table in the corner of the kitchen with four chairs around it. As Bessie took one of them, Martha came over and joined her.

"Aren't you eating?" Bessie asked.

"I've been nibbling on everything as I've been helping," Martha laughed. "I'm quite full up now."

"She does that every time," Lora said. "You two chat. I'm going to go and check on everyone else."

"Has Mum asked you to come to try to find out who blocked up the vent for the gas fire?" Martha asked as Lora left the room.

"Not at all, although she did mention that it had been blocked. She credited the carbon monoxide detector you gave her with saving her life."

Martha shrugged. "I saw something on telly about the dangers. Getting detectors seemed a good idea. I've given them to my brother and sister and to Ethel and Marie, too. I think Mum is the only who could be bothered to put batteries in, though."

"I'd have thought, after what happened with your mother, that the others would take it much more seriously."

"Mum can, well, overreact to things sometimes. I don't think anyone truly thinks she was in any danger. Charles reckons that she'd have started to feel unwell and realised what was wrong long before anything awful happened."

"Do you think the vent was blocked deliberately?" Bessie asked.

Martha glanced at the door and then sighed. "I don't know what to think. Mum seemed to think it had been, when she first told me about the alarm going off, but now she's insisting that she was overreacting.

From what I've heard, the man who came out to repair the problem didn't think there was anything suspicious about what had happened."

Bessie took a bite to give herself time to think. "Can you think of anyone who might want your mother dead?" she asked eventually.

Martha looked shocked and then gave what sounded like a forced chuckle. "No, of course not. I know you've been caught up in a lot of murder investigations, but Mum is fine, and she's just an ordinary person. No one wants to kill her."

"But you think someone might have blocked the vent. That would have killed her if she hadn't had the alarm."

"It probably wouldn't have done anything more than give her a headache," Martha argued. "Anyway, she did have the alarm and everyone in the family knew about it, so they would have known that there was no point in trying to hurt her with carbon monoxide."

"You did say that no one else has bothered to put batteries in their alarms. Maybe someone assumed that your mother hadn't done so, either."

"What you're suggesting is crazy," Martha said firmly. "This is my family you're talking about. No one wants Mum dead, and even if someone did, he or she would never actually try to harm her. It's a crazy idea."

"What about the neighbours?" Bessie asked.

"Percy and Elaine? I mean, I know that ever since Dad died, Percy has been hoping that Mum will move away, but that's a long way from trying to kill her. Anyway, I understand he and Elaine are considering moving into a care home soon. They won't be neighbours for much longer."

"And the neighbours on the other side?"

"Brian and Jill? They're horrible, but even so, I can't see them killing anyone. Maybe they've hired someone to kill my mother. That would be how they would do it. They hire someone to do just about everything for them, from cutting their lawn to cleaning their house. I'm expecting them to use a surrogate when they decide to have a baby."

"Does anyone in the family need money?"

"Don't we all?" Martha sighed. "Tony and I have two kids to put through university. We're doing okay at the moment, but we've had some extra expenses this year. We used to have money saved up for the kids, but we've had to spend some of that. I'm sure it will all work out in the end, though."

"Is there more shepherd's pie?" a man asked as he walked into the kitchen.

"Of course," Martha told him. She got up and helped him find the right container. "Bessie, did you meet Carl?" she asked as the man turned away from the table.

"We did meet," Carl answered for Bessie. "Although I've no idea why you're here."

"I met Lora at a party yesterday and she invited me," Bessie explained.

Carl frowned. "I must remind her not to invite strangers back to the house," he said. "No offense, of course, but she does have this bad habit of inviting anyone and everyone to her home. Then she's surprised when things go missing or get damaged. As if Linda would spill half a bottle of bath oil and not mention it to anyone."

"As if Linda would actually attempt to clean up a mess if she did spill something," Martha muttered under her breath.

Carl either didn't hear or chose to ignore Martha's words. He nodded at Bessie. "Anyway, welcome," he said as he walked out of the room.

"I don't believe I met Linda," Bessie said thoughtfully.

"She's probably not here yet," Martha told her. "She's nearly always late, but she'll turn up eventually because the food is free. Zack won't miss out on a free meal."

That tied up with what Lora had said about Zack, anyway, Bessie thought. She finished her last bite and then washed it down with a fizzy drink. "You must let me help with the washing-up," she told Martha.

"Oh, no, Christy and Daniel are responsible for the washing-up. At least April is here this weekend. I'm sure she'll help. Linda won't, but that's down to Doreen not ever making her daughter do a single thing."

"I'd like to think we've raised April better than that, anyway," a voice said from the doorway.

Bessie smiled at Marie Becker. "I met April earlier. She seems like a lovely girl."

"She tries hard, anyway," Marie replied. "She's terribly shy and she finds these occasions something of an ordeal, but she'd never miss one when she's on the island because she'd hate the idea of upsetting her Aunt Lora."

"She filled a plate for your mother, but Ethel didn't want it," Bessie said.

Marie frowned. "Mum can be difficult sometimes," she sighed. "That's probably why April is hiding in the spare bedroom with a book."

"A girl after my own heart," Bessie laughed.

Marie chuckled. "I'm sure you think our family is very odd."

"Not at all. I think it's probably the same as every other family," Bessie replied.

"Nathan's family isn't the same," Marie told her, referring to her husband. "They barely speak to one another. We get a card at Christmas from one brother and not even that from the other."

"What a shame," Bessie said.

"They all live on the same street, too," Martha interjected.

Bessie was surprised as Marie nodded.

"Their parents owned a large piece of land and built houses all along the road, one for each of their sons. I see Nathan's brothers nearly every day going in and out of their houses, but they don't even wave or acknowledge my existence."

"How very sad."

"We're used to it, really. I never liked any of them, anyway, and I have enough family of my own so that we don't feel as if we're missing out."

Marie took several biscuits from the table and then left the room.

A moment later a young woman strode in. She glanced at the table and sighed deeply.

"All the same things, yet again," she said in a dramatic voice.

Bessie studied her. Her hair was dyed an unattractive black. She was dressed all in black as well, aside from a few silver studs on the black leather jacket. Her eyes were rimmed in black eye liner. Even her lipstick was black. Bessie suspected that she would be stunning if she washed her face and changed her hair colour.

"It's fine," a sullen voice said from behind the girl.

"Bessie, meet Linda," Martha said brightly. "This is Doreen's daughter."

"It's nice to meet you," Bessie said politely.

The girl raised an eyebrow and then shrugged. "Whatever," she said.

"And this is Zack Payne," Martha added, nodding towards the young man who'd followed Linda into the room.

He was also dressed in black from head to toe. He had three earrings in one ear and Bessie could see part of a tattoo going up his neck. His hair was shaved on one side of his head but long on the other. He scowled at Bessie.

"Hello," she said.

"Let's eat and get out of here," Zack said to Linda.

"Yeah, that," Linda replied.

"I'm sure my mother would prefer if you stayed for a short while," Martha said. "She goes to a lot of trouble having these gatherings so that the family can spend time together."

"I never asked her to invite me around," Linda snapped.

"No, but since you're here, you could sit and chat with her for a minute or two," Martha replied.

Linda rolled her eyes. "We have things to do."

Martha sighed. Zack cleared his throat and then looked at Linda. Linda started eating shepherd's pie right off the serving spoon as Zack coughed loudly.

"Oh, yeah, right," Linda muttered. "Auntie Martha, I was wondering if you could lend me like fifty quid?"

73

Martha raised an eyebrow. "I told you the last time I lent you money that I wasn't going to do it again until you started paying me back."

"Yeah, I know, but Zack's car isn't running, and he can't find a job if he doesn't have transportation," Linda whined.

"Douglas has buses," Martha told her.

Zack laughed. "That's not going to happen," he said haughtily.

Martha shrugged. "I thought you were working," she said to Linda.

"The job didn't work out," Linda replied with a shrug. "They had unrealistic expectations. Expecting me to turn up at nine every single morning wasn't fair."

Bessie had to bite her tongue, and from the look on Martha's face, she was doing the same.

"Anyway, how about it?" Zack asked.

"I'm sorry, but no. If you want money, you're going to have to find a job and work for it yourself," Martha said firmly.

"You sound just like Aunt Lora," Linda sighed. "She's such a pain."

"You should appreciate her more," Martha suggested.

"We'll appreciate her a lot more when she drops dead and leaves Linda a big chunk of money," Zack replied.

CHAPTER 6

$\mathcal{M}$artha gasped while Bessie frowned at the young man. "What makes you think Lora is going to leave anything to Linda?" she asked.

He stared at her for a minute and then shrugged. "Linda is her granddaughter. Of course she's going to leave her something."

"I believe most people leave their estates to their children and let those children make their own choices about the next generation," Bessie said.

Zack shook his head. "Lora's kids are doing okay. They don't need the money. Linda, Christy, and Daniel need it more, anyway. Christy and Daniel want to go to university. Lora should leave everything to be divided between the grandkids."

"Perhaps Lora would prefer to leave her estate to charity," Bessie said. "It is her money. She can do whatever she'd like with it."

"She won't do that," Zack said confidently. "Right?" he asked Linda.

Linda shrugged. "I've no idea what she'll do. I'm sure she's the one who's behind everyone refusing to lend us any money, though. Isn't that right, Auntie Martha?"

Martha shook her head. "Not at all, actually. I believe we all reached the same conclusion on our own. Lending you money isn't a loan, it's a gift, and not one that most of us can continue to make, not when we have children of our own to worry about."

"Let's go and ask Bob," Zack suggested. "He's usually very generous."

Linda shrugged. "Did you want anything else to eat?"

Zack grabbed what was left of a large loaf of bread off the counter. "This will do," he said, taking a bite out of the middle of the loaf.

Linda giggled and then followed him out of the room with crackers in one hand and a banana in the other.

"They aren't trying to kill Mum," Martha said as soon as the pair was gone.

"I never suggested that they were," Bessie replied.

"No, but I wouldn't blame you for thinking that they might," Martha sighed. "They're short of money and they do seem to think that they're in line to inherit something when Mum dies, but in spite of appearances, Linda wouldn't hurt a fly."

"And Zack?"

"I don't like him, but I'm not ready to believe that he's capable of murder."

"People have been murdered for less."

Martha nodded. "It was clever of you to suggest that Mum might not have included Linda in her will. If they were thinking of killing her for the money, maybe they'll think again."

The words seemed odd to Bessie, coming immediately after Martha had insisted that there was no way Linda or Zack was behind the attempts on Lora's life. If they actually were attempts on her life, Bessie added to herself.

"I really need to go and find Bob," Martha said a moment later. "I'm probably too late, but I should warn him that Linda is going to hit him up for money yet again. He's promised before to stop giving in to her, but he has trouble saying no to the girl."

Martha walked out of the kitchen, leaving Bessie on her own. She got to her feet and started to tidy up. The first thing she did was wash the spoon that had been in the shepherd's pie, then she began to wash every cup, plate, bowl, and utensil that she came across. Most of the food bowls were empty or nearly empty, so she was able to move some things into smaller containers, which she refrigerated. While she knew it was good for the grandchildren to help with the chores, it didn't seem fair that Christy and Daniel were going to get stuck with the washing-up while Linda was excused. Anyway, Bessie was feeling a bit overwhelmed by the whole afternoon. She was happy to have some time on her own in the kitchen.

After she'd washed everything that she could, she started trying to put things away. She was holding a large casserole dish, wondering where it might go, when Ethel walked back into the room.

"That one goes over the refrigerator, but you might not be able to reach," she told Bessie as she headed for the table.

Bessie frowned at the cupboard that was over her head. It had to be the one out of which the knife had fallen, which made her hesitant to open it, especially as she knew she couldn't possibly put the casserole inside without being able to see what she was doing.

"There's a step behind the door," Ethel told her as she reached for a biscuit.

Bessie found the small folding step and set it up in front of the cupboard. Aside from a few tea towels on one side, the cupboard was empty. Bessie slid the large casserole dish into place and then carefully climbed back down.

"You've been busy," Ethel remarked as she glanced around the kitchen.

"I was raised to help when I was fortunate enough to be invited to spend time with friends," Bessie told her.

Ethel shrugged. "Christy and Daniel will be pleased, anyway," she said before she took two more biscuits and left the room.

"My goodness, look how tidy," a man said from the kitchen doorway. "I know Christy and Daniel haven't been in here."

Bessie shook her head. "I thought I should do a little tidying up, as everyone else is busy."

The man laughed. "Busy sitting around drinking and talking," he said as he walked into the room.

"And being chased into the kitchen," the second man added as he joined them.

"Chased?" Bessie questioned.

The first man laughed. "He's exaggerating. Martha just suggested that we might want to stay out of the way until Linda and Zack leave. Apparently she's skint again and is asking everyone in turn for yet another loan."

"Loan?" the other man asked. "How much have you lent her in the past year? Has she ever given you a penny back?"

"We really shouldn't air all of our dirty laundry in front of Aunt Lora's guest," the first man admonished. "I'm Milton Hayes," he told Bessie. "I'm Ethel's son, and one of her biggest disappointments in life."

Bessie frowned. "That's very sad."

Milton shrugged. "I suppose, to be fair, I was more of a disappointment to my father than to Mum. Compared to him, she's almost been supportive, really. Anyway, this is Bob, my partner."

"It's very nice to meet you both. I'm Bessie Cubbon."

"Laxey's Bessie Cubbon?" Milton asked.

"I do live in Laxey."

"My goodness, Bob, you should be impressed," Milton said. "Aunt Bessie is an island institution. Not only has she been an honourary auntie to every child in Laxey for the last fifty or sixty years, but now she's an amateur detective as well."

Bessie flushed. "I wouldn't say that," she protested.

"I've heard of you," Bob said. "You're in the paper all the time. You've found dozens of dead bodies, haven't you?"

"I don't know about dozens," Bessie said, determined not to try to count them.

"But why are you here?" Bob demanded. "Is someone going to get murdered here?"

"What an idea," Milton said excitedly. "Who do we think could be murdered in our little group?"

"Maybe someone is tired of lending money to Linda, so they're going to kill her," Bob suggested.

Milton shook his head. "I think it's more likely that Linda has decided to speed up her inheritance. She's probably going to get rid of her father and mother."

"That seems a bit extreme, even for Linda," Bob suggested.

"Maybe for Linda, but not for Zack. He's probably behind it all," Milton replied.

They both turned and looked expectantly at Bessie. She sighed and then shook her head.

"I'm only here because I met Lora at a party yesterday and she was kind enough to invite me. I certainly don't expect anyone to get murdered here today."

"Well, that's kind of disappointing," Milton said. "I mean, I'd hate for any of the family to die, but no one would miss Zack, not even Linda after a day or two. I've never been involved in a murder investigation, but they look fascinating on telly."

"They aren't," Bessie said flatly. "If I'm never involved in another one again, that would be fine with me."

"Maybe one of the neighbours is planning to do away with Lora," Bob said. "I don't understand why they keep coming to these parties month after month, when they so clearly can't stand any of us."

"They come so they can eat Lora's food and drink her drinks," Milton replied. "Brian and Jill come so that they can feel superior to us, and Percy and Elaine come out of habit. I can't imagine any of them wanting Lora dead, though, in spite of the fact that they don't like her."

"Murder is a serious business," Bessie said. "I'd like to think that most people would need a very strong reason for attempting to kill another person."

"So you're really just here for the party?" Bob asked.

"Yes, and it's been lovely," Bessie told him. "I'm getting a bit tired now, I must admit. I'm not used to being around so many people for such a long time."

"Which is why you're hiding in the kitchen rather than socialising," Milton said. "Have you met everyone at the party?"

"Not everyone. I haven't met either set of neighbours, actually,"

Bessie admitted. "I thought everyone would come through the kitchen eventually, but they haven't come in while I've been in here."

"They were probably among the first to get their food," Milton replied. "Neither couple will want to stay long. They may not even still be here. Should we go and take a look?"

Bessie found that she was just curious enough to take the arm he offered. The sitting room felt far too crowded for her to feel comfortable, though.

"Let's go and meet Percy and Elaine first," Milton whispered. He led Bessie across the room to the couple. Percy was the man Bessie had spoken to earlier. His wife was a tiny grey-haired woman who looked much older than Bessie felt. Elaine was staring at the glass in her hand as if she wasn't quite certain where it had come from. She looked up and frowned at Bessie as she and Milton reached them.

"This isn't my usual wine," she told Milton in an angry voice.

"Perhaps Lora ran out of what you usually drink," he suggested.

"I don't know why we bother coming if we can't have what we like," the woman snapped.

"Percy, Elaine, this is Elizabeth Cubbon. She's one of Lora's friends," Milton said.

"Please, call me Bessie. It's nice to meet you both."

"You were outside earlier, looking at the vent for the fire," Percy said accusingly. "I told you then that we know who you are."

"But you didn't take the time to introduce yourself," Bessie countered, "and I didn't get a chance to meet your wife, either." She nodded at Elaine.

"I didn't want to meet you," Elaine said bluntly. "Too many people end up dead after they meet you. I'm not ready to die yet." She grabbed her husband's arm and began to pull him away from Bessie. "Come along," she said sharply. "We're going."

Bessie watched as the pair headed for the front door. Percy waved towards Lora as they went. "Thanks," he shouted as Elaine opened the door and dragged the man out of the house. As the door slammed shut behind them, an awkward silence descended on the room.

"What did you say to them, Bessie?" Lora called from across the room. "I've never been able to get them to leave early."

A few people chuckled and then conversations began again. Bessie looked at Milton and sighed. "That was unpleasant."

"So are Percy and Elaine. I said they've never liked Lora, but the feeling is mutual. I keep telling her to stop inviting them, but it's a tradition that was fifty years in the making. I've heard rumours that they're thinking about selling their house and moving into a care home. I hope those rumours are correct."

"Be careful what you wish for," Bessie warned him. "You could get someone even worse over there."

"I'm hoping maybe I can buy the place," Milton told her. "I wanted to buy the house on the other side, but after they accepted my offer, the sellers accepted a higher offer from Brian and Jill. I'd already sold my flat, so now Bob and I are staying with his parents, which is difficult at our age."

"Good luck to you. I understand that property prices are rising quickly at the moment," Bessie said.

Milton nodded. "It doesn't help that I'm set on moving into this neighbourhood. There are lots of houses available all over the island, but not very much on this street. It's become a weird obsession for me, really, which is quite sad. But come and meet Brian and Jill. I'd dislike them just because they bought that house out from under me, but every time I speak to them, they seem to do everything they can to keep giving me more reasons to hate them."

Even if Bessie hadn't met any of the others yet, she would have been able to pick out Brian and Jill in the crowd. They were standing together in one corner, wearing trendy clothes and matching sneers. As she and Milton approached, Brian said something to Jill that made her snicker.

"Good afternoon," Milton said loudly. "I wanted you to meet Elizabeth Cubbon. She's one of Lora's friends."

"How nice," Brian said, looking Bessie up and down and then looking away.

"This is Brian Cobb," Milton continued. "He and his lovely wife, Jill, live next door."

Bessie nodded at Jill, who smiled faintly and then began to study her fingernails.

"It's very nice to meet you both," Bessie said. "I only met Lora yesterday, but she was kind enough to invite me to join you all today."

Jill glanced at her and then looked at Brian, who yawned. "Perhaps we should be going," she said. "You're off to London tomorrow, after all."

"I've several important meetings about a major business merger," he said to Bessie. "Flying back and forth is draining, but it pays the bills, I suppose."

"I'll be getting a new car in the spring," Jill added. "Brian just had one, of course. We've loads we want to do to the house, too. We're so fortunate that Brian's job pays so very well."

"I can't imagine," Bessie said. "I've never worked."

The pair both stared at her for a minute. "You've never worked?" Brian echoed eventually.

"Not long after my eighteenth birthday, I inherited a small amount from the man I was planning to marry," Bessie told him. "My advocate was something of a genius when it came to investments. He was able to turn my small inheritance into enough income to allow me to live a life of leisure."

Brian and Jill exchanged glances. "Where do you live?" Brian asked.

"I have a cottage on the beach in Laxey," Bessie replied.

"How near the beach?" Jill demanded.

"It's right on the beach," Bessie told her, knowing full well that the land her cottage was sitting on was now worth a considerable sum.

"Laxey Beach is covered in holiday cottages," Brian said.

"There are several of them, yes, but my cottage has been there for much longer. It can be a bit of a bother in the summer months, when the cottages are fully booked, but at this time of year, I nearly always have the entire beach to myself," Bessie said.

Brian looked at his wife. "Maybe we should be going," he said. "I do have to be up early tomorrow."

She nodded. "Do thank Lora for us, won't you?" she asked Bessie before she and Brian quickly moved towards the door. As it shut behind them, Lora began to laugh.

"I wish I'd known how good you were at getting rid of people," she called to Bessie. "I'd have been having you at these gatherings for years."

Bessie sighed. "I didn't mean to chase anyone away," she told Milton.

"You've done all of us a favour," he told her. "I think we should try to get rid of Linda and Zack next."

Bessie shook her head. "I'd rather just chat quietly with you and Bob."

"Have you met my sister and her husband?" Milton countered.

"Surely you don't want to chase away your own sister," Bessie replied.

Milton laughed. "Not Marie, no, but Nathan might be another story."

They crossed the room to where Marie was standing with April. Nathan was sitting on a chair nearby, apparently lost in the book he was holding.

"I thought you all should meet Bessie," Milton said brightly when they reached the others.

"We met earlier," Marie replied.

"But she hasn't met Nathan," Milton countered. "Nathan, this is Lora's friend, Bessie."

Nathan didn't look up. After a few seconds, Marie touched his arm. He sighed deeply and kept reading until he turned the page. Then he looked up at his wife. "Yes?"

"This is Aunt Lora's friend, Bessie," Marie told him, gesturing.

Nathan looked at Bessie and then shrugged. "It's nice to meet you," he said before turning his attention back to his book.

"What are you reading?" Bessie asked quickly.

"It's just an old Sherlock Holmes story," he told her, flushing. "I like to read lots of different things."

"I used to read all of the Sherlock Holmes stories every spring,"

Bessie replied. "Eventually I began to feel as I knew them too well and I stopped. Now I only reread one or two stories each year and I always enjoy revisiting Sherlock."

"You'll have read this one, then," Nathan suggested, showing Bessie the front of his book.

Bessie sat down in the chair next to his and the pair had a lively conversation about the book in question. Marie looked slightly bemused when Bessie finally glanced up at her about ten minutes later.

"You don't like Sherlock Holmes?" Bessie asked the woman.

"I'm not much of a reader. I'm rather too busy with work and other things."

"If you find some spare time, many of the works are quite short and they're all worth reading," Bessie told her.

"I've read them all," April said in a low voice.

"You have?" her father replied. "Why didn't you tell me?"

April blushed. "I've been reading them at school. I was going to tell you when I was home for my next break. This trip home was just a last minute one."

Nathan nodded. "We'll talk over your break, then," he said.

"We still have to work out if she's going back," Marie said softly. "We have a lot to discuss later today."

"Yes, well, let's not worry about that right now," April suggested. "We'll work it all out eventually."

Marie opened her mouth to reply, and then pressed her lips tightly together. Nathan sighed.

"We'll make it work," he said firmly.

"Because you can just magic up thousands of pounds from nowhere," Marie shot back.

Nathan flushed. "We can take out another mortgage," he began.

"I think it's probably time for us to leave," Marie interrupted. "Lora looks tired," she added.

Bessie glanced over at Lora. She was standing next to Linda, and she did look quite tired. Bessie wondered if she might simply be tired of talking to Linda.

Nathan got up and he and Marie crossed to Lora. April trailed behind them. Nathan spoke to Lora and then Marie gave her a hug. The trio disappeared out the front door a moment later.

"You truly are chasing everyone away," Milton laughed. "Who do we want rid of next?" He glanced around the room.

"Fifty pounds isn't much," a loud voice said.

Bessie turned around. Doreen was talking to Lora. Linda seemed to be hanging on every word. Bessie took a few steps closer to them, hoping to overhear the rest of the conversation.

"If it isn't much to you, why don't you give her the money?" Lora countered.

"Carl wants her to learn to manage her own money," Doreen replied. "We give her a small amount each week to help her out, but Carl doesn't like it if I give her any extra."

"Carl is right," Lora replied. "It's high time she learned to manage her own money. She's not going to learn if she keeps borrowing from everyone all the time, though, is she?"

Doreen frowned. "It isn't easy, you know, being a young person on the island. Good jobs are hard to find, and no one wants to pay a fair wage, either. She's had three different jobs in the past three months, and none of them have worked out. Zack can't even really look for work, because he doesn't have a reliable car."

Lora sighed. "He has two good legs and he lives within reasonable walking distance of half of Douglas. There are regular buses to the other half. I'm sorry, Doreen, but both of them need to grow up and learn how to be adults. They can't simply keep borrowing money from other people, especially when they clearly have no intention of paying it back. That wasn't how your father and I raised you and your siblings."

"Never mind," Doreen said tightly. "I'll give her the money myself." She opened her handbag and pulled out a wallet. The room was silent as she counted out fifty pounds and then handed the money to Linda.

"Thanks, Mum," Linda said carelessly. She glanced around the room. Zack was standing near the window, staring out into the street. "Come on," she shouted at him as she walked towards the door.

Zack nodded and then followed Linda out of the house. For a moment, no one spoke.

"I thought we had an agreement," Carl said to Doreen.

"If Zack gets his car repaired, maybe he'll be able to find work," Doreen countered.

"You know they aren't going to use the money on Zack's car," Carl replied. "They'll just buy cheap wine and take it back to our house and get drunk. We have to stop helping them behave badly."

"At least if they're drinking at our house, they aren't driving," Doreen said.

"I'd prefer it if they weren't drinking at all," Carl said. "I don't object to anyone having a glass of wine after a long work week, or even after a long work day, but neither of them does anything but sleep and eat. I can't imagine needing a glass of wine to deal with a life of leisure."

"They're both looking for work. That has its own stresses," was Doreen's reply.

Carl shook his head. "You've more faith in our daughter than I have. I don't think she's done any job-hunting since she quit her last job, but maybe it's time we find out and start making some demands."

"What do you mean?" Doreen asked.

"I mean she applies for five jobs a week or she moves out. I mean she starts paying rent once she starts working again. I mean Zack starts paying rent now. If he doesn't have any money, he can ask for help from his family in the same way Linda is always asking everyone here. We've been supporting Zack for months now. It seems to me that it's high time his family helped out."

"Maybe we should finish this conversation at home," Doreen suggested, glancing around and then blushing when she caught Bessie's eye.

"Just when it was getting interesting," Milton murmured in Bessie's ear.

She grinned at him and then watched as Carl and Doreen said their goodbyes to Lora. Charles and Ann weren't far behind.

"You did the tidying and the washing-up, didn't you?" Martha asked suddenly.

Bessie jumped. She hadn't noticed the woman approaching her. "I found myself alone in the kitchen, so I did some tidying and a bit of washing-up," Bessie admitted. "There was plenty left to do, though, when I came back out here."

"Christy and Daniel couldn't believe their luck," Martha replied. "They'd been trying to look inconspicuous in the corner for the last hour, hoping I'd forget to make them do the work. They were thrilled when they saw the state of the kitchen."

"I was more than happy to help out," Bessie told her.

"Well, thank you," Martha smiled. "The kids have finished what little you left undone, and now we have to be going. I hope to see you again at one of these gatherings. It was very nice to meet you."

"It was nice to meet you, as well," Bessie replied.

Martha said a few words to Lora and then she, Tony, and the children left. Milton and Bob had been quietly moving chairs and tables around the room, putting everything back where it belonged. When they finished, they each hugged Lora in turn.

"I really must hug Bessie, too," Milton announced. "She made today much more fun than these things usually are."

Bessie laughed and then hugged both men. As they left, she turned to Lora. "What a fascinating group of people," she said.

A loud laugh startled her. Ethel stood up from one of the couches. "I'd never describe my family as fascinating," she said, "but at least they've all gone now."

"I need a cuppa," Lora announced. "Let's go into the kitchen and have tea and biscuits."

Bessie nodded and then followed Lora. Ethel took a few steps after them and then stopped.

"Maybe I'll just go home," she said.

"Oh, come on," Lora said. "We haven't had a proper chat in ages, and I want you to get to know Bessie, too."

"I have things to do at home."

"And they'll wait until you get home," Lora countered. "I feel as if I never see you at the moment. You're always busy."

"I have had a lot going on lately, but I won't for much longer," Ethel sighed. "But you're right. We should talk."

The trio made their way into the kitchen.

"It looks much better than it normally does," Lora said as she sank into a chair at the kitchen table. "Martha told me that you did some tidying and washing-up," she said to Bessie. "You were meant to be my guest."

Bessie sat down next to her and shrugged. "I was raised to help out whenever possible. It's been years since I've been to a big family gathering like this, but I wouldn't have felt right just sitting around not doing anything all afternoon."

Ethel laughed and then dropped into a chair. "I prefer to leave that to the younger generation. What is the point in having children and grandchildren if you can't rely on them to deal with the hard work?"

"Maybe that's why I was so quick to help," Bessie said with a grin. "I never had children."

The other two women both chuckled.

"I can't imagine my life without my children," Lora said.

"But maybe without your grandchildren?" Ethel suggested. "Or at least one of them."

Lora sighed. "I love that girl with all of my heart, but she really needs to do something with her life. The first thing she should do, of course, is get rid of that boyfriend of hers."

"I don't like him," Ethel said. "I'm sure he's a bad influence on Linda, although she wasn't exactly the model granddaughter before she met Zack."

"No, you're right, of course. I keep thinking that things would be better if she ended things with Zack, but she wasn't working or doing anything with her life before she met him," Lora agreed.

"Maybe she'd replace him with someone worse," Ethel added.

Lora gasped. "Is that possible?" She held up a hand. "Don't answer that," she said quickly. "Zack is lazy and irresponsible, but as far as I know, he's not a criminal. Things could be a lot worse."

"Her parents need to kick them both out," Ethel said.

"They need to do something," Lora agreed. "But this conversation is depressing me. We need tea and some proper biscuits to go with it. I have a box of special ones hiding in my bedroom. Ethel, please put the kettle on while I go and get them."

Lora walked out of the room as Ethel slowly got to her feet. She picked up the kettle and took it to the sink. As she was adding water, she made a noise.

"What's wrong?" Bessie asked.

Ethel set the kettle down on the table in front of Bessie. "This kettle is nearly as old as I am," she said. "Now the cord has pulled loose from the housing. It's dangerous."

She pointed to the cord next to the switch. Bessie could see exposed wires. It seemed likely, from the location of the damage, that anyone trying to switch on the kettle would get a bad shock, or worse.

CHAPTER 7

"*H*ere we are," Lora said from the doorway. "But what's wrong?"

"The cord on the kettle has pulled loose," Ethel replied. "I could have been killed if I'd tried to use it."

Lora sat down at the table and pulled the kettle across to her. "It wasn't like this earlier today," she said tightly.

"Clearly the cord has been wearing thinner and thinner every day," Ethel replied. "How old is it, anyway?"

"I've had it for years and it's always been absolutely fine," Lora told her. "There was nothing wrong with it earlier today."

"So one of the grandkids must have damaged it accidentally and not wanted to mention it," Ethel suggested. "Maybe Daniel accidentally pulled on the cord when he was tidying the kitchen. He may not have even noticed what he'd done."

Lora stared at her for a minute and then nodded slowly. "I suppose that's possible."

Bessie didn't say anything. She'd used the kettle herself earlier in the day and she was certain that there had been nothing wrong with it at that time. She also knew that the kettle had been safely tucked away in the corner before the children came in to do the tidying up. There was no way Daniel or anyone else had accidentally pulled on the cord.

"So much for tea and biscuits," Ethel grumbled as she took the kettle away from her sister. She poured the water down the drain and then dropped the kettle into the bin with a resounding crash.

"I can boil water on the hob," Lora countered. "It's old-fashioned, but it works."

She put a pan of water on to boil and then poured fancy chocolate-covered biscuits onto a plate.

"Enjoy," she said faintly as she put the plate in the centre of the table.

"You sound upset," Ethel said sharply.

"I'm starting to worry about my sanity," Lora replied. She tried to laugh, but the sound was strangled.

"What's wrong?" Ethel asked.

"There have been so many accidents lately, that's all. I'm starting to worry that I shouldn't be living on my own."

"Go and live with Charles and Ann, then," Ethel suggested. "They've plenty of room, after all."

"I don't want to impose on my children," Lora countered.

"Maybe you should look at some of the retirement communities around the island," Bessie suggested. "They have several different options, depending on how much or how little care you'd need."

"I don't like to think that I need care, but, well, as I said, accidents keep happening. Maybe looking after this house is too much for me now," Lora sighed.

"It does seem a lot to look after," Bessie said. "Having met your neighbours, I think I'd be looking at other options if I were you."

Lora nodded. "Yes, there is that, although I understand that Percy and Elaine are considering some different things. It would be just my luck to find a nice flat in a retirement community and then find those two living next door to me again."

"I'm sure Brian and Jill would love it if you'd go," Ethel said. "I've half a mind to encourage you to stay put, just to annoy those two."

"Yes, I'd hate to move and see those two buy my house. They'd probably build a long corridor between it and theirs and live in both houses at the same time."

"I can't see them getting planning permission for that," Bessie said.

"They'd probably just buy yours and tear it down," Ethel suggested. "Then they'd have a big garden to enjoy and no neighbours on one side."

"Yes, I suppose so," Lora sighed.

"You could move in with Carl and Doreen," Ethel said. "They'd have to throw Linda out, then, wouldn't they?"

"Doreen wouldn't throw her own daughter out, not even for me," Lora told her. "My moving in might give them an excuse to get rid of Zack, though."

"So it would be worth it," Ethel said darkly.

"Maybe, or maybe it would just cause even more trouble. I think I'll stay where I am for now."

"What about Tony and Martha? I'm sure Martha would love to have you," Ethel said.

"Martha probably would, or at least she'd pretend that she would. Tony would hate it, and it would be difficult for Christy and Daniel."

"They won't be around for much longer, though. They'll be off to uni in a few years, right?" Ethel asked.

The water was boiling, so Lora got up and made tea before she answered Ethel's question.

"They are both planning to go to uni across, but nothing is definite. I might think about moving in with them after the kids are both gone, if Martha is lonely, but not now," she said as she sat back down.

"You could move in with Milton and Bob," Ethel suggested. "They both like you better than me, anyway."

"That isn't true," Lora said quickly. "They both love you, but you know things weren't always good in the past."

"My husband didn't approve of Milton's choices," Ethel told Bessie. "He wanted Milton to get married and have children to carry on the family name."

"A lot of men of that generation felt that way," Bessie said.

"Yes, well, sadly, Henry never did reconcile with Milton. There were years when I didn't see my son at all, although he was always welcome at Aunt Lora's house."

"Cecil didn't approve, either, but I didn't listen to him," Lora said with a chuckle. "I wouldn't have been as fortunate if it had been one of our children, I'm afraid."

"What about Nathan and Marie?" Ethel asked. "April is gone now. They have an extra room."

"I would never impose on Nathan in that way," Lora replied. "He doesn't like his own family. I'm sure he isn't fond of any of us."

Ethel nodded. "I've never understood what Marie saw in him."

"I thought he was interesting," Bessie said. "We talked about Sherlock Holmes for a few minutes and he had some very interesting things to say."

"I suppose if you like to read, he might be appealing," Ethel conceded. "Marie doesn't read, though."

"Opposites attract," Lora said. "Have we eliminated everyone, then? There really isn't anyone with whom I can go and stay."

"Except me," Ethel sighed. "You know you'd be more than welcome," she said flatly.

Lora laughed. "You couldn't sound less enthusiastic if you were talking about having all of your teeth pulled. No worries, dear sister, I won't be coming to stay with you, either."

"I have a spare bedroom, if you simply wanted to get away for a few days," Bessie suggested. "Laxey Beach is lovely and quiet this time of year."

"I don't think that's a good idea," Ethel said. "I'd miss you if you were all the way up in Laxey."

"It's a ten-minute drive away," Lora laughed. "As I understand it, people in big cities often commute for an hour or more. We're incredibly spoiled on our tiny island."

"Still, I don't like the idea of you being in Laxey," Ethel said. She glanced at Bessie and then looked down at the table. "I'm not sure I'm happy about your new friend, either. It's nothing personal, but Bessie does have a reputation on the island."

"What sort of reputation?" Bessie asked.

Ethel shrugged. "You do seem to attract more than your fair share of murderers and murder victims, that's all. I'm sure it isn't anything you're doing, but it is worrying. I don't want anything to happen to my sister."

Bessie nibbled her way through a chocolate biscuit while she considered her reply. "I have had the misfortune to be involved in a few murder investigations in the past year or two," she said eventually. "As you say, none of what has happened has been my fault, of course. Nearly all of the victims have been strangers to me, anyway. Perhaps becoming my friend is one way to protect yourself."

Lora clapped her hands together. "What a wonderful idea," she exclaimed. "In light of all of the accidents that have been happening around here, I'm probably lucky that I met you when I did."

Ethel made a face. "I'm sorry, but knowing Bessie isn't going to protect you if another bird decides to nest in your fire vent."

"I have a carbon monoxide alarm for that," Lora laughed. "Maybe knowing Bessie will keep murderers away, though. No one will want to kill me if they think Bessie would be on the case."

"Sorry, dear sister, but I find it hard to believe that anyone would want to murder you. No offense, but you're just a rather ordinary old woman," Ethel said.

"I hope you're right," Lora replied. "I'm quite happy being ordinary if it means I never attract a murderer."

"Some of the cases I've been involved in have included victims that seemed unlikely," Bessie said. "People get murdered over things that seem stupid or frivolous to everyone else."

"But why would anyone want to murder my sister?" Ethel demanded.

"Many murders are to do with money," Bessie replied.

Ethel sat back in her chair. "Money," she repeated thoughtfully. "Charles and Ann are fine, of course. Maybe Carl and Doreen want her inheritance so they can pay Linda to get rid of Zack. I can't see

Martha and Tony killing you, not even for money. Martha's too soft."

"You say that as if it's an insult," Lora replied. "I'd like to think all of my children are too soft to murder someone."

Ethel shrugged. "I can't see my children killing you, not for money, anyway. You aren't leaving them anything, are you?"

"I've left them each a small amount, just a token, really," Lora replied. "I've also left April some of my jewellery. She's always admired a few of my nicer pieces. There's still plenty left over for the other women, anyway."

"Cecil loved buying Lora jewellery," Ethel told Bessie. "I was fortunate that Henry bought me a wedding band. That was the only jewellery he ever bought me, though. Lora was showered with gems for every birthday and Christmas while Cecil was alive."

"Not quite, but he did buy me a lot," Lora said. "Anyway, I'm not leaving your children enough that they'd want to kill me for it, although I'd like to think that they'd not want to kill me even if I were leaving them millions."

"My children have always loved you," Ethel said, sounding slightly bitter. "You were much more fun than I was. They loved going to Aunt Lora's to have pudding for dinner and watch telly until the wee small hours of the morning."

Lora laughed. "It was a treat for my children, too. We never did those things unless your children were here for a visit. We used to have great fun, although it made Cecil crazy."

"And Henry didn't approve, of course. He used to complain every time the children stayed with you because they'd come home exhausted, having eaten nothing but cake and biscuits and crisps."

"And then he wouldn't let them come again for weeks or months, until you'd finally convince him to let me have them again," Lora said with a smile.

"It was a nice break for me, sending the children here for the weekend. Henry worked most weekends, especially when the children were small. If they were here and Henry was at work, I could have the house to myself for a few hours. It was wonderful," Ethel said.

"And now it's lonely," Lora suggested.

"Not at all," Ethel replied. "I'm quite happy on my own."

"I've lived on my own since I was eighteen and I've never been lonely," Bessie said.

"It's just me, then," Lora chuckled. "I miss Cecil and I miss the kids. When the grandchildren were small, they used to stay over on weekends, but now that they're older, they're all too busy to spend time with me."

"They still come to your gatherings," Bessie pointed out.

"Even Linda," Ethel interjected. "Although I believe she thinks of them as her personal piggy bank, rather than as family gatherings."

"I enjoyed it very much," Bessie said. "I sometimes wonder how my life would have been different if I'd married and had children. Today gave me a chance to see what might have been, in a way."

Ethel looked at the clock and sighed. "I should be going," she said. "It's past time for my dinner, although I'm not at all hungry, not after everything I've eaten here."

"Oh, that reminds me," Lora exclaimed. "It's time for my evening tablets. I'll be right back." She got up from the table and left the kitchen. When she came back, she was carrying a small metal box. "Now I just have to remember which tablets to take," she sighed as she opened the box.

Bessie was surprised to see many different prescription bottles inside the box. "My goodness," she said. "Are you okay?"

"I'm mostly fine," Lora replied. "I just have to remember to take all of my tablets at the right time every day. There isn't anything seriously wrong, but my doctor is watching my blood pressure and my cholesterol and half a dozen other things that might be a problem if he doesn't keep a close eye on them."

She took several bottles out of the box and read each label in turn. "No, no, no, no, yes," she said happily, waving one of the bottles in the air. "This is an evening one. Now, is it the one with food or on an empty stomach?"

Ethel shook her head. "I don't have time to sit here and watch you work out your medications. I keep telling you to get one of those little plastic carriers that let you divide what you need by days of the week. Then you could be sure that you'd taken everything at the end of the day."

"But I need the bottles because they have the instructions on them," Lora told her. "If I just had a pile of different tablets, I'd never remember if the blue ones were for breakfast or bedtime."

She opened the bottle in her hand and tipped out a tablet. "With food," she read off the label. Grabbing another biscuit, she winked at Bessie. "This is a medicinal biscuit, so the calories don't count."

Ethel got to her feet. "I'm going to go home," she said. "Thank you for another lovely family gathering. It was mostly lovely, anyway."

"It was nice to meet you," Bessie said.

"Likewise," Ethel said with a nod at Bessie. "It seems odd that we've never met before, really, since we've both been living on the island for so many years, but even though it is a small island, I suppose it isn't as small as that."

"I often feel as if I don't know very many people at all," Bessie told her. "That's especially true when I get outside of Laxey. All of the new arrivals in the past few years have complicated things, as well. Even in Laxey, there are new people just about everywhere."

"I suppose we can't complain about progress," Ethel said. "Or rather, we can complain, but it does no good. I'll see myself out," she told Lora.

Lora stood up. "Don't be silly. I'll walk you out. I'll be right back," she told Bessie.

Bessie nodded and then picked up another biscuit. As she nibbled her way through it, she stared at the box on the other side of the table. If someone truly did want to kill Lora, surely it wouldn't take much effort on their part to tamper with her medications.

"That was exhausting," Lora said as she sank back down in her chair. "I know Ethel won't believe me if I tell her that I think someone is trying to kill me, so I didn't bother, but surely whoever tampered with the kettle was trying to electrocute me?"

Bessie got up and pulled the kettle out of the rubbish bin. She sat down at the table with it and studied it carefully. After a minute, she looked up at Lora and shrugged. "I know the kettle was fine when I used it. When I tidied the kitchen, I tucked it away in the corner, which is where Ethel found it when she went to make the tea. Of course, everyone at the gathering had access to the kitchen. It probably wouldn't have taken more than a few seconds for someone to do this damage, either accidentally or on purpose."

"I simply can't believe that it was an accident," Lora said tightly.

"I'm going to give this to John," Bessie said, waving the kettle in the air. "Maybe he can have some tests run on it to determine if the damage was deliberate."

"What if he discovers that it was deliberate? I don't want him questioning my family about it."

"Let's cross that bridge when we come to it. At this point, I very much doubt that he'll be able to find anything. I simply think it's worth trying."

Lora hesitated and then nodded. "I suppose it won't hurt for him to try. I just don't know what to think. Who would want to kill me?"

"There's no point in going back through all of the possibilities yet again," Bessie said firmly. "It's getting late and I still need to get back to Laxey."

"I can drive you home," Lora offered. "It's the least I can do after today."

"I'd appreciate that, but I'm happy to take a taxi if you're tired."

"I am tired, but I could do with getting out of the house for a short while. I think a stroll on Laxey Beach is just what I need."

"Where do you keep your box of medications?" Bessie asked, trying to sound casual.

"This?" Lora replied, looking surprised. "It sits on my bedside table in my bedroom. I take one of the tablets when I wake up each morning and another is just to help me sleep if I need it."

"What would happen if the box went missing?"

Lora stared at her for a minute. "I don't know," she said eventually. "I mean, the tablets aren't necessary to keep me alive, but they help keep me healthy. I don't think anything horrible would happen to me if I missed taking them for a few days, though."

"What if some of the tablets were switched around so you ended up taking the wrong ones at the wrong times?"

"I don't know. I don't think the consequences would be horrible, but some of them can upset your stomach if they aren't taken the right way. I suppose there could be an issue if I took two of something too close together or too far apart, as well. I really don't know."

Bessie nodded. "Until we work out what's going on, I suggest you try to find a very safe place to keep that box."

"It should be safe enough now that today's gathering is over, at least until the next one, which probably won't be until Christmas week. I hope we've managed to stop the accidents from happening before Christmas."

"Do you have any way to check the tablets now?"

Lora frowned. "You mean someone might have tampered with them today."

"I don't know. The thought just occurred to me, that's all."

Lora sighed and then looked down at the box. "I probably should check them, shouldn't I?"

She read the label on the first bottle. "These should be little red tablets," she said before she opened the top and poured the contents into a small bowl. Bessie was relieved to see the small pile of red tablets that had come out.

Ten minutes later, Lora had checked every bottle, and they all seemed right. "I never thought about my medications, but now that you've mentioned it, I'm going to be paranoid," she said as she put all of the bottles back into the box.

"You shouldn't have to worry, not if you aren't having another gathering for a while."

"Except just about everyone who was here today has a key to my house," Lora sighed.

"Even the grandchildren and the neighbours?"

"The grandchildren each received his or her own key as a tenth birthday gift. It's sort of a strange family tradition now, but it started when Linda turned ten. Right around her birthday, Doreen had to have some surgery, so Linda came and stayed with me for a few weeks. We wanted to make it seem like a special treat, and tried to downplay the significance of the surgery, so we made a big deal out of giving her the key to my house and making her my extra-special guest." Lora shook her head. "It made sense at the time, anyway."

"And you did the same with the other two?"

"We were rather too successful, I believe," Lora chuckled. "Linda had a wonderful time while she was here, and she filled Christy and Daniel's heads with stories of late-night movies and endless supplies of chocolate. By the time Christy was nine, she was already planning for her fortnight stay with me. Actually, I had April to stay when she was ten, too, now that I think about it. Ethel wasn't going to do anything special for April's birthday, so I stepped in and had her stay here."

"Maybe I should have just asked who doesn't have a key," Bessie said.

"I think everyone who was here today has a key, except for you," Lora replied after a moment's thought. "We gave Percy and Elaine a spare key when we first bought the house. The neighbours on the other side had one as well, and they never gave it back to us when they moved. I suspect it's in a drawer somewhere in Brian and Jill's house. They may not even know they have it."

"So find somewhere safe to store your medicine box," Bessie repeated her earlier advice.

"I'm afraid if I hide it, I'll forget to take my tablets," Lora sighed. "I'm going to have to think about this later. For now, I need to get you home, though."

"I can get a taxi."

"No, no, I can take you home. I think I'll take the box with us, though. Give me a minute to get ready."

Bessie washed up the tea things while she waited.

"My goodness, you didn't have to do that," Lora exclaimed when she walked back into the kitchen. "I didn't invite you so that you could do my housework for me."

"I didn't have anything else to do while I was waiting. Ready?"

Lora nodded. She picked up her box and dropped it into a large carrier bag. "Let's go."

Bessie collected her handbag and the kettle and followed Lora out of the house. The drive to Laxey didn't take long.

"Is it okay if I leave my car here while I take a walk on the beach?" Lora asked Bessie as she parked next to Bessie's cottage.

"Of course. I don't have a car and I'm not expecting any visitors tonight."

They climbed out of the car and Bessie headed for her door.

"Would you like to walk with me?" Lora asked before Bessie had gone far.

While Bessie was eager to walk on the beach, feeling as if she'd been stuck indoors for most of the day, she didn't feel up to spending any more time with Lora at the moment. "I have a few things to do, actually, sorry," she replied, turning around to look at the other woman.

Lora looked disappointed. "Let me know what the police think about my kettle, then. Maybe you could ring me tomorrow?"

"I'll do that, although I don't expect to have any answers about the kettle that quickly."

"That's fine. I just, I don't know, want to keep in touch. You're the only person I've really talked to about what's been going on. If something does happen to me, you might be the only person who doesn't think my death was just an accident."

"Nothing is going to happen to you," Bessie said with more confidence than she felt. "I'll talk to John again and we'll work something out. Where did you take your car to get the petrol tank repaired?"

Lora gave her the name of the garage she'd used. "This afternoon, before you arrived, I'd convinced myself that I was imaging things. If it weren't for the kettle, I might have kept believing it, too."

"I'll tell John all about today and then he can decide what to do next. I believe he'll turn everything over to Pete Corkill, as he works in Douglas. Don't be surprised if Pete turns up on your doorstep."

"Maybe he could ring me and we could meet somewhere else. I'm

DIANA XARISSA

not sure I want the police knocking on my door. I don't want to worry the neighbours."

"Maybe it would warn them off, if one of them is behind the attacks."

"Maybe, but more likely they would assume that Linda has been arrested or some such thing. I'd rather keep the police as far away as possible."

"I'll tell John, but Pete might want to look at your gas fire, and maybe the rest of the house as well."

"I wish I had never asked Ethel to make tea," Lora sighed. "If she hadn't noticed the kettle, I could at least have spent tonight thinking that everything was okay."

"It's lucky she did notice. You might have missed the damage when you went to make tea tomorrow morning."

"And if I had spotted it, I probably would have rung you in hysterics. This was probably better."

"Enjoy your walk," Bessie told her as she turned around again. If Lora tried speaking to her again, she thought she might just ignore the woman. Once she was safely inside Treoghe Bwaane, she locked the door and then leaned against it. Perhaps if she'd married and had children, she would have become accustomed to being around large groups of people for hours on end. As it was, however, she found gatherings like the one at Lora's exhausting both physically and emotionally.

"And you still aren't done for the night," she muttered to herself as she crossed the kitchen. She still needed to ring John.

The light on her answering machine was blinking repeatedly. She sighed as she pressed the message button.

"Bessie? It's Hazel. What were you doing at Lora White's house today? I didn't know you knew Lora."

Three more messages, all almost exactly the same, followed. News travelled fast on the small island. Feeling almost as if she were being watched, Bessie paced around her kitchen for several minutes. Eventually she decided not to ring anyone back. People were just being nosy and she didn't have to satisfy their curiosity. When she reached for the phone, it was to ring John.

"I'll send someone over to collect the kettle," he told her when she was done telling him everything about her day. "Expect someone in the next half hour or so."

"Okay."

"I'd like to talk through the whole thing with you again, maybe including Pete this time. Are you available tomorrow evening?"

"Come for dinner. I can make spaghetti, with garlic bread and salad," Bessie offered.

"I'll bring a pudding. I may invite Doona and Hugh, as well, if you don't mind."

"Of course I don't mind. I hope Doona is feeling better."

"She was almost back to normal when I saw her this afternoon. That may be an exaggeration, actually, but she was pretty poorly last week. Today she said she's actually looking forward to living."

Bessie chuckled. "The poor girl. I should have taken her some chicken soup."

"I've been keeping her fed, and I keep bringing her different medications from the chemist, as well. Thus far she hasn't found anything that truly makes a difference, but at least she feels as if she's doing something. She didn't want you to catch anything, but she was pretty sure I'd already been exposed to the germs since they probably came from my kids."

"I'll see you all tomorrow, then," Bessie said with a laugh. She put the phone down and then found a large bag for the kettle. There wouldn't be any point in the police trying to get fingerprints from it, as any on there could easily be explained away, but Bessie still felt it was best if the constable who took it away didn't touch it.

While she waited, she found the box of books she'd recently received from the bookshop in Ramsey. She had a list of favourite authors on file with them and they sent her any new books that arrived by those authors. This saved her from making too many trips into Ramsey for books.

The book on top was a new one in one of her favourite cosy mystery series. Bessie grinned as she read the blurb on the back. It always amazed her how the heroine kept finding herself caught up in the middle of murder investigations. She settled into her chair and opened the book. Before she could read the first paragraph, she frowned. What was happening in her life was very different, she told herself. There weren't any parallels between the fictional world and her own very real one.

She was still trying to convince herself of that when someone knocked on her door.

CHAPTER 8

"*H*ugh, I didn't realise you were working nights," Bessie said as she opened the door to the young constable.

"I'm not exactly working tonight, but John asked me to pop over and grab a kettle from you."

"It was kind of you to agree."

Hugh flushed. "I get a bit of overtime pay. We need every penny, really, even though all of our friends and family members were incredibly generous at the shower."

"That baby will have an abundance of love, which is much more important than money," Bessie told him. "Come and have a cuppa, if you have time."

Hugh hesitated and then nodded. "I can spare a few minutes. Grace is at her mother's tonight. She's actually sleeping there."

"Oh?" Bessie said, not wanting to ask any rude questions, but feeling concerned.

"I'm on call tonight, which is why I'm here," Hugh explained. "Grace would prefer not to be home alone, not with the baby due in less than a month. She's worried about going into labour and not having any help."

"That makes sense."

"Her mother has been coming and staying at our house sometimes, but Grace thought it would be better if she went and stayed with her mother this time. She said something about really looking forward to sleeping in her childhood bed again." Hugh shrugged. "I'm not sure why, but maybe it was because I complain when she tosses and turns all the time. I know she doesn't mean to keep me awake, but she does."

Bessie filled the kettle and then piled biscuits onto a plate while she thought about all of the things she wanted to say to Hugh.

"Maybe she wanted to sleep in her old bed so that she could feel as if she were a child again," she suggested as she put the biscuits on the table. "I'm sure that she's more than a little worried about becoming a mother herself."

"She doesn't act worried," Hugh said around a mouthful of biscuit. When Bessie frowned, he flushed and then swallowed before he spoke again. "She seems to be taking it all in her stride. I'm the one who's worried all the time."

"I suspect she's just as worried as you are, but she's trying to act otherwise."

Hugh seemed to give the idea some thought. When the kettle boiled and snapped off, he jumped.

"You could be right," he told Bessie as she got up to make the tea. "She's said one or two things about being nervous about different things, but I haven't really been listening, I suppose."

"I'm sure it's difficult. We all know that you and Grace are going to be brilliant parents, but it's only natural for you to be concerned about the new responsibilities the baby will bring."

"I think I'm mostly worried about the money he or she will cost."

"Which will make Grace feel as if she needs to go back to work right away."

"I don't want her to do that. We both want her home with the baby until he or she is old enough for nursery. We've gone over the budget a dozen times and we should be able to afford for her to stay home until Baby is two if we're frugal."

"Which you both are."

"I'm getting better. Grace is much better than I am, though. I don't believe I've thanked you nearly enough for the baby shower, by the way. We had several hundred pounds budgeted for all of the things that we were given, which means we can now tuck that money into our savings account instead."

"Excellent. I'm glad Mary and I were able to help."

"You've both done so much for Grace and me and now Baby Watterson. I thought the honeymoon you arranged and funded for us was the best thing ever, but the baby shower meant so much." He stopped and then cleared his throat. Bessie hid a smile as he took a sip of tea and then ate a biscuit.

"What else do you need before Baby arrives, then?" Bessie changed the subject.

"Grace wants a rocking chair for the nursery. We have the money for it, but we're taking our time looking around at the various options. Grace wants something traditional that will last through our children and our grandchildren, if possible."

"I have just the thing upstairs," Bessie said. "You and Grace are welcome to it, if you want it. It actually came with the house, and I've never been fond of it."

Hugh looked surprised and then shook his head. "You can't keep giving us things. You've already been too kind."

"Come and see the chair before you accuse me of kindness," Bessie laughed. "You may dislike it as much as I do."

Hugh followed Bessie up the stairs and into one of her spare bedrooms. While she had a bedroom that she used as a guest room, this one was more of a catch-all, mostly for books, although there were a few pieces of furniture crammed into the small space as well.

"Goodness, I'd quite forgotten that it was covered in books," Bessie said from the doorway. "They'll have to go somewhere else if you want the chair."

Hugh crossed over to the wooden chair. It was plain, with a large blue cushion over the seat. Stacks of books had squashed the cushion fairly flat.

"The cushion is only tied on the back," Bessie told him. "You should be able to find a replacement, if you like the chair."

Hugh carefully removed the piles of books, stacking them neatly on the floor in the corner. After giving the cushion a quick plump, he sat down gingerly. "It's surprisingly comfortable," he said as he rocked back and forth slowly.

"Take it home and see what Grace thinks," Bessie suggested. "If she doesn't like it, take it to a charity shop. I truly don't want it back."

"If Grace does like it, you must let me pay for it," Hugh said.

"I'll take ten pounds for it," Bessie told him. "That will cover the cost of the bookshelf that I bought last week at one of the charity shops in Ramsey. They're going to deliver it tomorrow morning and it will fit nicely into the space that chair is occupying."

Hugh hesitated and then sighed. "It's worth more than ten pounds," he said.

"A charity shop wouldn't ask much more than ten pounds for it," Bessie replied. "Let's wait and argue after you've shown it to Grace, though. She may hate it."

"She may, but I think it's exactly what she's been wanting," Hugh told her. "It's just like the one her mother has, you see. Her mother offered to let Grace have hers, but Grace wants her mother to be able to rock her grandbaby in it at home, so she wouldn't take it. We've been all over the island twice, trying to find something just like it, but no one seems to make chairs like this anymore."

"As I said, it came with the cottage. It's very old, but it seems to have been well made."

"It feels sturdy enough, even for me," Hugh laughed.

He stood up and then carefully lifted the chair. "It isn't as heavy as it looks," he said happily. "I can probably manage it on my own."

Bessie walked behind him, trying to make helpful suggestions as he negotiated his way down the steep and narrow stairs. She and Hugh were both relieved when they finally reached the ground floor.

"It won't be nearly as much trouble getting it up to the nursery," Hugh laughed. "Our stairs are a good deal more accommodating."

"The cushion isn't as old as the chair," Bessie told him after he'd loaded the chair into the back of his car. "I believe I bought that about four years ago, when I decided I was going to force myself to learn to like the chair. That lasted about a fortnight before I banished it to the spare room again."

"Grace may want to put a different cushion on it, to match the nursery, but I'll let her decide about that. What am I taking to John?"

Bessie handed him the bag with the kettle. "Has he told you anything about this?" she asked.

"Nothing. He just told me to come and collect this and that we're meeting tomorrow night to discuss a case that isn't a case."

"That's one way of putting it," Bessie grinned. "If you have time, I'll tell you the story now. Otherwise, we can talk tomorrow night."

Hugh glanced at the clock and then shook his head. "I need to get this to John before it gets too late. I don't want to wake his kids, not on a school night."

"So I'll see you tomorrow, then," Bessie said as she walked the man to the door.

In the doorway, he gave her a huge hug. "I can't believe I let you talk me into taking that chair," he sighed. "Grace will be furious, delighted but furious."

"I genuinely don't need it or want it," Bessie said. "I should go through the rest of the house and clear out a few more things. Whoever inherits my cottage is going to have quite a job clearing it out."

"That isn't going to be a problem for many years to come," Hugh said firmly.

Bessie touched his arm. "You're going to be a wonderful father," she said, staring into his eyes. "Grace is going to be fabulous as well. Stop worrying so much about money and material things and remember that the baby will have two parents who love him or her and one another. That's what he or she needs most. I understand the baby will also be riding around town in a particularly smart pushchair."

Hugh laughed. "Thanks to you. We spent half an hour last night trying to work out how to open and close that pushchair. I pinched my fingers so many times that Grace left the room. She didn't want Baby hearing some of the phrases that were coming out of my mouth."

Bessie grinned. "Just wait until those phrases start coming out of Baby's mouth."

"And I'm sure they will," Hugh sighed. "It's difficult, sometimes, with what I do. I see the kids who get themselves into trouble and I can't help but worry about my own child." He shook his head. "John's going to be furious with me if I don't get over there soon. Thank you for the tea and biscuits, and thank you for the rocking chair." He reached into his pocket and pulled out his wallet. "I may as well give you this now. I know Grace will want to keep the chair."

He handed Bessie a ten-pound note and then quickly walked to his car. Bessie was pleased to see that Lora's car was no longer parked outside the cottage. Too bad it was too late to take a walk on the beach, she thought as she shut the door behind Hugh.

For years she'd walked on the beach whenever she'd felt the urge, regardless of the time of day. After her cottage had been broken into recently, however, she'd become more cautious about leaving the cottage empty after dark. Now she stood in the kitchen and stared at the starry sky through the window.

"I just can't stay indoors," she said eventually. Rather than walk, she let herself out the cottage's back door and settled on the large rock on the beach behind her home. If anyone approached the cottage, she'd spot them, she told herself as she took several deep breaths. Watching the waves by moonlight helped to clear her head. When she went back inside an hour later, she felt refreshed but ready to sleep.

John rang her mid-morning the next day.

"I've had a good look at the kettle. I can't say anything conclusive because of the age of the device. I'm sending it to an expert in the UK who may be able to discover more, but at this point, I simply don't know."

"I'll let Lora know," Bessie said. "She seems to be wavering between thinking she's overreacting and thinking she's going to be killed tomorrow. I promised that I'd ring her today."

"Pete is talking to the garage and the fire people today. He'll give us a full report over dinner tonight."

"Or as much of one as he can."

"This isn't an official police investigation," John pointed out. "Right now, we're just talking to a few people to help alleviate Mrs. White's concerns."

"Let's hope that's all this ever ends up being."

"Yes, let's."

Bessie rang Lora immediately, wanting to get that chore over with as quickly as possible.

"Bessie, how kind of you to ring," Lora said in a bright voice when she answered.

"I just wanted to thank you again for yesterday," Bessie began.

"I'm so pleased that you enjoyed our little family gathering. You'll be more than welcome at the next one, of course. It probably won't be until Christmas week, but I'm not planning that far ahead at the moment."

"No, well, do let me know when you make your plans. I can't promise I'll be able to attend, but I'll certainly try," Bessie said, feeling as if the fib was justified. "John looked over the kettle, but couldn't tell anything. He's sent it to a crime lab in the UK."

"How nice," Lora replied.

"Is there someone there with you?" Bessie asked, feeling confused by the woman's reply.

"Martha and Tony just popped in for a short visit. Maybe we could finish this conversation later?"

"Of course. Ring me when you have a chance."

"I'll do that."

Bessie put the phone down and then frowned at it. She should have realised that Lora wasn't acting naturally from the first words of the conversation. When they'd spoken yesterday, Lora had suggested that she didn't expect to see her family again until the next gathering. Why were Martha and Tony at her house this morning? After pacing around the kitchen for several minutes without being able to reach any conclusions, Bessie went and found her book from the previous evening.

By the end of the second chapter, the heroine had found two dead bodies and stumbled across a complicated drug-smuggling operation across international borders. Bessie smiled. She was right. These books were nothing like her life.

She dragged herself away from the book at midday to make herself some lunch. As she'd promised to cook that evening, she kept lunch light. She'd been slender her entire life, but sometimes when she was involved in an investigation with John, her clothes began to feel a bit tight. No doubt the pudding that John was bringing tonight would be both irresistible and fattening.

The afternoon passed quickly as the book's heroine talked to suspects, interviewed witnesses, and generally made a nuisance of herself with the police. She was confronting the killer when Bessie's phone rang.

"I'm sorry about earlier," Lora said when Bessie answered. "Martha and Tony surprised me and I was, well, upset when you rang."

"I hope everything is okay."

"It isn't, really."

Bessie waited for the woman to elaborate. Eventually she lost patience. "Do you want to talk about it or should we focus on other things?"

"I'm sorry," Lora said. Bessie could tell that she had been crying. "Ethel rang Martha last night and suggested that I need looking after. It seems she's been keeping track of all the things that have been happening and she thinks that they indicate that I'm no longer capable of looking after myself."

"Oh, dear."

"She did a good job persuading Martha of the same thing," Lora added. "Martha wants me to sell my house and move somewhere where I can be looked after."

"And you don't want to do that."

"This is my home. I don't want to leave it. I didn't realise quite how much I love it here until Martha started talking about different options. I don't want a flat in a building with neighbours all around me. The whole idea makes me feel claustrophobic."

"I understand that."

"I didn't know what else to do, so I told Martha and Tony that I think someone is trying to kill me."

"What did they say to that?"

"They didn't say much, but I could tell they thought I was either making things up out of desperation or that I was losing my grip on reality. Either way, they don't agree that the things that have been happening are anything other than accidents."

"Pete is investigating very discreetly. I'll see what he has to say tonight. John is sending the kettle across to be examined by a specialist there."

"I'm sorry, Bessie. Maybe Martha is right. Maybe I'm not fit to be left on my own any longer. Maybe I should look at the brochures that Martha brought."

"Have a look, by all means," Bessie replied. "Maybe even go and visit a few places. It can't hurt to see what your options are. Just don't agree to anything, not until the police have investigated the things that have been happening to you."

"Maybe I'll find somewhere that I actually like. I mean, it would be nice not to have to worry about looking after the house and the garden any longer. I just don't want to live in a flat with people all around me."

"I'll ring you tomorrow and let you know what Pete and John have discovered. It may be a few days before they manage to reach any conclusions, though. In the meantime, be careful."

Lora sighed. "I feel as if I'm just waiting for the next bad thing to happen. Maybe whoever is behind all of this isn't trying to kill me. Maybe they just want to slowly drive me insane. I have to say, if that's their plan, they're succeeding."

"You can't let them win," Bessie said firmly.

"I was thinking of going away for a few days. Cecil's sister lives in Birmingham. I haven't seen her in ten years or more. Maybe I could go and stay with her for a week or two, just to get away."

"We all need a holiday now and again."

"I really can't stand the woman, though," Lora sighed. "She never liked me and she never approved of my marrying her brother. She spent our entire married life muttering darkly about how it would never last. She's had six husbands, so I suppose she knows something about marriages not lasting, but Cecil and I were together for thirty-odd years. It wasn't all smooth sailing, but we stuck it out."

"Maybe you should visit a different friend," Bessie said dryly.

Lora chuckled. "The thing is, Cecilia has a huge house in the country with staff and everything. It would be like staying at a luxury resort, really, aside from having to have a few meals with Cecilia. Knowing her, she'd make sure she was too busy to spend much time with me, though." She sighed. "I don't know what to do. There's a little bit of me that's afraid that Ethel and Martha are right, too."

"I know I only met you a few days ago, but for what it's worth, I don't think you're incapable of looking after yourself. In your place, I'd be just as concerned about the number of odd incidents that have happened in such close proximity. I'd ring the police and have them investigate, but I can understand why you're less willing to do that."

"I don't mind them investigating. I just don't want them questioning my family. I don't want anyone to think that I suspect him or her of trying to murder me."

"But right now you do suspect them all," Bessie pointed out.

"But they don't know that," Lora retorted. "I know, I know, now I do sound crazy. I'm sorry. I need to go and lose myself in a good book or watch some mindless television and try not to think about anything for a few hours. The problem is, every time I reach into a drawer or turn on a light switch, I'm afraid it's been booby-trapped."

"Go and stay in a hotel for a few days," Bessie suggested. "Go across or just go to Ramsey or somewhere else on the island. Tell your family that you need to get away for a few days. You shouldn't have to make excuses, really."

"Cecil passed away twenty years ago this week. Martha suggested that I'm probably not myself because of the anniversary. It was funny, because I hadn't really noticed. Oh, I'll never forget the day he died, but I hadn't counted the years, not in a long time. Anyway, maybe I should tell everyone I'm going away to spend the anniversary on my own."

"I highly recommend the Seaview in Ramsey," Bessie told her. "If you ring, ask for Jasper Coventry and tell him that I suggested the hotel."

"I may just do that," Lora said.

"Let me know if you do. I need to know how to find you if John or Pete discovers anything."

"I'll ring you tomorrow," Lora promised. "Thank you for everything."

Bessie put the phone down and picked up her book. That was another difference between herself and the fictional heroine, she thought as she found her place again. She'd tried confronting a killer once and had done everything she could to avoid doing so again. She'd found herself listening to more than one confession since then, but not through design.

Half an hour later, after the heroine had been held at gunpoint for six pages, the police detective had burst through the door to save her. Bessie frowned as the heroine and the detective shared a kiss. The heroine might have forgiven the man for suspecting her of murder and doubting every word she said, but Bessie wasn't so easily swayed by his rugged good looks or his bulging biceps. "You can do better," she told the heroine as she shut the book and dropped it onto the table next to her.

When she looked at the clock, she was surprised to see that it was nearly time for her to start doing some cooking. Her guests were due in less than a hour. She only had time for a ten-minute stroll along the beach before she needed to be in the kitchen.

"I don't want to hug you," Doona said when Bessie opened the door to her a short while later. "I'm not contagious any longer, or so the doctor says, but he could be wrong."

Bessie laughed. "I haven't seen you in ages. I'm prepared to trust the doctor on this one." She pulled her closest friend into a hug. "Come in and tell me how you are."

From what she could see, Doona didn't look as bad as Bessie had feared. She was wearing her glasses rather than her brightly coloured contact lenses, but her brown, highlighted bob was perfectly in place and she'd taken the time to apply some makeup.

"I'm doing okay, I think. I haven't had a cold this bad in years, but the doctor assured me that it was simply a cold and not some sort of deadly flu or double pneumonia with extra virulent germs. I suspect I picked up something from one of the children. They're exposed to everything at school."

Bessie nodded. "I'm sure you're right. I was going to try to come and visit you once or twice, but John assured me that he was looking after you."

Doona blushed bright red. "He was terrific. I'm sure he thinks the kids gave me the cold, too. That's why he was so, um, attentive. He brought me food every day, and he brought me books and movies and all sorts of things."

"He's a good man."

"Yes, he is at that," Doona sighed.

"Why the sigh?"

Doona shrugged and then sat down at Bessie's table. "Do you think he'll ever get over Sue?" she asked in a low voice.

"I think he's well on the way to recovering from her. They've been divorced for a while now and she's married to someone else."

"Yes, but they have children together. They'll always have a connection that nothing can break."

"That doesn't mean that John can't find love again."

"I hope not, for his sake, I mean." She added the last bit quickly.

"You two could be good together," Bessie said. "If you're prepared to take on the children."

Doona sighed again. "That's the worst part. If it were just John, I would probably have already suggested that we try being more than friends. If it didn't work out, I could always find a new job if I didn't want to work with him anymore, but the children are a huge complication."

"And a huge blessing."

"There is that," Doona admitted. "I really love them both a lot.

They're great kids. I can't even bring myself to hate Sue, even though I want to, because she's their mother and they're terrific."

"You might feel differently if you and John did get involved."

"About Sue or about the kids?"

"Yes."

Doona chuckled. "I'm finding Sue less and less likeable every day that she stays in Africa. Not that I want her back, exactly, but I can see what her absence is doing to the children. They miss her and they feel abandoned. I don't blame them. They have been abandoned in a way."

"John said that she feels needed in Africa."

"She's needed here," Doona replied. "Amy needs her mother in a million different ways. Being a teenaged girl today is totally different to how it was in my day. I'm doing my best, but I'm still an outsider. And Thomas? Thomas needs his mother almost more than Amy does. John is wonderful with both of them, but sometimes teenaged boys need hugs and reassurances from their mums and John can't give him that. Again, I'm trying to help, but again, I'm an outsider."

Bessie switched on the kettle. "Maybe you'd be better off keeping John as a friend, then."

Doona nodded. "I'm sure that would be the easiest thing to do, anyway. Getting involved with him also means getting involved with the children, and breaking up with him would also impact them. I'm not sure I'm ready to break their hearts, not after everything that they've been through."

"And there's little chance that you and John would be able to make things work long term. Not with three divorces between you," Bessie said, watching Doona's face closely.

Doona winced. "That's harsh, but maybe true. I just don't know. As I said, if it were just John, I wouldn't hesitate. I like him a lot, but I don't know if that's enough."

"If you aren't sure, you're probably better off keeping your distance," Bessie suggested.

"You're probably right," Doona sighed. "I just keep thinking about how much fun we all have together. John is funny and smart and he's an amazing father. I feel so lucky to have had a chance to be a part of his family, if only for a short time."

Bessie smiled to herself as she made tea. Doona was finally starting to argue back. "What have you enjoyed the most about it?" she asked.

"The nothing evenings," Doona said after a sip of tea. "When I go to John's and we all sit around and watch telly and eat popcorn or play board games and cards. Those evenings aren't anything special, but they feel special to me. I'm going to miss them."

"But think about what you'll be gaining," Bessie suggested, playing devil's advocate yet again. "You'll be free to go out and have nice dinners and drinks with any man you meet. You'll be able to take holidays without having to worry about the children or John's work schedule. You won't have to worry about GCSE results or A levels or whether the children will get into a good university or not."

"Stop," Doona said with tears streaming down her cheeks. "I know what you're doing and you can just stop. I already know that I don't want to have dinner with random men or holiday without the children. I'm stupid crazy about John and I love his kids almost as much as if they were my own. Whatever happens, I'm going to worry about their GCSE results and their A levels and every little thing that happens to them. If I let myself, I could love them more, although I'm not sure I could be any more crazy about John. "

Bessie patted her arm. "I'm sure you'll get over him," she said.

Doona stared at her and then shook her head. "You win," she said softly. "One of these days, soon, I'm going to tell John how I feel."

"Good for you," Bessie said. "For what it's worth, I've thought you were perfect for one another since the day I met John."

Doona just looked at her. "He was married to Sue then."

"Yes, I was disappointed when I learned that, but it was quickly obvious that the marriage was failing. I think you were both smart to take things slowly, but maybe it's time to have a discussion about how each of you feels."

"What if he doesn't feel the same way?"

"He spent the last fortnight taking care of you when you were sick. If nothing else, he cares deeply for you as a friend. I'm not suggesting you ask him to marry you, I'm just suggesting you test the waters a little bit."

"You're right, of course, but I think I may wait until I'm feeling a bit better before I do anything. If he does want to, well, test the waters, I'd rather find out when I'm definitely not contagious anymore."

Bessie laughed. "That first kiss will tell you a lot."

"No doubt," Doona said, blushing.

A knock on the door ended the conversation. Bessie let Hugh into the cottage. He handed her a large bakery box.

"John was held up at the office, so he had me pick up the cake. He'll be here soon."

"Who's watching the children?" Doona asked.

"They both insisted that they're quite capable of looking after themselves," Hugh countered. "That was when I dropped Grace off on my way here. I agreed with them and asked them to watch Grace. She's anxious about staying on her own at the moment."

"I don't blame her. She's going to have a baby any day now," Doona laughed.

Bessie added the pasta to the boiling water. A moment later, John knocked on the door.

"Everything smells wonderful," he said. "Pete isn't coming until after dinner. Apparently his lovely wife was making something special tonight and he didn't want to miss it."

Bessie grinned. Pete and Helen had met during a murder investigation in which Bessie had been involved. Pete had just gone through a difficult divorce and wasn't looking for a new partner. Helen had fallen for the grumpy man in spite of his efforts to push her away. Bessie and John had been the witnesses at their recent wedding and it sounded as if the couple were still enjoying the honeymoon phase of their new life together.

"Maybe we should eat, then," Hugh said, making everyone laugh at the always hungry constable.

CHAPTER 9

"We should probably wait to cut the cake until after Pete arrives," Doona said a short while later.

"Maybe we should get our pieces now to save time when he gets here," Hugh suggested.

Bessie laughed. "I'm sure Pete won't mind if we cut the cake without him. I was hoping you might be full after two helpings of spaghetti, though," she told Hugh.

He flushed. "Grace's pregnancy has made me extra hungry, too," he said sheepishly. "Although she's not so hungry these days, because she's pretty uncomfortable most of the time. Baby Watterson is getting bigger really quickly and Grace reckons he or she is squashing her stomach."

"It won't hurt you to put on a few pounds now," John said. "Once the baby arrives, you'll miss a few meals here and there."

"And Grace won't be up to cooking, so make sure you're ready to take over that job," Doona added.

Hugh nodded. "We've been cooking together a lot lately. She's taught me how to make all of our favourite things so that I can make them for us once the baby arrives. Her mother will probably stay with us for a while, though, and she's already insisting that she'll do all of the cooking and cleaning so we can focus on the baby."

"After that, she can come and stay with me for a few weeks," Doona offered. "I don't have a baby to look after, but I'd love to have someone do my cooking and cleaning."

"Surely you can afford to hire someone now," John suggested.

Doona flushed. "I probably could," she said softly. "It isn't something I've ever really considered, though."

"Cake," Bessie said loudly. She cut slices for everyone, passing around plates. "Should I cut one for Pete?" she asked.

The words were barely out of her mouth when he knocked on the door. "I hope I'm not too late," he said after he'd hugged Bessie and greeted the others.

"Not at all. Would you like a slice of cake?"

Pete looked at the chocolate layer cake and nodded. "I shouldn't, as Helen made us a lovely dinner tonight, but we're both trying to eat more healthily, so pudding was an apple. That cake is too much to resist."

Bessie put his plate on the table while Hugh was moving a chair from the dining room into the kitchen for him.

Pete sat down and picked up his fork. "Did I miss anything?"

"We haven't talked about the case at all yet," John replied. "We thought it was best to wait for you."

"It isn't even a case," Bessie interjected. "I'm not sure what to call it."

"I don't think it much matters what we call it," John said. "Hugh and Doona haven't heard any of the details yet, so let me summarise things before we begin."

Bessie ate her cake slowly while John told the others about Lora and her recent misfortunes. When he was done, she repeated everything she could remember happening at Lora's house when she'd been there. She also reported everything that had happened since.

"Have you learned anything more about the kettle?" Bessie asked John when she was done.

"At first glance, there are no obvious signs of deliberate tampering," John replied. "That's what the technician at the lab said, anyway. He's going to take a closer look tomorrow, but he wasn't optimistic. His tentative conclusion is that it is possible the damage was deliberate, but equally possible that it was accidental, especially considering the age of the device."

Bessie sighed. She wanted to believe Lora and to find proof for the woman that she wasn't imagining things.

"I'm afraid I can't do much better," Pete said. "The technician at the garage where Lora had her car towed said that he never even considered that the petrol tank puncture was anything other than an accident. He's been repairing cars for twenty-seven years and he felt that Lora's puncture wasn't any different to any of the others that he's repaired in that time."

"So that one was almost definitely simply an accident," Bessie sighed.

"The man who sorted the gas fire said much the same thing, but he did admit that it was possible that the damage was deliberate. It wasn't so much damage as a buildup of material in the vent. While he nearly always assumes it was simply nesting birds, he did agree that it would be relatively easy for a person to cause the damage."

"And we've no way to investigate the other incidents," Bessie said. "I did take a look at the bathtub. If someone had spotted the bath oil and decided to take a closer look, he or she probably would have had to climb into the tub to reach it. I couldn't reach the shelf behind the tub any other way, anyway."

"I can picture it," Doona said. "Someone uses the loo and then spots the bath oil. Wondering what it smells like the person slips off his or her shoes and climbs into the tub. No point in climbing back out, not if you just want to smell the stuff."

"Not even if you decide you want to use a bit of it," Bessie suggested. "Linda seemed the type who would decide to help herself to her grandmother's bath oil if her hands felt dry or some such thing."

Doona nodded. "So whoever it is opens the bottle, spills a ton of it and then puts the bottle back and climbs out of the tub. Cleaning up the spill probably didn't even occur to him or her."

"And if Lora had showered before her next bath, depending on how long it takes her water to warm up, the oil might have all washed away before she got into the shower. She might never have noticed," Hugh suggested.

"She did notice that the almost new bottle was half-empty, but someone using your bath oil isn't the same as someone trying to kill you," Bessie replied.

"The issue here isn't whether the things that happened might have been accidents or not," John said. "What's odd is the pattern that's developing. Accidents happen every day, but not usually this many to one person in such a short space of time. Even if we eliminate one or two as genuine accidents, there are still several incidents that are worrying."

"I also had a look at the cupboard over the refrigerator," Bessie said. "The knives aren't still being kept in there, but I can tell you that it's a deep cupboard that's just a bit too high to reach from the ground, at least for me."

"Is Lora taller than you?" Doona asked.

"Yes, by a few inches," Bessie told her. "I used a step to get into the cupboard, but if I were Lora's height, I might have been tempted to simply stretch. Getting the step out was more hassle than I'd probably have bothered with, especially if it were my home and I knew what was in the cupboard."

"I'd like to go and talk to her, preferably at home," Pete said. "It might be helpful for me to have a walk through her house. I may be able to spot other potential issues. I'd also like to check that cupboard and take a look at the knives."

"Lora doesn't want the police visiting her at home. She's worried about what the neighbours will think, and also that word will get back to her family."

Pete nodded. "I understand, especially if some members of the family are suggesting she might not be capable of living on her own any longer, but it does rather tie my hands."

"Bessie, you're the only one who knows Lora," Doona said. "Is it possible that she does need looking after now?"

Taking another drink of her tea gave Bessie time to think. "When I first met her, I absolutely believed her that her life was in danger. The more I get to know her, the more I wonder, though. She seems to be as uncertain as I am, really. I'm sure she doesn't want to believe that anyone would want her dead, of course."

"Maybe I should arrange to meet her somewhere other than her home," Pete said. "Just having a chat with her might tell me enough."

"There is another possibility," Hugh said. "I've been doing a lot of reading about different types of criminals. Is it possible that she's behind the accidents herself? Might she be seeking attention?"

"Attention from whom?" Bessie questioned. "As far as I can tell, I'm the only person she's told about any of this. She's doing everything she can to avoid telling her family what's happening. She told me that when she tried to discuss it with Martha, Martha didn't seem to believe her anyway."

"Some people do cause their own accidents as a means of generating sympathy or support," John said. "Her family are certainly aware of the various things that have happened, just not what she fears might be behind those things. Everyone knows about the carbon monoxide alarm, for example."

"That's true," Bessie agreed. "Someone made a comment about the bath oil, so she's talked to at least some people about that, too. Everyone knows about the railing, as well, as that's very obvious."

"We haven't really discussed that, but since the evidence was destroyed, there isn't much to say," John said.

"Does that move Charles up the list of suspects?" Doona asked.

"I don't think so," John replied. "If he'd suddenly insisted on having a bonfire for the first time ever this year after the incident with the railing, I might wonder, but Lora told Bessie that Charles has a bonfire every year."

"It might be best if Lora moved out of her house for a short while," Doona said. "Surely she has friends with whom she could stay?"

"I suggested a stay at the Seaview," Bessie told her. "That seemed the safest option, really."

"Let's run through the suspects, then," Hugh suggested. "Means, motive, opportunity."

"I believe everyone had the means and the opportunity," Bessie told him. "Having been to one of Lora's gatherings, I can assure you that any one of the guests could have rearranged the kitchen cupboards, spilled bath oil, gone outside and blocked up the fire vent, and taken a saw to the front railings, all without anyone else paying any attention whatsoever."

"I hope you're exaggerating," Pete said.

"Maybe somewhat, but the day was a bit overwhelming. There seemed to be people everywhere inside the house. Lora said that some people had spent some time outside during the previous gathering, which would have helped, but it also would have made it easier for someone to tamper with the kitchen cupboards or the bathtub."

"With everyone indoors, how difficult would it have been for someone to damage the kettle?" Hugh asked.

"I was alone in the kitchen for at least half an hour," Bessie said. "Before and after that stretch, people were wandering in and out regularly. I can't imagine it would have been that difficult to pull the kettle's cord partly out of the housing. I was busy trying to tidy up when I was in there. Someone could have done it right under my nose, really."

"Is there anyone who didn't visit the kitchen that day?" John asked.

"I doubt it. The food was in the kitchen, and I'm pretty sure that everyone had something to eat. April brought food to Ethel, her grandmother, but Ethel decided she wanted to get her own food. The food was out for hours, too, which meant people kept going in to get more."

"The neighbours all had food?" Pete asked.

"I don't remember them specifically, but I probably would have noticed if they didn't get food, if you see what I mean," Bessie told him. "I wasn't watching anyone in particular, I was just interested in meeting everyone."

"So let's get your impressions of all of them," Pete said. "You're an excellent judge of character."

Bessie flushed at the unexpected praise. "Where shall I start?"

"Tell us about Lora's children and their spouses," John suggested.

"I barely spoke to Charles and Ann," Bessie replied. "They seemed nice enough, but not overly friendly. I rather liked Doreen and Carl until Doreen gave Linda money."

"I can't believe she did that," Doona said. "The girl is never going to take responsibility for her own life if her mother keeps helping her every time she needs money."

Bessie nodded. "I agree. I didn't like Linda in the slightest, and Zack was even worse."

"But Linda doesn't have any reason to believe that she's going to inherit anything if her grandmother dies, does she?" Hugh asked.

"No, but maybe she thinks her mother will be more generous if she inherits from Lora," Bessie suggested.

"What about the other daughter?" John asked after a moment.

"I thought Martha seemed nice and genuinely concerned about her mother. I rather liked her and Tony until Lora told me that they're trying to convince her to move house."

"I think that's just a further indication of how much she does care for her mother," Doona said. "Lora is seventy-three. That's quite old for a woman to be living on her own."

Bessie bristled. "I don't think so," she said tartly.

Doona chuckled. "Not everyone is as good at being alone as you are," she told Bessie. "You said yourself that Percy complained that Lora wasn't looking after the house properly."

"Percy is a complainer," Bessie countered. "The house wasn't any more rundown than any other in the neighbourhood."

"If all of the incidents have genuinely been accidents, then maybe Martha has a point," Hugh said. "You said that Lora told Martha that she thinks someone is trying to kill her. It will be interesting to see if Martha contacts the police."

"From what Lora said, Martha didn't take her seriously," Bessie told him. "If she had done, surely she would have suggested that Lora ring the police."

"I suppose so," Hugh said.

"What about Martha's children?" Doona asked.

"They're still fairly young. Christy is sixteen and Daniel is fourteen. I'd hate to think that either of them would want to kill anyone."

"Maybe one or both of them are just trying to cause some mischief," Hugh suggested. He flushed. "I had friends who used to do silly things, just looking for a reaction."

"What sort of things?" Pete wondered.

Hugh looked down at the table. "Just dumb stunts like going into restaurants and filling the salt shakers with sugar, that sort of thing."

"I suppose that's a possibility," Pete conceded. "Blocking the fire vent was quite serious, but some of the other things could just be mischief by bored teens, I suppose."

"In a way, I prefer that to thinking that someone wants to kill Lora," Bessie said. "On the other hand, some of the things that have happened could have been quite serious."

"The expert who has been examining the kettle did confirm that if someone had tried to switch it on, especially with wet hands, there could have been serious consequences," John said. "Lora was lucky Ethel noticed the damage."

"Let's talk about Ethel," Doona suggested. "Might she be trying to kill her sister?"

"I can't imagine a motive," Bessie replied. "She knows that she isn't going to inherit anything, or at least that's what Lora told me. All of Lora's children have money as a motive, although none of them seem to need it, at least not desperately. Ethel doesn't even have that."

"Which suggests that Ethel's children are equally lacking in motives," Hugh sighed.

"Unless there's something else going on, other than money," Bessie said.

"I wonder if Lora inherited anything from their parents that Ethel has always wanted," Doona said. "Maybe she's finally decided to get rid of her sister so she can have the family silver or the family chamber pot." Everyone laughed.

"I'll ask Lora about that," Bessie promised. "Beyond the family, we've only the neighbours to discuss."

"If Percy and Elaine have been living next door to Lora for that many years, I can't see why they'd want to kill her now," Doona said.

"Maybe he's just had enough of her letting her grass get too long or not painting her house often enough," Hugh said. "He did say he feels that she's letting down the neighbourhood."

"Well, it didn't appear that way to me," Bessie said. "All of the houses are starting to show their age now. I didn't think Lora's was any worse or better than any of the others, not even Percy's."

"That just leaves Brian and Jill Cobb," Pete said, after glancing at his notebook.

"They'd like Lora to go, wouldn't they?" Hugh asked. "Maybe they're trying to make her miserable so she'll sell them her house."

"That's one possibility, certainly," Bessie said. "I'm not sure either of them is clever enough to come up with the various incidents that have taken place, though. If they truly have been murder attempts, our killer is quite cunning."

"And not very successful," Doona added.

"But that may be part of his or her plan," John said. "It's possible that our troublemaker isn't trying to kill Lora, simply upset her or make her feel unsafe in her home. If that is the case, it makes the neighbours seem more likely suspects. I can't see any advantage to her family if Lora moves into a flat elsewhere on the island."

"I feel as if we're just going around in circles," Doona said. "This is easier when someone is murdered."

"I, for one, am awfully glad no one has been murdered," Bessie told her.

"Oh, I know, but we don't even know if anything criminal is happening this time," Doona replied. "Accidents do happen."

"As I said earlier, it's the frequency with which they keep happening that is worrying," John told her. "I'd be happier if Lora would let Pete visit her and look over the house. Hearing that she'd moved into a hotel for a short while would be a good temporary measure, but she can't stay in a hotel forever. We need to get to the bottom of what's happening before anything more serious takes place."

"Do you think things are escalating?" Hugh asked.

"I think the bathtub incident and the tipped-over knife block were minor concerns," John told him. "Tampering with a petrol tank and a gas fire are more serious. The railing is also worrying, as is the kettle. From what Lora said, everything aside from the kettle could have been tampered with at the previous gathering. If that's the case, I'm concerned that Lora might have other unpleasant surprises waiting for her from this last one."

Pete nodded. "Another reason why I want to go through her house," he said.

"I'll try to persuade her again when I talk to her tomorrow," Bessie promised.

Hugh's mobile phone buzzed. He glanced at it and then laughed. "How late is the shop at the top of the hill open?" he asked Bessie.

"Until nine, I believe," Bessie replied.

"Grace is craving toast with raspberry jam. We only have straw-berry at home. Lots and lots of strawberry, because she craved that for six months. I thought the cravings were supposed to go away later in the pregnancy," Hugh said.

"Don't say that to Grace," John suggested. "Just get her the jam and back away slowly."

Hugh laughed. "She's been good about it all, really. I don't mind indulging her cravings. She's doing all the hard work."

"And don't you forget it," Doona told him.

"You should go," Bessie told Hugh. "I'd hate for you to get to the shop too late."

He glanced at the clock and then nodded. "Were we done?"

"I think so," John said. "Until Pete can talk to Lora, I don't think there's much else we can do."

"Except wait for the next accident," Pete suggested.

Bessie shivered. "I'm hoping there isn't going to be a next accident."

"If someone truly does want to kill Lora, he or she is going to keep trying. If being a nuisance is the goal, he or she may feel as if it's time to stop," John said. He got to his feet. "I need to get home so that Grace can head for home in time for her toast with jam."

Hugh and John walked to the door together. Bessie was right behind them, and she let them out with a hug for each of them.

"I should go, too," Pete said when Bessie turned around. "Now that I have someone to go home to, I don't like to stay out late."

Bessie gave him a hug and then opened the door for him. "Give your lovely wife a hug from me as well," she told the man as he walked away.

Doona was starting the washing-up as Bessie shut the door. "Do you think that John will ever be comfortable with my money?" she asked as Bessie grabbed a tea towel and started drying dishes.

"You aren't comfortable with your money," Bessie pointed out.

Doona looked at her for a minute and then laughed. "You're right, of course. I wish Charles had left everything to charity or to his crooked partner or even to that awful woman he was cheating on me with when we were married."

"You don't mean that."

Doona shrugged. "Okay, not to her, but maybe to charity. It's odd. I've always dreamt of not having to worry about money, but now that I have a small fortune, it worries me more than being more or less broke ever did."

"And it complicates things with John."

"Yes, exactly that. I don't know if he's just uncomfortable with the fact that I'm wealthier than he is or if he has issues with the source of the money. If I truly believed that Charles had acquired any of it through illegal means, I'd give it all to charity, you know that."

"I do. Maybe you should have this conversation with John."

Doona nodded and then blushed. "It's difficult to talk about money with John, and it's even harder to discuss Charles with him."

"Do you talk about Sue?"

"Only when we have to, with regard to the children, mostly. He's as concerned as I am about how they feel, of course." She shook her head. "Of course, he's more concerned than I am. You know what I meant."

Bessie nodded. "It's only natural that you're both worried about the children. If you and John want to make your relationship work, though, you need to be able to talk to him about everything, even the uncomfortable topics."

"I know, but as I don't know exactly where I stand with John, well, it's easier to ignore the hard stuff."

"Promise me, if you do decide to give a relationship a try, that you'll talk through all of the awkward things."

Doona nodded. "We're going to have to, I suppose. We're both adults. It shouldn't be that difficult, really. If he really hates the money, I could give it all away. That might be the easiest solution for both of us."

"Except think what it could do for Thomas and Amy," Bessie suggested.

Doona smiled at her. "You know me too well. It would be wonderful to be able to help them with uni and whatever they want to do with their lives. Getting on the property ladder is harder and harder every day. It would be lovely to be able to give them a boost when they're ready to buy their first homes." She sighed. "I'm getting ahead of myself. John may be secretly planning to ask our new receptionist out for dinner. I know she'd go in a heartbeat."

"The station has a new receptionist?"

"She just started last week. She's only working part-time, and I don't like her one bit."

"Tell me about her," Bessie suggested.

"Her name is Suzannah Horton," Doona said, spelling Suzannah carefully. "Her mother named her after some American folk song, but spelled it differently, apparently. I know that because she tells everyone who comments on her name the entire story. As nearly everyone who rings comments on it, I get to hear the story at least a dozen times an hour."

Bessie chuckled. "I am sorry," she said.

"Not as sorry as I am," Doona shot back. "She's probably thirty, although she tries to look and act younger. Her hair is long and blonde, probably dyed, and her eyes are blue, probably fake. Her figure is all her, though, and I have to admit that it's just about perfect. She's thin but still has enough curves to attract looks from the younger constables. She tends to wear low-cut shirts and short skirts, which helps, of course."

"I'm starting to think you don't like her," Bessie said dryly.

"She's annoying, mostly. She flirts with every man at the station, from the cleaning crew to the constables to John, not to mention the members of the public who wander in from time to time. I'm not suggesting that she's set her sights on John specifically. I get the feeling she'd be happy to go out with every single man on the island at least once."

"There's nothing wrong with that, if she confines herself to single men," Bessie suggested.

Doona shrugged. "She flirts with the married men just as much as the single ones, but I've never been there when anyone has actually asked her out. Maybe she's after any man, no matter what."

"Or maybe she's just a flirt," Bessie suggested. "Maybe she's in a happy relationship, but she enjoys flirting."

"Oh, she's definitely single. She makes a point of mentioning that in just about every phone conversation, too."

"I'm going to have to visit the station and meet this woman."

"I wouldn't advise it. You won't like her."

"Did she grow up on the island?"

"No, she's from London. She came over for the TT last year and allegedly fell in love with the island. She decided she wanted to come over and join the police so that she could work at the TT and help keep the island safe, or some such thing. Anyway, this receptionist job is the closest she could get to her dream."

"I'm sure she can volunteer to be a marshal when the TT comes around again."

"No doubt she will," Doona sighed. "I shouldn't dislike her so much, but she's so much younger than I am and so much prettier. I'm sure John is going to fall for her if he ever really notices her. I suppose I'm lucky he's so busy with the kids that he hasn't really paid much attention to Suzannah."

"Are you really worried about her?"

Doona thought for a minute. "I suppose not. I'm just finding excuses, really. I'm really worried about talking to John about how I feel. If I cared even a tiny bit less, I'd probably never say a word. As it is, I almost asked him if I could drop in later tonight so that we could talk."

"You should have."

"Maybe. And on that note, I'm going to go home to my germ-infested house and maybe do a bit of tidying up. It needs it quite badly."

"Get to bed at a decent hour," Bessie told her. "Your body still needs extra rest."

"It feels good to have had a chance to get out of the house. It's been ages since I've been able to get out, or at least it feels as if it's been ages. I feel better for it, too. I should have dragged myself out yesterday."

Bessie walked her friend to the door. "Take care of yourself. If you want to talk, you know where I am. If you want to have your chat with John on neutral ground, I suggest the beach. It's very quiet this time of year."

"Quiet and cold," Doona laughed as Bessie opened the door. "We'd have to make it a short conversation."

"That might not be a bad thing."

Bessie watched as Doona walked to her car. She had high hopes for the woman's future with John, assuming they could work out what to do with Doona's money. Sue was another problem, one that they had no control over. If she wanted to cause chaos in their relationship, she only had to come back and demand that John let the children go back to Manchester with her immediately. Bessie could only hope that Sue would be sensible when she returned and do what was best for the children. At this point in the school year, it would be better if they were allowed to stay on the island until the summer holidays at least.

Still thinking and worrying about Thomas and Amy, Bessie checked her locks and then climbed the stairs to the first floor. She got ready for bed and then climbed under the covers, sighing as she dislodged a few cuddly toys. Being everyone's honourary auntie had meant that she'd been given hundreds of the silly things over the years. She'd always been unwilling to throw any away in case she might hurt some child's feelings. Now however, the toys had more or less taken over Bessie's bedroom. They were tucked on shelves and in corners and they covered her bed. She was used to rolling over on them in the night and to picking up dozens of them every morning. Just occasionally, she thought about moving every single one of them into one of the spare rooms. Tonight was one of those nights. Sighing, she shut her eyes and fell asleep immediately.

CHAPTER 10

*T*he next morning, as she collected toys from the floor, she picked up a small cuddly purple kitten and smiled to herself. She didn't remember every toy in her collection, but she remembered this one. A very young Hugh Watterson had brought her this kitten one Christmas morning. He'd saved up his pocket money to buy her a present because he was sure that she didn't have anyone to give her anything and he was worried that Father Christmas might not bring her anything since she was so old.

Bessie remembered being slightly offended by the thought, but also very touched by his kindness. As Hugh had grown older, he'd spent more and more time at Bessie's, and he'd given her other gifts over the years. None had meant as much to her as that oddly coloured kitten that he'd bought all those years earlier. She tucked the kitten under the covers and gave it a pat. There was no way she could move the cuddly toys anywhere else. They were part of her history, and they would be part of her estate one day.

She made herself breakfast and then set out on a long walk across the sand. A cool, almost cold breeze was blowing, but Bessie just buttoned up her coat and marched onwards. Once she was past Thie yn Traie, she slowed her pace. When her cheeks began to feel slightly numb, she turned for home. Her phone was ringing as she unlocked her door.

"Hello?"

"Bessie? It's Lora. I just wanted to let you know that I'm going out to the Seaview this afternoon. I've booked myself in for a week. The very nice man I spoke to told me that they aren't busy this time of year, so I can extend my stay if I choose."

"Excellent. Did you ask for Jasper?"

"I did, and he was lovely. I'm sure he's giving me a very special rate, as it seemed far too inexpensive. When he told me the price, I thought he meant for each night and I was a bit unsure, but then he said the price was for the full week and it seemed a tremendous bargain."

"That's good to know. They are quiet this time of year, so they can afford to give people good rates, especially for longer stays."

"Yes, I suppose so. Anyway, I've a million errands to run this morning, and probably this afternoon, too. The house needs a good cleaning before I go, as well. I expect I'll be checking into the Seaview around five. Would you meet me there for dinner tonight? My treat, of course."

Bessie hesitated and then swallowed a sigh. "That sounds lovely," she said politely. "What time?"

"Let's say six, as that will give me time to get settled in my room before we meet. I'll see you in the dining room at six, if that works for you."

"That's fine. I haven't eaten at the Seaview in ages. The chef there is excellent."

"So I've heard. I've never eaten there. I've never even been there, actually. I've always heard that it's frightfully expensive, but that doesn't seem to be the case at all. I asked Jasper about the prices in the dining room and he assured me that they're very reasonable during the low season, too."

"I'll see you at six, then."

"You can tell me what your police friends have discovered about my accidents," Lora said. "Now that I'm planning to get away, I'm feeling so much better, though. It's hard to feel worried when you're going on holiday."

Bessie put the phone down and sighed. Lora had sounded incredibly cheerful on the phone and not at all worried. Maybe the stay at the Seaview was just what she needed. She quickly picked the phone back up and rang John.

"I just wanted you to know that Lora is moving to the Seaview," she told him. "I'm meeting her there at six for dinner."

"I'll let Pete know. Maybe I could drop in around seven for a chat."

"That's an idea."

"It would be best if you were surprised to see me there, so I won't make definite plans now," John told her. "I may see you later, though."

Bessie put the phone down and then tried to decide what to do with her morning. She hadn't done any historical research in quite some time. A few days earlier, she'd received a large envelope from Marjorie Stevens, and she'd set it to one side without opening it. Now, with nothing else to do until time to meet Lora for dinner, she sat down at her desk and opened the envelope.

I found this collection of old letters in the archives and I thought you might be interested in transcribing them. They're from a young woman called Onnee, who moved to America in the nineteen-twenties. She sent letters back to her mother on the island every month for the next fifty years. When her mother passed away in the early eighties she left the entire collection to the library, where they've been gathering dust ever since. I'm enclosing the first two years of letters, and I'll be happy to send you more once you've read through these. They should give an interesting picture of life in the US at the time and may be worth some analysis. Let me know your thoughts, Marjorie.

Bessie read the note from Marjorie twice before she put it to one side and began to read the first letter. She could immediately see why Marjorie had suggested that the letters needed transcribing. The writer wrote with a flowery handwriting that was nearly impossible to read.

"Dear Mother," she read aloud. That much was easy. Having deciphered those two words, Bessie began the painstaking process of transcribing each remaining word in the document. After the first sentence, she found a blank sheet of paper and carefully printed out her transcription. When she'd finished the first page, she sat back and took a few deep breaths. Her head was pounding and her eyes felt strained. She got up and stretched for several minutes before she sat back down and read through her transcription.

By the time she'd reached the bottom of the page, she was in tears. The letter's author was only eighteen years old. When a cousin had visited the island from the US, bringing along an American friend, she'd fallen in love with the friend. They'd agreed to marry, and within weeks of the wedding, they headed for the US aboard a freight carrier rather than a passenger ship. The first page of the letter detailed the difficult sailing. The cousin had fallen ill almost as soon as they'd left Liverpool, and by the time they'd reached New York, he'd passed away. Onnee was on her own in a strange country with only her husband, a man she'd known for not much more than a few months, for support.

Bessie was torn between her desire to find out more and an unwillingness to read further. The letters were clearly very personal and had been intended for Onnee's mother, not Bessie. She slid everything back into the envelope. She'd think about it later, she decided. Now she found a book and curled up, eager to forget about Onnee and her problems.

Knowing how delicious the food at the Seaview was, she kept her lunch very light. A second brisk walk cleared her head and let her think more clearly about Onnee. While she felt odd about reading the woman's letters, she was beginning to think that Onnee's story deserved to be told. That Onnee's mother had left the letters to the museum suggested that the family agreed with that sentiment. When she got back to Treoghe Bwaane, Bessie decided to give herself another day to make a final decision. Mostly she wasn't feeling up to the struggle of deciphering Onnee's handwriting any more for today. It would get easier as she did more of it, but that wasn't a reason to rush back to the job.

Instead, she read more of her book, did some tidying up around the house, and took another short stroll on the beach. She chose a pretty green dress for her dinner with Lora. It wasn't one she wore often, and as she studied herself in the mirror she wondered why that was, as she liked it a great deal. She moved her necessities into the matching handbag and then headed down to the kitchen to wait for her taxi. Dave arrived a short while later.

"I haven't seen Mark in ages," Bessie said once they were on their way to Ramsey. "That isn't a complaint, as I don't like the man, but I do hope that he's okay."

"He's fine. He and his wife decided to move to Port St. Mary, so he's trying to limit his driving to the south of the island as much as possible," Dave explained.

Bessie grinned. "Their loss is our gain," she said lightly.

Dave laughed. "He isn't that bad, really, if you get to know him."

"I'll take your word for that," Bessie replied. They chatted about the weather and Dave's wife on the short drive to Ramsey.

"Do you want me to collect you at a certain time?" he asked as he pulled into the hotel's car park.

"I've no idea how long dinner will take. I'll ring the office when we're done."

"Ring me directly," Dave suggested. "You have my card, don't you? We're pretty quiet at the moment, so I'll probably just be sitting around doing nothing. If I am with a customer, I'll get the folks in the office to send someone else to you."

"That sounds good," Bessie told him.

He pulled up to the hotel's front door. A uniformed doorman pulled open the car's passenger door and helped Bessie from the car.

"Miss Cubbon?" he asked.

"Yes, that's right," she replied, slightly surprised.

"Mr. Coventry told me that you were expected," he replied. "He's waiting for you in the lobby."

Bessie grinned. The man escorted her into the huge, gorgeously decorated lobby and then left her as Jasper rushed towards her.

"Bessie, how lovely to see you," the short and rather plump man said as he pulled her into a hug. "You look stunning, as always. Green suits you, and I'm not certain I've ever seen you in green before."

"It's an old dress and not one that I wear often," Bessie replied.

"You should wear it more. I love it."

"Thank you," Bessie laughed.

"But tell me about Lora White," Jasper said in a whisper as he led Bessie across the lobby. "Very few of our overnight guests actually live on the island, aside from those who come to celebrate weddings or anniversaries or the like. When I asked her if she was celebrating anything, she became incredibly vague, almost evasive. Tell me everything."

"I'm sorry, but I'm not sure I should be sharing Lora's secrets," Bessie said primly.

Jasper laughed. "Of course you shouldn't, but I had to ask. At least now I know that she has secrets, which is quite exciting in its own way. She seems very nice, anyway, and very happy to be here."

"That's good to hear. I'm sure she needs a holiday."

"Don't we all," Jasper drawled. "Although I mustn't say that, as Stuart and I just shut the Seaview for an entire weekend and went to Barcelona. It was wonderful to get away, and as we didn't have any guests booked for the weekend, we saved money by not being here, paying staff to sit around hoping someone might decide to have lunch with us or something."

"You should shut for longer and have a proper holiday," Bessie suggested.

"Maybe one day. It's difficult, because we have some incredibly slow periods when we could shut and go away without upsetting very many people, but we really can't afford the holiday. If we're successful and get busier, we'll have the money for a holiday but no time to take one."

While they'd been talking, Jasper had escorted Bessie through the building to the large and luxurious restaurant at the back. A party of ten were sitting at a long table on one side of the room. Lora was on her own on the opposite side.

"As it's lovely and quiet, we're able to separate our guests," Jasper said. "You'll have privacy so you can chat easily."

Lora stood up as Bessie approached. She gave Bessie a hug before she sat back down. "I love it here," she said excitedly. "My room is huge and gorgeous with stunning views of the sea. I'm just sorry I didn't do this years ago. It would have been nice if Cecil and I could have sneaked away once in a while, maybe."

"The Seaview was shut for many years," Bessie told her. "Jasper and Stuart have only been running it for a year or so, I believe."

"It's been a bit longer than that, but not much," Jasper said. "We have high hopes of becoming the island's first choice for special events, but it's taking time to get there."

"Well, I shall be recommending it to all of my friends," Lora told him. "You may struggle to get rid of me after my week, too."

"You may stay as long as you like at the rate I quoted you," he told her. "At least until TT fortnight, anyway. I believe we're already fully booked for TT fortnight."

Lora grinned. "We'll see how I feel at the end of my week. Right now I feel as if I'm sixteen again and just out of school for the summer holidays."

"It's nice to see you so happy," Bessie remarked as Jasper walked away.

"I just feel, I don't know, as if I'm a million miles away from all of my problems. I was starting to feel afraid of everything at home, but here I feel safe."

The waiter brought menus and the wine list.

"Oh, let's get a bottle of wine," Lora giggled. "I never drink. I'm not supposed to, not with my medications, but the doctor did say that one glass now and again wouldn't hurt."

"In that case, let's just get a glass each, rather than a bottle," Bessie replied. "You don't want more than a single glass, and I can't drink the rest of a bottle by myself."

After they'd ordered drinks and food, Bessie told the other woman what the police had found thus far.

"So all of the incidents could have been accidents," Lora sighed. "That should make me feel better, but it doesn't. I was hoping they might reach some definite conclusions on one or two of the things that happened."

"They're still examining the kettle," Bessie reminded her. "John was disappointed that the railing has been destroyed. He thought they might have been able to tell something from that."

"I actually rang Charles to make certain that it was gone. He confirmed that it went up in the bonfire."

The conversation moved on to more general topics. The women discussed their childhoods, with Bessie talking about growing up in the US.

"It sounds much more exciting than my childhood here," Lora sighed.

"I don't think it was that different," Bessie countered. "I went to school and did chores at home and fought with my sister. Not much different to what you were doing on the island."

"Except you were doing it in Ohio, which sounds incredibly exotic to me."

Bessie laughed. "You wouldn't consider Ohio exotic if you'd ever been there. It's lovely, and I feel fortunate to have had the childhood that I had there, but as I said earlier, it wasn't that different to your childhood."

"Would you like to see the pudding menu?" the waiter asked eventually.

"Oh, yes, please," Lora said. "I am on holiday, after all."

Bessie grinned. "It doesn't hurt to look," she said.

Once they'd both ordered their puddings, Bessie asked for coffee while Lora ordered herself a second glass of wine.

"I never drink," she told Bessie, "or not much. Today is special, though." As the waiter walked away, a man walked into the room.

"He looks familiar," Lora said. "I'm sure I've seen him somewhere before."

"Maybe you've seen his picture in the local paper," Bessie suggested. "That's Inspector John Rockwell from the police."

"I have seen his picture in the paper," Lora agreed as John walked towards them. "It didn't do him justice, though."

Bessie smiled. John was looking very handsome that evening in a dark grey suit. His hair appeared to have been cut that day, as it was noticeably shorter than it had been the previous evening. He greeted Bessie with a smile.

"Good evening," he said. "What a lovely surprise."

"It is a surprise," Bessie agreed. "John, this is Lora White. Lora, my friend John Rockwell."

"It's nice to meet you, Inspector," Lora replied.

"Please, call me John. I'm not working tonight. I'm meeting a friend for dinner."

Bessie nearly asked whom he was meeting, but it was possible John was just saying that as an excuse for being there. "We're just getting pudding," she said instead.

"I understand their puddings are delicious. I've only been here a few times, and it's been a while since my last visit," John replied.

"I know Bessie has told you all about my problems," Lora said as the waiter delivered their coffee and sweets.

"She has, yes. I was pleased when she told me that you were going to stay in a hotel for a short while. Whatever is going on, a break from home might be just what you need."

Lora nodded. "I've been telling Bessie that I feel much safer here. I love my little house, but it almost feels as if everything there is a danger at the moment."

"Have you told your family and friends where you're staying?" John asked.

"Oh, yes, of course," Lora replied. "I'm not hiding from them, just from everything that's been happening."

"But one of them might be responsible for it all," John said.

"They can't do anything to me here. They can't get into my room, and I'm sure the hotel looks after the heating and every little thing," Lora told him.

"What are your plans for the week, then?" John wondered.

"I'm not sure, really. Today I was just worried about actually getting everything I needed into suitcases. Then I came up here and checked into my gorgeous room. I've started unpacking my bags and making myself at home. I've no idea what I'm going to do tomorrow, though."

"You could do some sightseeing around the north of the island," Bessie suggested.

Lora shrugged. "I've seen all of the sights dozens of times. I really just want to relax. I'll probably sit in my room and stare out at the sea all day, at least for a day or two."

"Is anyone planning to visit you while you're here?" was John's next question.

"Oh, goodness, I don't believe so, but I don't know. No one mentioned coming to visit, but that doesn't mean one or another of them won't decide to come up, I suppose. I can't imagine why they would, though. Aside from my monthly gatherings, none of them make a habit of visiting me."

"Except Martha and Tony visited you yesterday," Bessie pointed out.

"Yes, but that was just because Ethel rang them. They were both terribly worried by the time they came to see me, but I think I was able to reassure them that everything is okay. I don't think they believed that anyone is trying to kill me, but by the time they left I hope I'd convinced them that I'm still fine on my own."

"I hope your stay here is uneventful, then," John said.

"I brought my latest knitting project and a book, but as I said earlier, I may just sit and stare at the sea all day, every day," Lora replied. "I imagine Martha will ring me at least once a day, but I don't know that anyone else will even really notice that I'm gone."

"If anyone does come to visit you here, maybe meet with them in the lobby or one of the lounges, rather than in your room," John suggested. "We've no evidence that anyone wants to hurt you, but I'd rather be extra safe."

Lora nodded slowly. "I'm trying not to think about someone from my family wanting to kill me," she said. "What you say makes sense, though. My room is too small for me to entertain guests in, anyway." She shook her head. "As I said, I'm sure no one will bother with visiting me here. They're all busy with their own lives."

A quiet but persistent buzzing noise interrupted the conversation. Lora frowned. "Martha set an alarm on my phone," she said. "I'm not sure I know how to make it stop." She dug around in her handbag and then pulled out a mobile phone. It kept buzzing as she turned it over in her hands.

"Any ideas?" she asked John.

He took the phone from her and pressed a few buttons. The noise stopped. "You only need to press here and then here," he said, showing Lora the phone.

"I hope I remember that tomorrow," Lora sighed. "Martha is ever so worried that I'll forget my tablets. She thinks that changing my routine is going to end up confusing me. Maybe she truly doesn't think I should be on my own any longer."

"She's only fussing because she cares," Bessie suggested.

"I suppose so. And she's quite right, really, as I had completely forgotten about my tablets," Lora laughed. "I've left them up in my room. I shall have to go and get them." She got up and walked away, leaving Bessie with John.

"How is she?" John asked.

"She seems incredibly happy to be here," Bessie told him. "The break from home might do her some good, beyond keeping her safe."

"If she truly is in any danger," John sighed. "I must say I prefer more clear-cut cases. I'd like some hard evidence that what happened in at least one of the incidents was deliberate, whether it was a murder attempt or not."

"You still think it might just be someone trying to cause mischief?"

"Or get Lora to move out of her house."

"So one of the neighbours," Bessie mused.

"Not necessarily. If Lora decides to move, what will she do with her house?"

"I'm sure Milton would love to have it. He told me as much. I can't see him doing anything to hurt Lora to get the house, though."

"There are many options. Maybe she'd be willing to let Linda stay there, for example," John said.

"Which would make Carl and Doreen likely suspects," Bessie suggested.

John shrugged. "Or Linda, with or without Zack's help. Everything

I've heard about the pair of them makes me think that they'd like to get out of Carl's and Doreen's house."

"Undoubtedly, they simply don't want to have to do any work in order to accomplish that."

John made a face. "I don't understand people sometimes. I hope I'm doing a better job with my children. I think they appreciate the value of hard work, anyway."

"From what I've seen, they do," Bessie told him. "They're great kids, both of them."

"So far, anyway," John sighed. "They'll both feel better when Sue gets back from Africa, although neither of them wants to go back to Manchester before the end of the school year. They've both hinted that they'd like to live with me, even after Sue is back, but that's something I'm going to have to discuss with Sue and Harvey."

"From what they've said in front of me, I'm not sure Harvey would mind if they stayed here."

John grinned. "From what I've heard, he isn't exactly excited about becoming a step-father. One of the reasons that he and Sue split up in the first place was because she wanted children and he didn't. I do believe that he's done his best to deal with the situation, but the kids don't feel as if he likes them or wants them around."

"Maybe that's why he and Sue are still in Africa. Maybe he doesn't want to come back."

John shrugged. "According to Sue, this trip has been a lifelong dream of his. He originally became a doctor because he wanted to work in developing countries, helping the people who needed him the most. At university he became interested in cancer treatment, and ended up becoming an oncologist instead. I think this trip is probably his version of a midlife crisis."

Bessie chuckled. "It's better than buying a fast car, I suppose. I'm sure he's genuinely doing good things out there. It's just unfortunate that Thomas and Amy have to suffer because of it."

"They probably wouldn't mind as much if they liked Harvey better. As I said, I do believe that he's trying his best, but it's been a challenge for everyone. I talked to Sue this morning and she now thinks they'll be back before Christmas, but maybe not much before. She said she has a big surprise for the children, too. That's worrying."

"That is worrying," Bessie said. "I don't suppose she gave you any clues as to what she was talking about."

"She just laughed and then asked to speak to the children. She didn't say anything to them about a surprise, though, or they would have mentioned it to me."

"Maybe she's decided to divorce Harvey," Bessie speculated.

"I'm pretty sure that isn't it. He was with her on speakerphone when she rang."

Bessie thought for a minute. "You don't think she's pregnant, do you?"

John sighed. "That was my first thought, actually. Pregnancy at her age can be tricky, though. I hope she and Harvey are prepared for all of the possible outcomes, if that is her surprise."

"If Harvey isn't ready to be a stepfather, how will he cope with being a parent?"

"Good question. Aside from her age, I worry about her dealing with a pregnancy without access to proper medical care, too. Harvey's a doctor, of course, but he isn't a specialist in pregnancy and baby care. If that is her news, I think she's being irresponsible by not coming home immediately."

"Maybe they've adopted a puppy or an orphaned child," Bessie suggested.

"Either of those would be preferable," John said. He sighed. "It isn't really my problem, of course, except that whatever she's planning will impact my children. They've been through a lot in the past few years and it upsets me that she seems oblivious to what she's put them through."

Bessie opened her mouth to reply as Lora walked back into the room. She reached over and gave John's hand a sympathetic squeeze as the other woman sat back down at the table.

"That took ages," Lora sighed. "I'd unpacked most of my things, except for my blue suitcase this afternoon. I was sure that was where this box was, but it wasn't there after all. I ended up having to unpack the whole case in order to be certain and then I couldn't work out where the box had gone." She took a sip of water and then sighed.

"Where did you find it in the end?" Bessie asked.

"It was in another bag, the one with my makeup and things that I'll need in the morning. I hadn't bothered to unpack that one as I didn't think I'd need any of it tonight. I was sure I'd packed carefully and organised everything, but clearly not." Lora took another drink and then opened her box of medications. She worked her way through the various bottles, reading each label in turn. John watched, seemingly fascinated by the woman's behaviour.

"Ah, here we are," Lora said triumphantly as she held up the very last bottle. She opened it and tipped out a tablet.

Bessie frowned. "Is that meant to be the same tablet you took the other night after the party?" she asked quickly.

"Yes, it's my after-dinner-take-with-food, tablet," Lora replied.

"I'm sure that tablet was white," Bessie said.

Lora looked at the tablet in her hand. It was green with white lines across it. "This isn't the right one," she said softly.

"Are you quite certain?" John asked.

Lora looked at the bottle in her left hand and then at the tablet she had in her right hand. "Bessie is right. The tablets that should be in this bottle are plain white. They're for my cholesterol, I think. This one is to help me sleep, and I only take them when I need them."

"Maybe you should check all of the bottles," Bessie suggested.

"Maybe we should have them all dusted for prints," John said quickly.

"Even after I just handled them all?" Lora asked.

John sighed. "It would probably be a waste of time, but it's still worth doing, at least for the bottles that we know have been tampered with. Let me see if Jasper can find me some gloves."

He walked away from the table, leaving Bessie with a visibly upset Lora.

"We were just talking about someone tampering with my medications and now someone has," she said.

"Where was the box today?"

"After you warned me about it, I put it inside another box and then inside of a drawer. I thought that would keep it out of sight. It was in there until I started packing to come here."

"And were you home from then until you drove up here?"

Lora frowned. "I packed everything, but then I had to run out to get some things I needed, extra shampoo and a new hairbrush. I left the box of medications in my suitcase while I was gone."

"How long were you gone?"

"Maybe half an hour. It may have been a bit longer, actually. One of my friends was at the shop and we started talking. It may have been closer to an hour."

Which gave someone plenty of time to let themselves into Lora's house, switch the tablets, and then leave again unnoticed, Bessie thought.

John came back with a pair of kitchen gloves and several small bowls. "Here we are," he said. "You can check each bottle. Let's see what's happening."

Lora tipped out the bottle she was still holding. All of the tablets were the same green ones. After slipping on the gloves, she opened each bottle in turn. "These should be red," she said as she poured out small white tablets. "These should be brown," came next as she tipped out blue capsules. When the box was empty, she stared at John.

"Every single bottle was wrong," she said, "and I don't even recognise some of these tablets."

CHAPTER 11

*J*ohn frowned. "I'm going to have to take all of them for analysis. You'll need to ring your doctor and have him write new prescriptions for everything that you take."

Lora nodded. She looked at John with tears in her eyes. "I thought I could get away from all of my problems here."

"Where were the bottles during the day?" he asked.

"In this box. Bessie warned me about leaving it lying around, so I was hiding it, but when I started packing, I put the box into one of my suitcases."

"Who visited your house while you were packing, then?" was John's next question.

"I don't know," Lora sighed. "I ended up having to go out and I left the suitcases on my bed. As I said before, when I went up to get my tablets, the box wasn't in the suitcase where I thought I'd put it, but I just assumed that I'd forgotten where I'd left it. Someone must have put it back in the wrong place after they'd switched my tablets around."

John pulled out his mobile and rang someone. When he was done, he patted Lora's hand. "I'm going to have everything in that box, and the box itself, gone over carefully. We'll check for fingerprints, so I'd like to take yours so that we can eliminate them."

"I don't mind," Lora replied. "I'm not sure it will make much difference, though. You won't have anyone else's fingerprints, will you?"

"Maybe not at the moment, but we may be able to find a reason to ask for them at some point," John said. "Right now I'm interested in seeing if we find any prints other than yours, though. If someone switched the tablets and then wiped the bottles clean, that would be telling."

Unless it was Lora who tampered with the bottles herself, Bessie thought.

"Most of my family have probably handled at least some of the bottles in the past," Lora said thoughtfully. "I often used to ask one of the grandchildren to go and fetch the box for me during a gathering. A few months back, Daniel dropped the box and the bottles rolled all around the room. It took ages to find them all and I think everyone helped in the end, even the neighbours."

"So we should find a few odd prints on each bottle, but only yours on every single bottle," John suggested.

Lora nodded. "I suppose so. I wish I'd remembered to keep them hidden until I was ready to leave, but I was so excited about my holiday and worried that I might forget the box that I behaved foolishly."

"Never mind. We can't rewind time, so we'll just have to deal with the situation," John said. "If you have tablets that you need to take tonight, I suggest you ring your doctor's emergency number now. They may have a lot of work to do, getting everything you need ordered as soon as possible."

Lora nodded. "I'll go and ring him from my room, I suppose."

A uniformed constable walked into the room. He looked around and then nodded when he spotted John.

"This needs to go to the lab in Douglas," John told the man. "I've already rung Inspector Kelly. He's expecting it, and he knows why it's coming."

The constable nodded. He slid on gloves and then carefully put the box into a large carrier bag. "Was there anything else?" he asked John.

"If you could take Mrs. White's fingerprints, that would save me a job," John replied.

The young man grinned and then nodded. "I have everything in the car. I'll be right back," he said before he left with Lora's medication box.

"He seemed awfully excited about taking my fingerprints," Lora said.

"The young constables don't often get to do such jobs," John explained. "They're usually writing traffic tickets most days."

The man was back a moment later. Bessie tried not to laugh as he somewhat clumsily took Lora's fingerprints.

"Did you need anyone else's?" the constable asked eagerly as Lora tried to wipe the ink from her fingers.

"No, thank you," John replied. "Give the card to Inspector Kelly."

He nodded and then bowed and left the room.

Lora was frowning at her hands. "I need to wash this off," she said.

"You were going to go and ring your doctor anyway," Bessie reminded her.

"Yes, of course," Lora sighed. "I don't suppose you'd like to come with me? I'm not sure I want to be alone right now."

Bessie didn't really want to go with her, but she couldn't very well refuse. "Of course," she said, getting to her feet.

"As I said, I'm meeting someone for dinner. I'll be here if you need anything," John said.

Bessie and Lora headed for the door. Bessie stopped their waiter as he walked past. "I'll come back and pay the bill on my way out of the hotel," she told him. "I'm sure Jasper won't mind."

"Mr. Coventry has already taken care of the bill for you," the waiter replied. "He's instructed me to refuse to accept a tip, as well."

Not wanting to keep Lora waiting, Bessie just nodded. She'd argue with Jasper another time. Lora was waiting at the lifts.

"I didn't want to push the button," she said apologetically, frowning at her black fingertips.

"Which floor?" Bessie asked.

"Four."

The lift arrived quickly, and it only took a few seconds to whisk the women to the fourth floor.

Lora opened her handbag gingerly and looked inside. "Can you see the key?" she asked. "It isn't a real key, it's just a plastic card."

Bessie looked into the woman's bag and spotted the white card decorated with the hotel's logo. She pulled it out of Lora's bag and slid it into the slot on the door. A green light flashed and then the door opened as she turned the handle.

"Make yourself at home," Lora told her. "I'll only be a minute."

Bessie knew better. Having had her fingerprints taken more than once in the past, she knew the ink was difficult to remove. The room was larger than Bessie had been expecting. It had a sitting area that wasn't much smaller than Bessie's sitting room. Beyond that was a large bed and a huge built-in wardrobe on one wall. The door to the en-suite was on the opposite wall. Lora had shut the door behind herself and a moment later Bessie could hear water running.

The chairs in the sitting area faced huge windows that looked out on the beach. As it was dark outside, the lights in the room made the windows more like mirrors. Bessie switched off the overhead light that Lora had put on as they'd entered. After a moment, when her eyes had adjusted, Bessie could see the water and the waves as the moon illuminated them. It was very nearly a full moon.

When the door opened behind her, Lora gasped. "Bessie?"

"I switched off the lights so I could see the water," Bessie said, turning on the lamp at her elbow.

Lora looked pale as she crossed the room to sit next to Bessie. "I thought maybe you'd left," she said. "It took ages to get the ink off my fingers."

Bessie nodded. "Are you okay?"

"Not really," Lora sighed. "I know when we talked that I said I didn't need any of those medications, but I've come to rely on them. Taking them makes me feel better, if that makes sense. Now I feel as if something terrible could happen at any moment."

"Ring your doctor," Bessie told her. "He'll be able to get your medications sorted and set your mind at ease, too."

Bessie listened as Lora talked to her doctor's answering service.

"Yes, it's Lora White. I'm on holiday up in Ramsey at the moment and all of my prescription medications were, um, lost. I need everything replaced immediately."

When Lora put the phone down a few minutes later, she shook her head. "The woman who answered the phone didn't even sound surprised. I felt as if I were making an unusual request, but she acted as if she'd heard it a dozen times before."

"Maybe she has. People can be incredibly careless with their medications."

"I suppose so. Anyway, she's going to ring my doctor and he'll ring me back. I may not be able to get anything until tomorrow morning."

Bessie could hear the worry in the woman's voice. "I'm sure it will all be fine," she said quickly.

"Yes, of course," Lora replied mechanically.

A moment later the phone rang. Bessie heard nothing much more than a few short answers before Lora put the phone down.

"I need to go to Noble's," she said. "They're going to provide me with twenty-four hours worth of my tablets. My doctor will ring my regular chemist with the rest in the morning and I can collect the full prescriptions tomorrow afternoon."

"Excellent," Bessie said.

"I couldn't tell them on the phone that I can't drive, though," Lora said. "I'm not meant to be drinking with my tablets, and I've had two glasses of wine. How can I get to Noble's?"

"You'll have to take a taxi."

"Is that difficult? And is it expensive?"

"It's very easy and it isn't terribly costly," Bessie said. "I highly recommend the company that I use. They have very helpful drivers."

"Will they wait for me while I go into Noble's to get what I need?"

"If you ask them to wait."

Lora sighed. "I don't suppose you'd like to come along? I'm sorry to ask, but I've never needed a taxi before. I've been rather spoiled, really. When the children were small, we walked everywhere, and when they got a bit older, Cecil agreed that we needed a second car. I tried taking them places on the bus once or twice, but that was difficult. Is there a bus to Noble's?"

"I don't know that the buses run this late at night. I don't have any idea where you'd catch a bus near here or where it would take you. I can pay for the taxi, if money is an issue."

"It shouldn't be, but the week here is an incredible indulgence. I'm trying to be very careful with my money otherwise."

Bessie nodded. "Let's go down and tell John what we're doing before I ring for the car. He might have some other suggestion."

When they walked into the restaurant a few minutes later, Bessie very nearly changed her mind. John was sitting at a table for two in a dark corner of the room. It looked terribly romantic as he laughed at something the woman sitting opposite him said. Bessie was about to turn back around when John spotted her. He said something to his companion and then got up and crossed to Bessie and Lora.

"Did you need something?" he asked.

"We're going to get a taxi down to Noble's," Bessie told him. "They're going to provide emergency medication for tonight, and Lora will be able to get everything else tomorrow."

"Excellent," John said. "If you need anything, ring my mobile."

Bessie nodded. "Enjoy your dinner," she said, trying not to stare past John to try to see whom he'd left behind at the table.

"I'm sure we will," John replied.

Bessie watched as he walked back to the table. He said something that seemed to make his companion laugh. Her reply made John laugh loudly enough for Bessie to hear. As Bessie turned away to follow Lora out of the room, the woman at the table turned around and waved to her.

"Doona," Bessie said quietly under the breath. She felt a rush of relief and then happiness as she walked away.

She and Lora made their way to the front of the hotel, where Bessie pulled out her mobile phone. "I'll just ring the car service, then," she told Lora.

"Where are you heading?" a voice asked at her elbow.

Bessie smiled at Jasper. "Lora needs to go to Noble's to collect some medications. There was a problem with the ones she brought with her."

"That will be why the police were here," Jasper guessed. "I've just decided that I've had enough of dealing with guests and staff for tonight. Why don't I take you to Noble's and then bring you back," he suggested.

"We can't impose in that way," Bessie protested.

"It's no imposition," Jasper insisted. "I've just had a bit of an altercation with the head chef and I need to get away for half an hour or so to calm down. If I stay here, I'll end up saying something I shouldn't and then the guests in the restaurant probably won't get any dinner. If I'm going to fire the man, I need to wait until everyone is fed."

"Are you going to fire him?" Bessie asked. "My dinner was delicious."

Jasper laughed. "So that's one vote for keeping him, anyway. I'm probably not going to fire him, but I do need to talk to him later, after I've calmed down. Let me take you on your errand. It will be a favour to me, really."

"Yes, please," Lora said eagerly.

Bessie frowned. "You didn't let me pay for dinner, either," she protested as Jasper led them out to his car.

"No, I didn't," he replied easily. "You're one of my favourite people and you never come and have dinner with me. This way I got to buy you dinner, anyway."

"I'd rather you hadn't," Bessie told him.

"You've just sent us a guest who is staying for an entire week," he told her. "I can't tell you how excited we are to have a paying guest. Buying you dinner is the least I can do."

Bessie would have argued further, but Jasper stopped suddenly in front of a huge antique car.

"This is your car?" Lora asked.

"This is mine," he laughed. "We had a very successful summer, so I treated myself to my dream car."

"It's gorgeous," Lora told him. "My Cecil loved cars and he would have loved to see this one."

"I love cars, too," Jasper replied. "Anyway, Bessie, you can see that I can afford to treat you to dinner once in a while now."

Bessie laughed. The car had clearly been very expensive. The Seaview must be successful, even if they were mostly empty at the moment.

Lora sat in the back and Bessie joined Jasper in the front. They chatted about the hotel and the island as he drove across the mountain road into Douglas.

"We're fully booked for TT fortnight, and for the Manx Grand Prix as well," he told Bessie. "We've only a few rooms available for odd nights between the two events. Beyond that, our ballroom has been booked for about a dozen charity events throughout spring and summer. I suppose I need to keep our chef, as he's designed the menus for all of them."

As usual, there weren't any empty parking spaces around Noble's. Jasper drove up and down the crowded side streets twice and then pulled up right in front of the hospital entrance.

"Jump out. I'll just keep driving around. You may have to wait a minute or two when you come out, but don't worry. I will be back."

Lora opened her door. "Bessie? You are coming, aren't you?"

Bessie swallowed a sigh as she opened her door. She'd only met the woman a few days earlier. It seemed odd how much Lora seemed to need her help.

"I'm sorry," Lora said softly as they walked towards the front of Noble's. "I'm usually quite independent, but everything that has happened has left me feeling rather vulnerable. I shouldn't keep relying on you for everything, though."

"I'm sure recent events have been quite unnerving," Bessie said. "I don't mind helping out for the short term."

They stopped when the automatic doors didn't open. "Now what?" Lora asked.

Bessie began to read the various signs on the door. There were several, with different instructions for different circumstances. Eventually she found the relevant one. "The sign says that we should ring the buzzer," she told Lora, gesturing towards the small button on one of the doors.

Lora pushed the buzzer and both women jumped when the loud angry noise filled the air.

"I didn't expect to be able to hear it out here," Bessie said.

"No, me either."

A moment later a uniformed security guard appeared in the door-way. He unlocked the door and pushed it open an inch. "Yes?"

"I'm meant to be collecting some medications," Lora told him.

"Your name?"

"Lora White."

"Wait here."

The man shut the door and locked it again before he turned and disappeared back into the building. A short while later, he returned. This time he unlocked the door and opened it a bit further.

"Ms. White, you can step inside," he said.

When Bessie went to follow Lora, he held up a hand. "I'm sorry, but only Ms. White is authorised, unless you're here for some other reason?"

"No, I can wait out here," Bessie replied, glancing up at grey skies. If it started to rain, she'd get back in the car with Jasper, she decided as the guard locked the door again.

Lora followed the guard into the building. Bessie counted slowly to a hundred and then back again to one. As a light rain began to fall, she turned to watch for Jasper. He came around the corner at the same time as the door behind Bessie opened again.

"Jasper is here," Bessie told Lora as she emerged from the building.

"What perfect timing," Lora said happily.

Bessie wasn't sure she agreed as she followed Lora to the car. If Jasper had been a few minutes earlier, Bessie could have stayed dry. As it was, she felt cold and damp all the way through, even though she'd only spent a few minutes in the rain.

"Back to the hotel?" Jasper asked.

"Would you mind terribly taking me home first?" Bessie asked.

"Oh, Bessie, I was hoping we could talk more," Lora said from the back.

After counting to ten in her head, Bessie replied. "We can if you feel we need to, but it's late and I'm getting tired."

"Maybe we could talk tomorrow," Lora conceded. "You could meet me for breakfast. It's included in my room rate."

But not in mine, Bessie thought but didn't say aloud. No doubt Jasper would have insisted that breakfast was his treat if she did say something. "What time?" she asked.

"I think I shall have a very lazy morning tomorrow," Lora replied. "Let's meet at ten."

"Okay," Bessie replied. There was no way she would want any breakfast that late in the morning, and it was too early for lunch, but she could have a cup of tea while she listened to whatever Lora wanted to discuss.

Jasper pulled up in front of her cottage a few minutes later. "I'll just be a minute," he told Lora as he climbed out of the car. Bessie had her door open, but Jasper was there in time to help her out.

"I'll just have a quick look around," he said as they walked to the door. "I know everything will be fine, but I'll sleep better tonight knowing I checked the cottage over."

Bessie wanted to argue, but the break-in had left her slightly anxious whenever she returned to the cottage after dark. She stood by the front door as Jasper walked from room to room. His footsteps overhead sounded loud and intimidating, and she had to hope that if anyone was hiding anywhere in the cottage, they'd feel the same way. He was back a moment later.

"No sign of anything untoward," he said. "I'll see you tomorrow for breakfast, which will be my treat, of course."

"I won't want anything to eat at ten o'clock," Bessie told him. "It's too late for breakfast and too early for lunch."

"I'll have tea and biscuits for you, then," Jasper replied. "You'll manage a biscuit or two, if only to sweeten what may be a difficult conversation."

"What makes you think that?"

"Nothing, really, it's just that your friend seems as if she needs a lot of looking after and handholding. That can't be easy."

"She's having some difficulties right now."

"I got that, and I can certainly understand why she's relying on you for help. You're ever so good to people."

Bessie shrugged. "I try, anyway."

Jasper gave her a hug. "You were a big help to me when I was a teenager, just as you've been to hundreds of teens over the years. I haven't forgotten."

He let himself out. Bessie checked the door behind him and then checked the back door as well. It was much later than she'd been expecting when she'd gone out. All she could think about was getting some sleep.

When her internal alarm woke her the next morning, Bessie wondered idly why she didn't have an internal snooze alarm. She felt as if she could do with about twenty more minutes of sleep, but after a moment she rolled out of bed and headed for the shower. The hot water helped wake her. She set coffee brewing and took a very short walk while she waited for it to finish. After her first cup, she headed out for a much longer walk.

The empty holiday cottages felt slightly eerie to her as she walked behind them. Glancing inside each one as she went, she noticed that a few were in particularly bad condition. Maggie and Thomas were going to have to do a lot of painting and redecorating before the spring season. All of the curtains were tightly shut in the last cottage. Bessie tried to picture it with an extra storey on top, but whatever Thomas and Maggie decided to do with the cottage didn't matter much to her.

A few minutes later she walked past the stairs to Thie yn Traie. The coffee was working its magic now, so she kept going, picking up her pace in spite of the brisk wind. When the row of new houses came into view some time later, she decided to walk past them before she'd turn around.

"Hello, Bessie," a friendly voice called as she walked.

"Grace, how lovely to see you," Bessie replied when she spotted the girl sitting on a chair on the patio at the back of the house she shared with Hugh.

"It's nice to see you, too. I was feeling a bit lonely," Grace replied as Bessie walked up the beach towards her.

"Lonely? Isn't Hugh home?"

"Oh, yes, he's home, but he's fast asleep. His alarm will be going off soon, but I couldn't sleep, so I got up and came out here. Sometimes the sea air seems to help the baby sleep."

Bessie smiled as Grace rubbed her tummy. It was probably just her imagination, but to Bessie the woman looked noticeably larger than she had at the baby shower just a few days earlier. "I'm sure the baby is hard work."

"Yes, but worth it," Grace said quickly. She sighed. "That's what I keep telling myself, anyway, and I know I'm right, too, but some days I do wonder what I was thinking."

"He or she will be completely worth it," Bessie assured her.

"I'm not sure I'm going to be able to get through another month of this, though. I feel as if I haven't slept properly in six months or more. The worst part is that everyone keeps telling me that I won't get any sleep once the baby gets here. When am I going to be able to sleep again?"

"He or she will leave home at eighteen," Bessie said helpfully.

Grace stared at her and then burst into tears.

"I was only teasing," Bessie said quickly. She sat down next to the girl and pulled her into a hug. "It's okay. You'll get sleep once Baby arrives. You can make Hugh take the baby for a long drive and you can sleep for hours and hours." She kept talking, repeating the same things over and over again while Grace cried for several minutes.

"I'm so sorry," Grace said eventually. She sat back and wiped her eyes on her jacket's sleeve. "I'm so embarrassed."

"Don't be. I shouldn't have teased you when you're so clearly exhausted."

"I am exhausted, but I can't sleep. Baby seems to think that night is day and day is night, and whenever I try to get comfortable he or she wants to dance. I get kicked in the bladder, the ribs, everywhere. Hugh can't sleep while I'm tossing and turning, so I end up getting up and lying on the couch or coming out here for some fresh air, which means he gets to sleep, but I still don't."

"I'm sorry."

"I love this baby so much, but it's so much harder than I realised it would be," Grace said with tears in her voice. "I didn't think the sleepless nights started until after the baby arrived."

"Maybe you should talk to your doctor," Bessie suggested. "Maybe she could suggest some different things for you to try."

Grace laughed. "I've had three pages of advice, everything from sleeping with extra pillows to napping in the daytime. Nothing seems to work for very long, although I did have a nice nap yesterday, I will admit. It would be easier if I didn't care about disturbing Hugh, but he has an important job and I know he needs his sleep."

"You're doing an important job, too, growing his baby. It won't hurt him to miss a bit of sleep now and again, if you need to toss and turn for a bit."

Grace nodded, but she didn't look convinced.

The sliding door behind Grace opened and Hugh walked out in his pyjamas.

"Bessie? I didn't know you were here," he said, blushing bright red.

"Grace and I were just talking about how tired she is," Bessie replied. "She needs more sleep, but she doesn't want to wake you when she's tossing and turning."

"Ah, sweetheart, don't worry about me. Toss and turn as much as you have to until you can find a comfortable position. If I'm tired enough, I'll sleep through it anyway," Hugh said.

Grace sighed. "I'm just a big soppy mess today."

Hugh took her hand and pulled her into an embrace. "Come back to bed now," he said. "I don't have to be at work for two hours. We can snuggle up together and I'll rub your back until you fall asleep. You can sleep all day if you want."

"Good night," Bessie told the pair as they walked back into the house.

Hugh waved as he shut the door behind them.

Shaking her head, Bessie turned towards home. While she had no regrets about how her life had turned out, today she felt hugely grateful that she'd never had children. Her sister had had ten, something that always amazed Bessie, especially when she saw firsthand how difficult pregnancy was.

Back at Treoghe Bwaane, she changed her clothes and then combed her hair. A touch of lipstick was all that she added to her face. She wasn't looking forward to breakfast with Lora, but having been dragged into Lora's problems, she felt obliged to try to help her work out what was happening.

"The Seaview again?" Dave asked when he arrived at half nine to collect her.

"Yes, my friend is staying there," Bessie explained.

"Did he or she give you a ride home last night, then?" he asked.

"Oh, goodness, that's a long story. I hope you weren't waiting for me to ring. We ended up having to go into Douglas and back. Jasper drove us in the end."

"It sounds as if you had an interesting evening, then."

"That's not necessarily how I'd describe it, but it all worked out eventually."

He pulled up to the Seaview a few minutes later. "We're still really quiet, so you can ring me directly when you're done, if you'd prefer."

"My friend might take me home," Bessie said. "Don't worry if I don't ring."

Dave laughed. "I never worry about you," he told Bessie.

CHAPTER 12

"How are you this morning?" Bessie asked Lora as she took the seat opposite the woman in the Seaview's dining room.

"I'm fine," Lora replied. She smiled, but the expression didn't reach her eyes.

"You look tired," Bessie told her.

"I didn't sleep well," Lora admitted as the waiter crossed to the table.

"Just tea for me," Bessie told him.

Lora ordered a full English breakfast and coffee.

"I'm sorry you had trouble sleeping," Bessie said as the waiter walked away.

"I'd just about convinced myself that all of the accidents were just that, accidents. There's no way all of my tablets were switched by accident, though, is there? Especially not since I had the box hidden from the day we checked them all until yesterday. Someone must have let themselves into my house and deliberately switched the tablets."

Bessie nodded. "That seems the only explanation." Unless you switched them yourself, she thought. Bessie had been giving the matter a great deal of thought. That the woman had discovered the switch very publicly, in front of both Bessie and John, made Bessie somewhat more suspicious. Surely it would have been much more natural for Lora to go to her room and simply take whatever tablet she'd needed before rejoining Bessie. Why had Lora brought the entire box of tablets to the restaurant unless it was so that Bessie could notice that the tablets had been changed?

"That seems more like a murder attempt than any of the other things," Lora said.

"I suppose a good deal depends on what was actually in the bottles that John took away last night."

"Whatever was in them, they weren't what they were meant to be. If I hadn't noticed the switch, I could have taken the wrong tablets for days. That might have killed me."

"Once John has worked out what was actually in each bottle, he'll have to talk to a doctor to find out what effect the changes could have had on you," Bessie told her.

"Whoever did the switch may not have known about the possible effects, though," Lora replied. "He or she was probably just hoping to cause as much damage as possible."

Bessie nodded. "And everyone in the family has a key to your house?"

"I believe so. As I said before, the neighbours have keys, too." Lora sighed. "I should have been more careful with my tablets."

"Let's not worry about that for now. We need to work out what you're going to do next."

"I've been thinking about that. I want to have a party."

Bessie sat back in her seat, stunned by the woman's words. "A party?" she echoed as the waiter approached.

He delivered Lora's breakfast and coffee and then put a cup of tea and a large plate of biscuits in front of Bessie. "With the compliments of Mr. Coventry," he told her.

Bessie might have argued, but the biscuits looked delicious, and Jasper had been right the night before. She needed a sugary treat to get through the conversation with Lora. The waiter walked away as Bessie took her first bite.

"I want to invite everyone who was at the gathering," Lora told her. "I want to confront them all with what's happening to me. I'm sure they'll all laugh and tell me that I'm imagining things, but the tablets have pushed me past caring. There isn't any way that was an accident. Even Ethel will have to admit that."

Bessie nodded slowly. "Confronting everyone would warn the perpetrator that you've noticed what he or she is doing. Maybe it would make him or her think twice before trying anything else."

"I'm going to tell them all that I'm staying here until Christmas. No one will try anything while I'm here, surely."

"I would hope not."

"The hotel staff won't let anyone into my room and I won't let anyone in either. If anyone wants to talk to me, we can talk in the lobby or in here. I should be safe at the Seaview."

Bessie could hear doubt in Lora's voice, but she nodded encouragingly. "Let's talk to John," she suggested. "Let's see what he thinks about you having a party."

"I hope he likes the idea. The party is tomorrow night."

"Tomorrow night?" Bessie repeated. "That's rather short notice."

"I want to make sure everyone knows what's been going on. Then, if anything does happen to me, everyone will know that it was murder."

"You're having the party here?"

"Jasper is going to let me use the small room at the back," Lora told her. "We're going to have a three-course sit-down dinner. I'm meeting with the chef at eleven to go through the menu options. I've already invited everyone, although mostly I've left messages on answering machines. I can't imagine anyone will turn me down, though. Everyone knows that the food here is delicious."

Bessie nodded. "You're inviting everyone who was at the last two gatherings?"

"Yes, which includes you. You will come, won't you?"

"I suppose so, if John doesn't mind." Bessie's mind was racing. She wasn't sure what John was going to think of the party idea. He'd probably like the idea better if he could find a way to attend himself, but that didn't seem likely. His face was too well known on the island now, after the number of high-profile murder investigations he'd been involved in over the past two years.

"You'll ring him?"

"Yes, right now." Bessie pulled out her mobile phone.

"Laxey neighbourhood policing, this is Suzannah. How can I help you?"

"I'd like to speak to John Rockwell, please. It's Elizabeth Cubbon."

"I'm sorry, Mrs. Cubble, but Inspector Rockwell is busy. What exactly is the nature of your problem?"

"It's Miss Cubbon," Bessie said through gritted teeth. "I'd prefer to discuss my problem with John, if you don't mind."

"Inspector Rockwell is a very busy man. I can't put just anyone through to him, no matter how important you may think you are, Mrs. Bubbon."

Bessie took a deep breath. "Can you ask John to ring me back, please?"

"I can leave him a note, but it may be some hours before he sees it. As I said, he's a very busy man, Mrs. Cuban."

"Is Doona there?"

"Doona? Do you mean Mrs. Moore?"

"Yes, Mrs. Moore. Is she there?"

"She has the morning off. I can leave her a note that you rang, though, Mrs. Cubby."

"It's Miss Cubbon, but never mind. I'll ring John's office directly."

"Inspector Rockwell isn't in his office. As I said, he's very busy, Mrs. Clubbon. Would you like to speak to the constable on duty?"

"Which constable is on duty?" Bessie asked, counting to ten after each word.

"Constable Watterson is dealing with phone concerns at the moment. I can put you through to his desk if you'd like."

"Yes, please," Bessie said tightly.

"Ah, good morning. This is Constable Watterson. How can I help you, Mrs. Bubble?"

"It's Miss Cubbon," Bessie exploded.

There was a moment of silence and then Hugh laughed. "Bessie? Is that you?"

Bessie took a sip of tea before she replied. "I'm sorry. I didn't mean to shout at you. That horrible woman on reception got my name wrong half a dozen times in two minutes. She's dreadful."

"She's very new and I think she's a bit overwhelmed, but I'm sure she'll get better."

"That's very kind of you. I don't think she will, but time will tell," Bessie replied. "I really need to speak to John. Can you get him a message and have him ring me when he has a minute?"

"I can put you through right now if you'd prefer. He's in his office."

Bessie swallowed a dozen angry retorts. "That would be good," she said after a moment.

The line went quiet for a moment and then John picked up. Bessie gave him an earful about the new receptionist.

"I'm sorry," he said when she was done. "I'll have a word with her about people's names and also make her aware of the list of people who are meant to be put through to me without question. You're on that list, obviously. Doona knows the job so well that I often forget that others aren't as well acquainted with the island and with Laxey."

Bessie took a deep breath and then sighed. "I'm sorry. I didn't ring you to complain, I truly didn't."

"So what can I do for you, then?"

It only took Bessie a moment to tell him all about Lora's party plans. When she was done, he was silent for a full minute.

"I'm not even sure where to start," he muttered eventually.

"Yes, well, it seems an interesting idea," Bessie said.

"Are you still sitting with Lora right now?"

"I am."

"Then I can't ask you to tell me what you really think, not directly. Do you think this party is a good idea?"

"Maybe."

John laughed. "I suppose it doesn't much matter what we think of the idea. She's having the party regardless, isn't she?"

"I believe so."

"So rather than try to stop her, I simply have to find a way to protect her," John mused. "I wonder if Jasper needs any extra waiters for tomorrow night."

"You've been in the local paper rather a lot lately."

"Yes, I suppose I have. Hugh hasn't, though. He might appreciate a bit of overtime, too."

And Grace might get some sleep before he gets home, Bessie thought. "That's a good idea," she told John.

"Let me ring a few people and see what I can arrange," he said. "I don't want you at that party unless I can get everything the way I want it, though."

"We can argue about that later."

John sighed. "Let's hope we don't have to argue." He ended the call.

"John's going to try to arrange to have someone here to keep an eye on everything," Bessie told Lora as she put her phone back in her bag.

"That's kind of him."

"He's worried about you confronting everyone."

"I'm worried about me, too, but I don't know what else to do. I want to feel safe again and I want to know why someone wants me dead. Maybe everyone will end up thinking I'm losing my mind and Martha will arrange to have me put into a care home. I might not even complain, not really, if it keeps me safe."

Bessie was struck again by how the woman kept changing her mind about things. Previously Lora had been adamant that she wanted to stay in her house. Now she was suggesting that she'd rather move into a care home. Keeping up with Lora's moods was exhausting.

"What are your plans for today?" she asked.

"I'm going to spend the day here, resting and relaxing, well, when I'm not planning for the party, anyway. That will take a lot of my time, I suppose. I have a book and my knitting, though. I don't plan on going out, except for one quick trip to the chemist's to get my medications."

"Which chemist?"

"My doctor just ordered everything from my usual chemist in Douglas." Lora frowned as she spoke. "I hadn't thought about that, actually. I'd rather not go into Douglas, not today."

Bessie bit her tongue. There was no way she was going to volunteer to go with Lora to Douglas. She was already sorry that she'd asked her about her plans.

"Did anyone need anything else?" the waiter asked.

"I'm fine," Bessie said.

"You've barely touched your biscuits," he replied. "Let me put them in a takeaway box for you."

He was gone and back before Bessie could object. As he piled the biscuits into the box, he smiled at Lora. "Chef is ready to speak to you whenever you're done here. He's made a few sample starters and sample puddings for you to try while you're deciding on your menu for tomorrow."

"Oh, yummy," Lora said happily. "I'm ready now, then." She got to her feet and looked over at Bessie. "So you'll be here at six tomorrow, then?"

Bessie nodded, and then made a face as Lora walked away with the waiter. Apparently Bessie was useful for late-night visits to Noble's but not so useful when there was delicious food to taste. Telling herself that if she'd stayed to help Lora with the menu, she would have found herself having to ride along to the chemist's as well, Bessie got up, collected her box of biscuits, and headed for the door.

Her phone was ringing when she got back to Treoghe Bwaane. "Hello?" she said, trying to catch her breath after having dashed inside to grab the phone.

"It's John. I was wondering if we could talk about everything over dinner tonight."

"Yes, please."

"I'll bring pizza," he offered. "I'm going to invite Hugh and Doona, too. I'll have one of them bring pudding."

"Perfect. What time?"

"Six should work. The kids are both going in different directions, but they both want to be out of the house by five. Once they're both where they need to be, I'll have a few hours before I have to round them back up again."

Bessie laughed. "Parenting sounds as if it's hard work at every age."

"I won't disagree."

After doing a bit of tidying up around the house, Bessie settled in with the second page of Onnee's first letter to her mother. This time she found the handwriting somewhat less difficult. She still had to work on each word, one at a time, but it took her less time to complete the page. Again, she found the transcribed letter emotionally difficult to read. Onnee wrote of her arrival in the US with her new husband, Clarence. From New York, they travelled to Wisconsin, where her husband's family lived. There, the young girl was met with an unenthusiastic welcome. She soon discovered that Clarence had left a fiancée behind in the US when he'd gone travelling. The girl in question, Faith, had been living with Clarence's parents while she'd waited for Clarence to return.

Bessie wiped away a stray tear. Poor Onnee found herself something of an outcast in her new home. Clarence's letter to his parents, telling them of his marriage to Onnee, arrived in Wisconsin several days after Clarence and Onnee's own arrival. His letter to Faith, breaking their engagement, had been enclosed with the letter to his parents. As Onnee struggled to adjust to her new life in a new country, she confided to her mother that Clarence had been rather happier to see Faith than she might have preferred. That was where the first letter ended, and Bessie quickly grabbed the next one, now eager to find out what happened next.

When the phone rang half an hour later, Bessie ignored it, focusing on her transcription. She didn't stop until just before six, when someone knocked on her door.

"Ah, John, Doona, come in," she said, her mind still very much with Onnee.

"Are you okay?" Doona asked as John put pizza boxes on the counter.

"I'm fine. I've been transcribing some letters and I'm completely caught up in them, that's all."

"Tell me more," Doona urged.

Hugh knocked before Bessie could reply. As they all piled pizza and garlic bread onto plates, Bessie recounted Onnee's story from her first letter.

"The second letter is dated a month later," Bessie said as she sat down with her dinner. "She and Clarence have been living with his parents while he's been looking for work. Faith is still living there as well, and Onnee finally decided that she'd had enough and is ready to demand that they find a place of their own."

"Good for her," Doona said.

"Maybe, or maybe not," Bessie sighed. "Clarence still can't find work. The letter ends with details of their efforts to find a flat, but without an income, they can't find anything. Onnee seems convinced that Clarence is seeing Faith behind her back, as well, and she's certain that his family is helping him get away with it."

"The poor girl," Hugh exclaimed.

"I hope things get better for her," Doona said.

"I'm finding myself oddly fascinated by her story," Bessie said. "She wrote to her mother monthly for fifty years, which means I have a lot more to learn about Onnee and Clarence."

"Maybe she got rid of Clarence within a year and found someone better," Doona suggested.

"I doubt it. Those sorts of things didn't usually happen in those days," Bessie reminded her.

"You will let us know what happened, won't you?" Doona asked.

"I will, but Onnee's handwriting is challenging. It's going to take me some time to get through even the first year of letters."

"Maybe we should talk about Lora and her party tomorrow," John suggested as they dug into apple crumble for pudding.

"Will you be there?" Bessie asked Hugh.

"I will," he replied. "I'm going to be a waiter, but Jasper has promised that I won't have to do too much actual waiting on tables. That's probably for the best."

Bessie chuckled. "I'm sure you'll do fine."

"We haven't had all of the results back yet on the tablets we sent to the lab," John told them. "Their preliminary check suggests that six of the eight sets of tablets were items that were prescribed for Lora, just in the wrong bottles. The other two sets of tablets were not ones for which there were prescription bottles in that box."

"But we don't know what the tablets actually were?" Bessie asked.

"Not yet. It will take a few days for the analysis," John replied.

"You talked with Lora about the tablets," Doona said. "Do you think there's a chance that you put the idea into her head and she switched them all herself?"

"I don't know," Bessie sighed. "I hate to think that she's doing all of this for attention, but it does seem odd that we'd just talked about the bottles and keeping a careful eye on them and then this happened."

"Can you check on the whereabouts of all of her family and friends yesterday while Lora was out of the house?" Doona asked John.

"Pete is doing some discreet checking into that, but it's difficult as we've no real evidence that a crime was committed, at least not yet. Once we learn what the substituted tablets actually are, we might have more reason to investigate."

"Whatever they are, someone switched them. Surely that's a crime?" Bessie asked.

"Under the circumstances, and at Lora's request, I should add, we're keeping our investigation low-key at the moment. Tomorrow night's party might change our thinking on what actually happened, but only time will tell."

"Do you think Lora is safe at the Seaview?" Doona wondered.

"If she follows my suggestions and refuses to let anyone into her room, she should be fairly safe," John replied. "If someone truly wants her dead and intends to keep trying, he or she is probably increasing the odds of success with every attempt."

Bessie frowned. "Maybe she should go further away than just Ramsey," she said softly.

"Maybe she'll consider that after tomorrow night," John replied.

They talked for a while longer about Lora, but Bessie was sure they were simply talking in circles.

"Tomorrow night may be interesting, but for now I think we should give up on Lora and her problems," Bessie said after a while.

"Let's talk more about Onnee," Doona suggested. "Let's read her next letter."

"You may try, if you'd like," Bessie said with a grin. She went upstairs and brought down the copy of the next letter.

Doona's jaw dropped when she looked at the sheet of paper. "Okay, I see why it's going to take you a while to read them all," she admitted. "I can't even read a single word."

"It starts 'Dear Mother,'" Bessie told her.

Doona stared at the sheet for a minute and then shrugged. "I'm going to have to take your word for that. I can't even make out that much from the scrawls on the page." She handed the sheet back to Bessie and then looked at the clock. "It's getting late."

"I have to collect the kids, but not for another ninety minutes," John told her. "I'll take you home now, though, if you'd like."

"I need to get home to Grace. She's going to spend tomorrow night at her parents' house, since I'm going to be working in the evening," Hugh said.

All three of Bessie's guests stood up at the same time. She walked them to the door and then watched as Doona and John got into John's car. They waved to Hugh as he climbed into his car. When they'd all driven away, Bessie locked the door behind them. Doona had done the washing-up, so Bessie simply did a bit of tidying before heading for the stairs. As she switched off the kitchen light, she noticed that her answering machine light was blinking.

"Ah, Bessie, it's Lora. I was just wondering if you'd like to come into Douglas with me. I have to visit the chemist. I suppose you've other things to do with your time, though. Never mind. I'll go by myself. I must stop..." the message cut off there. Bessie played the message twice, wondering at the abrupt ending.

"I'm sure Lora is fine," she muttered to herself as she switched off the kitchen light again. She hadn't even reached the bottom of the stairs when she decided that she needed to ring Lora to set her mind at ease.

"Hello?"

"It's Bessie. I was just ringing you back. Your message earlier cut off suddenly and I was a bit worried."

Lora laughed. "Would you believe I dropped my phone? I was trying to find the hotel room key while I was talking to you and I ended up dropping my handbag and my phone at the same time. I wasn't sure where the message cut off. I didn't want to ring back and simply repeat myself. I should have realised that you'd worry, though. Sorry."

"It's fine," Bessie assured her. "I'm just glad that you're okay. You didn't have any trouble getting into Douglas and back, then?"

"None at all. It was an odd trip, really. I stopped at home, since I was passing. I grabbed some extra clothes in case I do decide to stay longer. Brian from next door stopped me on my way into the house. He said it was because he was worried about me, but he managed to casually drop into the conversation that he and Jill have applied for planning permission to extend their house. He said something about good neighbours wanting everyone on the street to be happy with their homes, which I took to mean that he's hoping I won't object to whatever they've requested."

"Are you planning to object?"

"I'm going to have to go and see what they've actually requested. I have a feeling I might. Percy stopped me on my way out. He's already been to the planning office and he's very upset with Brian and Jill's plan."

"Oh, dear."

"They want to double the size of their house by building a second storey, but they also want to add a large conservatory at the back and a double garage. According to Percy, if they do everything they want to do, they'll have very little garden left. The entire plot of land will be nothing but house."

"That doesn't sound attractive."

"No, and it isn't in keeping with the neighbourhood, either. I did wonder if they'd requested all these things knowing that they'll get turned down for some of them. Maybe they're hoping that once they get turned down, if they resubmit something more reasonable, what they actually want, we'll all agree because it will seem like a fair compromise."

"I suppose that's possible."

"The worst part about all of this is that I'm probably going to have to side with Percy on this one. I truly don't like that man and I hate the idea of agreeing with him on anything."

"If you don't side with him, you'll have to side with Brian."

Lora made a noise. "I don't like him any better," she sighed.

"Was the rest of your trip uneventful?" Bessie asked.

"Ethel popped in while I was home. We just had a quick chat. She doesn't want to come to the party tomorrow night, but I think I've persuaded her to come anyway."

"Why doesn't she want to come?"

"She thinks I'm being overly dramatic, having a big party at the Seaview with all the family. It isn't something I've ever done before, you understand. She doesn't really appreciate the monthly family gatherings. I think she believes that the tradition should have stopped once both our mother and father passed away. I love our gatherings, but I don't believe that Ethel enjoys them very much."

"That's a shame."

"I'm a lot like my mother. She was the one who always insisted on family gatherings with the children and grandchildren. Ethel is more like our father. He loved all of us, of course, but was happy to do so from a distance. If he saw us all once or twice a year, that was plenty for him. I think Ethel would be fine with only seeing everyone at Christmas."

"Surely she doesn't have to come to every gathering."

"No one has to come, but I think she's afraid she might miss out on something interesting if she doesn't attend. I don't know, maybe she's right. Maybe it's time to stop having the gatherings every month."

"Let's see how tomorrow night goes," Bessie suggested. "Is everyone else planning to attend?"

"Charles and Ann will be there, as will Carl and Doreen. Doreen talked to Linda, but she can't promise that Linda and Zack will be coming. I suppose it depends on whether Linda needs to borrow more money or not."

Bessie frowned at the bitterness in Lora's voice. "She's young and foolish."

"Yes, I know. Anyway, Tony and Martha will be there with Christy and Daniel. They never miss anything. Ethel won't promise that she'll come, which is typical of her, really. I talked to Milton this afternoon and he and Bob are looking forward to it, though. Apparently, they like the food at the Seaview."

"Doesn't everyone?"

Lora chuckled. "You're probably right about that. Nathan and Marie will be here and they'll be bringing April. I'm not sure why she isn't at school right now, but she isn't. Percy and Elaine will be coming, although I worry that they might leave when they realise that I've invited Brian and Jill, too. They'll be here because they want to stay on my good side in the hopes that I'll agree to their planning permission."

"Is that everyone?"

"Goodness, I hope so. It seems quite a lot of people, really."

And quite a lot of suspects, Bessie thought. Any of them could be behind the various incidents. "What time should I arrive?" she asked.

"We'll be starting around six. There will be starters and then a sit-down dinner. I've asked for a short gap between the main course and the pudding so that I can talk to everyone. I want to tell them what's been happening and hear what they think of it all. I suppose it's too much to hope that someone might confess to being behind everything that's happened."

"I suspect it won't be that easy," Bessie told her. "It could be quite interesting, though. The food should be good, anyway."

"If you aren't doing anything tomorrow, maybe we could spend the day together," Lora suggested. "I don't have any plans, although I suppose I could read and knit, as I never found the time to do either today."

"I'm sorry, but I'm in the middle of a research project for the museum. I shall be spending most of tomorrow transcribing letters."

"My, that sounds fascinating."

"It is," Bessie replied. While she could have talked about Onnee all night, it was getting late and she was tired of speaking to Lora. "I'll be at the Seaview around six, then," she said. "Good night."

"Oh, good night," Lora said, sounding slightly surprised at the sudden end to the conversation.

Bessie put the phone down and headed for the stairs. As she put the letter she'd shown Doona back on the pile, she couldn't resist glancing at it. Half a hour later, she had to force herself to stop. Poor Onnee was now living in a tiny flat without electricity or running water. Clarence was staying with her some nights, but returning home to his parents' house several nights a week as well. Onnee was sure that he was spending far too much time with Faith. On top of all of that, Onnee was worried that she might be pregnant.

Crawling into bed, Bessie found herself thinking about how much the world had changed since Onnee had moved from the island to the US. As she drifted off to sleep, she remembered that her little cottage had been lacking in electricity and running water when she'd first purchased it. That hadn't been unusual for cottages like hers in those days and it hadn't seemed at all a hardship. She would have to remember, as she read Onnee's story, not to judge the woman's experiences by modern standards. The lack of electricity and running water would have been less of a concern to Onnee than her husband's fidelity and her possible pregnancy, Bessie thought as she plumped her pillow.

CHAPTER 13

She took another long walk the next morning, stopping just short of the new houses. While she felt like walking further, Onnee's story kept calling to her. When she returned home, however, her telephone was ringing. A dear friend had fallen at home and been rushed to Noble's. Bessie immediately rang for a taxi and headed to Douglas. She didn't get back to Treoghe Bwaane until it was nearly time to get ready for the party at the Seaview. Fortunately, her friend hadn't suffered any broken bones, but she was badly bruised and would need at least a few nights in hospital. Bessie had promised to return the next day and to bring her a handful of books to help her pass the time.

Now she stood in front of her wardrobe and wondered what to wear. After some debate, she settled on a simple blue dress. That decided, she changed clothes and combed her hair. A dinner party required a touch of makeup, she decided, so she did her best. "That will do," she told her reflection before she headed down to wait for her taxi. Dave was right on time.

"The Seaview again?" he asked. "Perhaps you should just get yourself a room there."

"I may, if only to get away for a few days," Bessie laughed. While the idea was tempting, Bessie had never worked, and there were those who would argue that she had nothing from which she needed to get away. A short stay at the Seaview was suddenly quite tempting, but Bessie pushed the idea out of her head. She could think about it again once Lora had gone home to Douglas.

The doorman helped Bessie from the car when Dave stopped in front of the hotel. "Mr. Coventry would like to see you in his office, if you don't mind," he told Bessie as he led her into the building.

"Of course not," Bessie said in surprise.

He nodded and then escorted her through a door marked "Staff Only." Jasper was standing in the corridor.

"Ah, Bessie, there you are. Thank you, Jason," Jasper said.

The doorman nodded and then quickly disappeared back through the same door. Jasper offered his arm.

"Inspector Rockwell wants a word before the party starts," he told her in a whisper.

"Why are we whispering?" Bessie asked in a low voice.

Jasper laughed. "Because it all feels quite cloak and dagger, even though it isn't really. The inspector doesn't want Mrs. White's guests to know he's here, of course, but they can't hear us back here even if we shout. I suppose I'm just being silly." He took Bessie to a small office along the corridor, knocking once and then opening the door for her.

Bessie smiled at John, who was behind the desk in the office. Doona was sitting next to him.

"Good evening," John said. "Hugh will be waiting tables and Doona will be helping out in other ways. If you see or hear anything worrying, don't hesitate to tell one or both of them."

"Where will you be?" Bessie asked.

"Probably sitting in here, wishing I were out there," John replied. "I'm hoping to find a vantage point that will allow me to hear at least some of the conversation, but barring that, Hugh is going to ring me on his mobile and leave the phone in his pocket. I should be able to hear some of what goes on, anyway."

Bessie nodded. "Was there anything else?"

"Have you spoken to Lora today?"

"No, not at all. I was in Douglas all day." Bessie quickly explained about her friend's accident.

"One of the mystery tablets has come back as a harmless placebo," John told her. "It's something that's commonly prescribed for low-level anxiety, but it isn't much more than compressed sugar and starch. Lora could have taken the entire bottle full and done herself no harm."

"I'm not sure what that tells us," Bessie said.

"Neither am I," John admitted. "Don't say anything to Lora at this point. I'll speak to her after the dinner party."

Bessie nodded. "I should get in there so I don't miss anything," she suggested.

"I don't believe anyone else is due before half six," John told her. "Lora may well be in the dining room now, though."

"I should go, too, and just be generally helpful," Doona laughed. "I'll start by escorting Miss Cubbon to the party." She offered her arm.

Bessie took it and smiled. "I can't wait to see how else you manage to be helpful."

Doona shrugged. "I'm really hoping I can help work out what's happening to poor Lora."

The pair walked back out into the lobby and then followed the corridor to the restaurant. The dinner party was being held in a small private room at the back of the building. Bessie had never been in the private room before. She stopped in the doorway and sighed with pleasure. "This is stunning," she said. It was decorated in a similar fashion to the ballroom, but on a smaller scale that suited the space. The chandelier that glittered above them was reflected in mirrors along one wall that made the room feel much larger than it actually was.

Hugh appeared from behind a door, carrying a tray of drinks. "Wine?" he asked Bessie.

She made a face and then took a glass. "I must look as if I'm having fun, mustn't I?" she asked.

Hugh winked at her. "I can make sure the rest of your drinks are nonalcoholic," he said.

"I'd appreciate that," Bessie replied.

"Bessie, thank goodness you're here," Lora said as she emerged from the same door that Hugh had used. "I'm getting cold feet and thinking about cancelling the entire thing."

"You can't cancel now. Everyone will be on the way here. You don't have to say anything about the incidents, though. It can just be a nice dinner party, if you'd prefer."

Lora nodded. "We'll see how it goes. Maybe after a few drinks, I'll feel braver." She grabbed a glass of wine from Hugh's tray and drank half of it in a single swallow.

"I thought you weren't meant to drink," Bessie said.

"I'm not, but I need a drink right now," Lora replied. "I'm slightly terrified that one of my guests might come after me with a knife tonight. Someone certainly seems determined to get rid of me."

"Do you know Angela Howard?" Bessie asked.

Lora thought for a minute. "I believe I do. Was she married to Henry?"

Bessie nodded and then told Lora all about Angela's accident and how she'd spent the day with her at Noble's. By the time Charles and Ann arrived, Lora seemed much calmer. How much of that was due to Bessie's inane chatter rather than the two and a half glasses of wine Lora had consumed was anyone's guess.

"Mother, I don't understand why you're staying here or why you've invited us all to dinner tonight," Charles said as a greeting.

"I'll explain everything as the evening goes on," Lora told him. "Thank you for coming."

Martha expressed a similar sentiment when she arrived a few minutes later.

"Where are Tony and the children?" Lora asked, ignoring Martha's words.

"Tony is parking the car. The car park is busy," Martha replied.

Bessie wondered how busy it could be, as the hotel was nearly empty, but there seemed no point in questioning the woman. She was determined to stay with Lora as the guests arrived, but that proved difficult as Lora kept rushing around the room, greeting new arrivals. Within minutes everyone had arrived, and Lora waved to Jasper.

He cleared his throat loudly. "Starters are available on the table at the back," he told everyone.

Several people immediately headed towards the tables at the back of the room. Bessie hung back, watching. Hugh and Doona were on either side of the table, ready to help if needed.

"At least the food will be good," Brian Cobb said to his wife as they slowly followed the others towards the back.

"It had better be good. I can't imagine anywhere I'd rather be less than right here, right now," Jill hissed back.

"We need Lora on our side," Brian replied. "If she objects to our plans, we'll never get permission for our extension."

"She's old. Surely she won't be around much longer," Jill countered.

"Probably not, but when she does go, one of her kids might decide to move into her house. We need them all on our side until the extension is approved. Then we don't ever have to speak to them again."

Bessie had followed them on their slow progress towards the food. They were keeping their voices low, but that didn't prevent her from hearing every word. As Brian grabbed a plate and began to fill it, Bessie wondered idly if she could object to their planning request even though she didn't live anywhere near them.

"I don't want anything," Elaine Quinn said loudly.

Bessie turned to see Lora standing with Elaine and Percy.

"You should try something," Lora said encouragingly.

"No, thank you," Elaine replied. "Percy and I prefer simple foods. This is all too fancy for our taste."

Percy shrugged. "I thought I might try a few things, just to be polite," he said. He moved to the table and began to fill a plate. Elaine frowned and then turned and walked across the room to the far corner, where she stood on her own, watching everyone eat. After a moment, Doona joined her.

"It's all good," Zack said loudly. He was holding a plate that had nothing but crumbs and smudges of food left on it. Linda was standing next to him.

"It was good. Let's get more," she suggested.

"Dinner will be served shortly," Lora told her.

Linda shrugged. "We're hungry now."

"And we have somewhere else to be," Zack added. "We may not stay for the whole thing."

Lora frowned as Doreen spoke. "I told you that you have to stay until after pudding," she said sharply to Linda. "We had an agreement."

Linda rolled her eyes and then flounced away. Zack quickly threw several things onto his plate and then followed her across the room.

"This is why you usually only do this once a month," Ethel said. "It's too much of a strain, asking everyone to get along twice in the same month."

"It's fine," Doreen said quickly. She grabbed a glass of wine from the table and then walked over to where Carl was standing. They had a short conversation that looked tense from where Bessie was standing.

"It looks as if your wonderful happy family isn't quite as perfect as you'd like to pretend," Ethel said to Lora. "Sometimes I wish Mum and Dad were still around so that they could witness some of this."

"I wish Mum and Dad were still around because I loved them and I miss them," Lora replied with tears in her eyes. "They knew my life wasn't perfect anyway. I wish you'd stop with all of that."

Ethel shrugged. "I need more wine," she said, taking a glass and downing its contents in a single swallow.

"Don't we all," Lora muttered. She reached for a glass and then stopped herself and shook her head. "Some of us can't, though," she said softly.

"Ladies and gentlemen, if you could take your seats, we're ready to serve the first course," Jasper announced from the doorway.

Again Bessie stood back and watched the others. There were place cards at each seat, and it seemed to take ages for everyone to find his or her place at the single long table that was being used.

Once most people were seated, Bessie found her own place across the table from Lora. She sat down and then smiled at the waiter who poured her a glass of wine. While she wasn't planning to drink it, she was too polite to refuse.

The hotel staff served soup, while Bessie amused herself by watching Hugh and Doona. Hugh was trying to pretend to be a waiter, but it quickly became obvious that he'd never carried a heavy tray full of soup bowls before. He did his best, but it was only down to luck that he didn't spill anything on any of the guests. Doona stood near the kitchen door, helping in a dozen different small ways and watching everyone. She finally took pity on Hugh, coming over to take the soup bowls from his tray and deliver them to the guests. Bessie nearly laughed at the relieved expression on Hugh's face as he was able to stop having to try to balance the tray while serving the soup himself.

The room was oddly quiet as everyone ate their soup. Bessie jumped when Lora finally spoke. "The soup is very good, isn't it?" she asked, glancing around the table.

"Very good," Milton replied.

"Excellent," someone else said.

A short while later, the staff cleared the bowls and then reappeared with the main course.

"I'm a vegetarian," Linda announced as her chicken dish was placed in front of her.

"Since when?" Doreen asked.

"Since yesterday," Linda replied. "It's the morally correct thing to do."

"Just eat the vegetables and potatoes," Zack told her. "I'll eat your chicken."

"You said you were going to be a vegetarian, too," Linda complained.

"Yeah, maybe, but not today," Zack replied.

Linda sighed deeply and then began to push her food around on her plate.

"Let me take that and get you a vegetarian meal," Jasper offered.

"What would that be?" Linda asked.

Jasper gave her three choices, all of which made her frown. "I'll become a vegetarian tomorrow," she sighed, picking up her knife and fork.

The food was delicious, but the tension in the room was high. Everyone seemed to be anticipating that something awful was coming. As the staff cleared the dinner plates, Lora finished the last swallow of her wine. When the waiters had all left the room, she got to her feet.

Bessie noticed that Doona was still in place near the door, and she smiled as Hugh reappeared beside Doona. Confident that they could handle whatever came next, Bessie sat back to listen to Lora.

"I know you're all wondering why I'm staying out here and why I asked you all to dinner tonight," Lora began. "I wasn't going to tell anyone, well, anyone other than Bessie, but after giving the matter some thought, I decided it would be best to tell you all what's happening. Maybe you can help me work out what I should do to make it stop."

"Make what stop, Mother?" Doreen asked.

"Someone is trying to kill me," Lora announced dramatically.

For a moment the room was totally silent. Suddenly, it seemed as if everyone began talking at once. Lora didn't speak as the others all shouted questions at her for several minutes. When the room fell silent again, she sighed.

"This is why I didn't want to tell you anything," she said. "I'm sure most of you don't believe me. I tried talking to Martha about it, but she wants to have me put into a care home."

"That might be a good idea," Ethel said.

Lora stared at her sister. "Are you ready to move into a care home?"

"Probably. I'm tired of looking after a house, that's for sure. I'm tired of a lot of things, though."

"Mother, what are you talking about?" Charles asked.

"In the last two months, there have been several attempts made on my life," Lora replied.

"Seriously? Like people are shooting at you and stuff?" Zack asked.

"No one is shooting at anyone," Ethel snapped. "Lora just loves the drama of turning accidents into murder attempts."

"Accidents?" Charles said. "You mean like the broken railing? I told you ten years ago that that railing was an accident waiting to happen. You ignored me and didn't get it repaired. You can't seriously believe that anyone deliberately damaged that railing, can you?"

"Maybe," Lora replied. She was already starting to look as if she felt defeated.

"What else has happened?" Marie asked.

"Someone spilled some bath oil in my bathtub. I nearly slipped and hit my head," Lora told her.

"Maybe someone just wanted to try the oil and spilled it accidentally," Martha suggested.

"Maybe," Lora admitted softly. "A knife fell out of the cupboard over the refrigerator."

"How did a knife get into that cupboard?" Tony demanded.

"It was part of a set that I kept in that cupboard, but the set was all the way at the back," Lora explained.

"Except you keep a bunch of junk in there and are always just opening the cupboard and grabbing things out without looking," Martha said. "I've seen you do it a dozen times and I always tell you to use the step because it's safer."

Lora nodded. "My gas fire vent got blocked and I nearly died of carbon monoxide poisoning," she said.

For a moment, no one spoke. "Did the man who repaired it say that he thought it had been deliberately blocked?" Ethel asked eventually.

"No," Lora sighed. "He said it was usually birds that blocked the vents."

Ethel laughed. "I'm sorry, dear sister, but even for you this is a new extreme. I know you love drama and being the centre of attention, but calling us all here and suggesting that someone is trying to kill you seems a bit, well, irrational."

"Have there been other incidents?" Charles asked.

"My petrol tank got a hole in it," Lora told him.

"Your car is pretty old," Doreen said.

Lora nodded. "And so was my kettle. The cord suddenly frayed very badly, though, and I nearly got electrocuted."

Ethel laughed. "That's my sister, always claiming the credit for everything. If you remember, I was the one who almost got electrocuted, because you'd asked me to make the tea that afternoon. Now I'm starting to wonder if maybe you were trying to kill me that day."

Lora flushed. "Of course I wasn't trying to kill you," she said quickly, "but someone is trying to kill me. Someone switched all of my medications, every single one of them. They put them all into the wrong bottles and even substituted some other drugs for some of my medications."

"You take too many things anyway," Ethel said dismissively. "I saw your box full of bottles of tablets. It was like your own chemist's shop in a box."

"My doctor thinks I need them all," Lora defended herself.

"Doctors can be wrong," Ethel shot back.

"We'll see what the police think," Lora said. "They're examining the tablets that were substituted for mine. They're taking me seriously, even if you lot aren't."

"You've told the police about your ridiculous notion?" Ethel asked.

"Yes, of course. That's what you do when someone is trying to kill you," Lora replied.

"Cool," Zack said. "So someone in here is probably an undercover cop. I saw something like this on telly once. Who might be with the police?" he asked, looking around the room.

Bessie followed his gaze. Doona and Hugh were standing together, seemingly having a whispered conversation. Hugh yawned and then looked over and seemed to notice that everyone at the table was staring at him.

"Did you need something?" he asked, sounding confused.

Zack laughed. "I suppose the police have the room under video surveillance or something. This is neat."

"It isn't anything of the kind," Doreen said tightly. "Mother, I don't know what's wrong with you. Why would anyone want to kill you?"

"There could be lots of reasons," Lora replied.

"Such as?" Doreen demanded. "You're a perfectly ordinary woman who's, let's face it, not exactly young any longer. If anyone wants you dead, they only have to wait a few more years."

Lora flushed as several people gasped. "As your daughter is on the top of the police suspect list, perhaps you should be more careful what you say," she snapped.

Doreen looked stunned. "Linda? A suspect? Why would Linda be a suspect?"

"You're all suspects," Lora said, reaching for another glass of wine. "Odd accidents only seem to happen to me right after one of our family gatherings. The police are looking at all of you."

Another stunned silence followed Lora's words. Bessie looked around the table and saw confusion, anger, and worry on the different faces.

"Mother, you aren't making any sense," Charles said eventually. "Are you actually suggesting that one of us is trying to kill you?"

"That's the only possible solution," Lora replied. "As I said, everything bad that has happened has taken place right after one of our gatherings."

"Anyone on the island could have damaged that railing," he retorted. "It wouldn't have taken them much time or any effort, as the railing was falling apart already."

Lora nodded. "But the bath oil, the knife, the kettle, my medications, those all needed access to my house."

"Have you had any tradesmen in lately?" Jill asked.

"Only after the accidents, to repair things," Lora told her.

"This is all fascinating, but I think that Jill and I should go now. This seems very much like a family matter," Brian said.

"Except you're suspects, too," Lora told him.

"We are?" he replied, sounding amused. "Why on earth would Jill or I want to kill you?"

"So that she doesn't object to your ridiculous planning request," Percy snapped. "if you time it just right, by the time the estate is settled, you could have your permission in place and be turning our neighbourhood into an eyesore."

"I hardly think that our small addition will turn the entire neighbourhood into an eyesore," Brian replied with a chuckle.

"It's not a small addition, though," Percy nearly shouted. "It's a monstrosity not at all in keeping with the rest of the street. It wouldn't surprise me at all to learn that you're prepared to kill Lora to get your way, either."

"Be careful about throwing around accusations like that," Brian said tightly. "I still remember how much you complained about Lora to me when Jill and I first moved into our house. Maybe the police should be looking closely at you."

"Preposterous," Percy yelled. "While Lora and I have never been friends, I've no reason to kill her."

"Unless you think she might side with me and tell the planning committee to approve my request," Brian suggested.

"Lora wouldn't do that," Percy said. "Right?" he asked Lora.

"I don't want to talk about that right now," Lora replied.

"No, she doesn't want anything to take the attention away from her and her crazy accusations," Ethel said. "She'll keep you both dangling for weeks or months before she'll choose a side, so that you'll both have to be extra nice to her until she finally does exactly what she's already planning to do."

"You can't believe that any of your children or grandchildren have any reason to kill you," Martha said.

"Money," Percy called out. "Every one of you would love to get your hands on your mother's money."

Martha flushed. "We're all doing okay," she said.

"That's why Linda is a suspect?" Doreen asked. "Because she always needs money?"

"Always needs money?" Tony echoed. "Isn't willing to work and insists on living with a deadbeat who sponges off of you and Carl for everything is more like it. I can see why Linda would be a suspect, although I'd put Zack at the top of the list myself."

Zack laughed. "I'm a suspect? How exciting. How much does Linda get when her granny goes? It must be a lot if I'm willing to kill for it."

"I think you'd kill someone for fifty quid," Tony said.

"Fifty quid? I won't do anything for fifty quid," Zack shot back. He looked at Linda. "This is hilarious," he said.

Linda shook her head. "It isn't at all funny." She stood up and walked to Lora. Taking her grandmother's hands, she stared into her eyes. "Do you really think that I would do anything to hurt you?" she demanded.

Lora blinked back tears. "I hope not," she whispered.

Linda looked as if she'd been slapped. "You think I'd kill you for money," she said, dropping Lora's hands and spinning back around. "I come to your crummy family gatherings every month and I put up with everyone looking down their noses at me because I'm not working or doing anything useful with my life all because I love you, and you actually think that I might hurt you." She burst into tears and rushed out of the room. After a moment, Doona went after her.

Doreen got to her feet. "I should go and see if she's okay," she said.

"I wouldn't, if I were you," Milton said, sounding amused. "You might be accused of attempted murder next and you wouldn't be here to defend yourself."

"I'm glad you find this all so funny," Doreen snapped. "I suppose you don't have a motive for wanting my mother dead, so you're off the hook."

He shrugged. "I can't imagine any reason why I'd want her dead. Can you?" he asked Lora.

She shrugged. "Not really, not unless you think you're in line to inherit something from me."

"Am I?" he asked.

"No."

"Then I suppose I shall have to give up on my rather pathetic attempts to end your life, or rather, I would, if I had been behind any of them. They have been rather pathetic, though. Surely it would be much easier for someone to simply stab you or choke you or something," Milton replied.

Lora shuddered. "Just because the attempts have been unsuccessful doesn't mean my life isn't in danger."

"As I'm sure Nathan and April and I aren't in your will, either, I hope we're off the suspect list," Marie said.

"Everyone has to be considered," Lora replied.

"Yes, maybe we're just tired of her cooking, or feel the need to attend a funeral and no one we know will cooperate," Milton said.

Lora sighed. "I wish you would all take this seriously," she said. "The police are, anyway."

"Are they?" Ethel asked. "What have they said, exactly?"

"They're investigating," Lora told her. "They have the kettle that was tampered with and they're speaking to the men who repaired my gas fire and my car. They're also having all of my tablets checked to see what was substituted for my regular medications. They're going to check for fingerprints, too."

"Well, when they find mine, make sure you tell them that I handled some of the bottles the day of the last gathering," Ethel laughed. "I'd hate to think that I'm on the suspect list."

Lora nodded. "You know you aren't in my will, anyway."

Linda walked back into the room and took her seat next to Zack. Doona returned to her spot next to Hugh.

"Are you okay?" Doreen asked loudly.

Linda nodded. "Sure, great," she said sarcastically.

"You should be enjoying this more," Zack said. "It isn't every day that we get accused of attempted murder. It's like on telly, only surprisingly boring."

"Shut up," Linda replied.

"Maybe it's all a big conspiracy," Zack suggested. "Maybe all three of your kids got together and decided to get rid of you. Now they're taking turns trying to bump you off, but none of them are very good at it."

"I think that's enough pointless speculation for today," Doreen said. "Mother, I'm not sure what you were hoping to accomplish by all of this, but I hope it wasn't what you have done, which is just upset everyone."

"I was hoping someone might have a suggestion for how I can keep myself safe," Lora told her. "Right now I'm staying here, which feels somewhat safer than home, but at some point I'm going to have to return to my house. I don't think I'll be safe there."

"Unless you're simply overdramatising a few accidents," Charles suggested.

Lora sighed. "We'll see what the police have to say about that."

"Maybe you're doing it all yourself," Brian said loudly.

"Why would I do that?"

"Perhaps you really were trying to kill me," Ethel said. "Perhaps you caused all the other accidents to make it look as if someone is trying to kill you, before you actually killed me."

"But you're still alive, and someone switched my medications after we found the broken kettle," Lora replied.

"Sure, because you have to keep making it seem like you're the target until you find another way to kill me," Ethel said. "I'm going home to lock myself in and hide. My sister is trying to kill me." She stood up and then began to laugh heartily.

"Why would I want to kill you?" Lora demanded when Ethel stopped laughing.

"I don't know, but my version of events makes as much sense as yours does," Ethel replied. She took a step towards the door.

"Would you like us to serve pudding now?" Hugh asked Lora.

Lora sighed and dropped back into her seat. "Yes, please," she said.

Ethel stopped. "Pudding? I really hope you haven't hidden the poison in pudding."

Lora frowned at her as the waiters began to serve crystal bowls of chocolate mousse to everyone.

The pudding course was eaten in complete silence. Bessie found it difficult to eat her mousse with the palpable tension in the room. As soon as Ethel emptied her bowl, she got up and left without saying another word. Brian and Jill were only a moment behind her. They shouted goodbye as they headed for the door.

A moment later the rest of the room seemed to empty at once as people muttered goodbyes to Lora and disappeared. Before the waiters even began to clear the pudding bowls, Bessie was alone with Lora.

"That was a disaster," Lora sighed. "I have a blinding headache and I'm going to bed."

She walked out of the room without waiting for a reply.

"I think she was right," Doona said as she sat down next to Bessie. "That was pretty disastrous."

CHAPTER 14

*H*ugh sat down across from Doona, and John joined them a moment later.

"I don't know what Lora was hoping to accomplish, but that wasn't it," Bessie sighed.

Several waiters came into the room to start clearing up as John opened his mouth to reply. "Let's move this conversation to Bessie's," he suggested.

"We can clear the room later," Jasper offered from the doorway. "If you need to talk, you're welcome to stay."

"We can talk just as easily at my cottage," Bessie assured him. "We don't want your staff to have to work late."

Jasper laughed. "They're happy to have the work at this time of year."

"You'll be doing my Thanksgiving dinner soon enough," Bessie reminded him.

"Yes, we're all looking forward to that," Jasper replied.

"I'll take Bessie," Hugh offered as the foursome walked out of the hotel.

"Doona can ride with me, then," John said, just slightly too eagerly.

Bessie grinned as the pair headed for John's car. "I think they're going to be very happy together," she told Hugh.

He shrugged. "I hope so. I remember when Doona first started at the station. Her marriage had just fallen apart and she was so sad all the time. When John came, it quickly became obvious that his marriage wasn't in very good shape, but he kept trying to work at it for the kids. I thought, way back then, that he and Doona would be good together. It seems to have taken them a long time to reach the same conclusion."

Bessie laughed. "It's always easier to see things more clearly from the outside. I thought you and Grace were perfect for one another from the first time I met her, but it still took you months to propose."

Hugh flushed. "I kept getting cold feet," he muttered as he opened the passenger door of his car for Bessie. "It all worked out in the end."

"It did, yes," Bessie agreed.

At Treoghe Bwaane, Doona, Bessie, and Hugh told John everything that he had missed. When they were done, he shook his head. "I don't blame Lora's family for being upset. I suppose it could have been worse. At least everyone ended up getting accused. I did worry that the family might blame one of the neighbours and that it would get ugly."

"I don't think we're any closer to working out what's happening, though," Bessie sighed.

"I should have more results from the lab tomorrow," John told her. "They've found many fingerprints on the bottles, but most are too smudged to be identifiable, even if they had fingerprints on record for everyone involved."

"And, as Lora said, almost everyone could find an excuse for having touched the bottles at some point in the past," Bessie sighed.

John nodded. "I'm hoping we might learn something from the contents of the last bottle. We know those anti-anxiety tablets are widely prescribed. Maybe whatever the other unidentified tablets are will be something more unusual. Then we'd just have to track down who might have been prescribed it among Lora's family and friends."

"Have you looked to see if any of them were actually prescribed those anti-anxiety tablets?" Bessie asked.

"Lora used to take them," John replied. "As did some others involved in the case. They seem to be a particularly favoured prescription at a surgery in Douglas where nearly all of the family go, or at least have gone in the past."

"Percy seemed incredibly angry," Bessie said tentatively. "I'm not actually accusing him of anything, but I think you should take a good look at him." She sighed. "I don't know, I just don't like the man, and that makes me suspicious of him."

John nodded. "You have excellent instincts about people. If you're concerned about him, I'll take a closer look."

They chatted for a few minutes longer, but no one had any suggestions for ways to move the case forward.

"At least I feel that Lora is reasonably safe at the Seaview," John said as he got to his feet. "The longer she stays there, the longer I have to work out what's happening."

"Is it possible she's doing some of these things herself?" Doona asked.

"Ethel's idea that Lora is doing all of this to seem like the victim while planning to actually murder someone was far fetched, but interesting," Bessie said.

"Why would she want to kill anyone?" Hugh asked.

"Maybe I need to ask her that question," Bessie mused.

"Make sure you talk to her in a public place," John warned her. "That goes for everyone involved in the case. If you decide you want to speak to any of them, do so in a public place. Let Hugh or me know about the meeting, too," he added as he headed for the door. "You have an uncanny knack for getting confessions out of people."

"I never mean to," Bessie replied.

He nodded. "I know."

Doona had followed John to the door. "Would you mind driving me home?" she asked.

"Not at all," he smiled. "It isn't that late. Maybe you could pop in to see the kids for a few minutes. Amy wanted to talk to you about something. I'm not sure what."

Doona nodded. "Sure."

They were still chatting together as Bessie shut the door behind them.

Hugh got to his feet before Bessie could speak. "I should go, too," he said. "I just wanted to let them leave together before I said anything."

"That was kind of you," Bessie smiled.

"They both seem a lot happier lately. I just hope they can work through all the issues. It might get uncomfortable when Sue gets back, I suppose."

"Yes, she may well be a problem, but she needs to come back for the sake of the children. I'm sure they feel rather abandoned at the moment."

Hugh shook his head. "I can't imagine. My baby isn't even here yet and I'm already insanely protective of him or her. I know I'm going to struggle to go to work every day and leave the baby at home. I can't imagine flying halfway around the world and leaving my child for months at a time."

"She knows the children are in the best possible hands with their father," Bessie reminded him. "I can understand her desire to support her new husband in pursuing his dream, I truly can. It's a difficult situation for everyone."

"John isn't complaining, really. He loves having the kids here."

"Yes, there is that."

Bessie let Hugh out and then checked that all of her doors and windows were locked. She was still thinking about John and Sue as she headed up to bed. Her dreams were all about elephants and safaris across Africa, but her first thought when she woke up in the morning was about medicine bottles.

As she made herself some breakfast, she tried to remember the scene at Lora's house after the gathering she'd attended. She remembered Lora getting her box of bottles, and Lora going through them. What she couldn't remember was Ethel handling any of the bottles. Why had Ethel said yesterday that she'd touched them? Was it because she knew her fingerprints were going to be on the bottles? Bessie headed out for her walk with her mind racing. Last night she'd been almost convinced that Percy was behind the accidents, but now she found herself wondering about Ethel.

As someone had pointed out last night, all of the attempts had been clumsy. That was one reason why Percy seemed a possibility. Bessie didn't think he was trying to kill Lora, just get her to move away.

Ethel doesn't have any motive, she told herself. She wasn't in line to inherit anything when her sister died. When Bessie reached Thie yn Traie, she turned back for home. Was it possible that Lora had something that Ethel wanted? Maybe Lora had inherited something when their parents died and now Ethel wanted to own the item herself as Doona had once suggested. It was all just blind speculation, of course.

If the perpetrator wasn't actually trying to kill Lora, just scare her, what motive might Ethel have for that? Bessie pondered that question all the way home. Ethel had said a few mean things about her sister at the party the previous evening. Was it possible that years of resentment had led the woman to try to harm her sister? The idea seemed bizarre.

"Ethel? It's Elizabeth Cubbon. I was wondering if you were available for lunch today," Bessie said a short while later. "I'm quite worried about Lora and I wanted to speak to you about her."

"We could have lunch," Ethel agreed. "Where?"

Bessie named a favourite restaurant on the Douglas promenade. She knew that Ethel lived near Lora, so it would be convenient for her.

"Sure, midday?"

"I'll be there," Bessie replied. She put the phone down and then paced around her kitchen for several minutes. Having promised John that she wouldn't talk to the people involved in the case without telling him, she knew she had to ring the station. What she didn't want to do was try to explain why she felt the need to talk to Ethel, but no doubt he was going to ask.

"Why Ethel?" was his first question after she'd told him about her lunch plans.

"She said something last night about handling all of Lora's medicine bottles after the last gathering, but I don't remember her doing so," Bessie explained. "I can't help but wonder if she isn't simply making trouble for her sister in small ways to get back at her for something."

"Attempted murder is pretty serious," John replied.

"But maybe none of the things that have happened were actually murder attempts," Bessie argued. "Maybe she's just trying to upset Lora, not actually hurt her."

"Blocking up a fire vent is pretty serious."

"But she knew that Lora had a carbon monoxide alarm."

"Switching her tablets could have been serious, too."

"Ethel doesn't seem to think that Lora actually needs any of her tablets, though. What did the doctor say about them? Would Lora have died if she'd taken the wrong ones at the wrong time?"

John sighed. "No, probably not. According to the doctor, she'd have been fine for a few days, anyway. After that, she might have begun feeling a bit off, but not terrible. If she had started to feel poorly, he would have had her bring all her medications with her when she went to see him and he would have helped her sort them at that time."

"My sister and I fought a bit when we were younger. When my parents insisted on dragging me back to the island, away from Matthew, she refused to take my side against them. I was furious with her about it for a very long time. I forgave her long ago, but maybe Ethel is still nursing a grudge from something that happened many years ago."

"And now she's trying to kill Lora."

"No, now she's trying to scare Lora."

"You could be right. We're still looking at Percy. He's had anger management issues in the past."

"Really?"

"I can't say anything more than that, but I'd be more concerned if you were planning on having lunch with him."

"I'll ring you after I get home from lunch," Bessie told him.

"I'd appreciate that."

Bessie was too distracted to read any more of Onnee's letters. Instead, she cleaned an already spotless house for a short while and then rang for a taxi. She could wander around Douglas until it was time to meet Ethel. That was better than scrubbing her kitchen floor for a second time. While she did her best to fill the time, she was still fifteen minutes early to the restaurant.

"Miss Cubbon, how lovely to see you," the man at the door greeted her. "Just yourself for lunch today?"

"I'm meeting a friend," Bessie replied. "I don't know if you know Ethel Hayes?"

"Oh, yes. Mrs. Hayes lives quite nearby. She and her sister, Lora, often have lunch here. Mrs. Hayes meets her daughter here for lunch occasionally, too."

"Well, today she's having lunch with me," Bessie told him.

"I'll show her to your table as soon as she arrives," he assured her after escorting her to a small table in the back corner of the room. "Would you like a plate of garlic bread while you wait?"

"Yes, of course," Bessie grinned.

She'd eaten two pieces by the time Ethel arrived. Ethel settled into her seat across from Bessie.

"Help yourself," Bessie told her, gesturing to the plate of garlic bread.

"This is the best thing about this place," Ethel said as she took a piece. "I could just eat this and nothing else."

"It's excellent," Bessie agreed.

They chatted about nothing much until the waiter took their order. When he was gone, Bessie took a deep breath.

"I only met Lora a short while ago, but I'm rather worried about her," she began. "Do you think someone is truly trying to kill her?"

"Can you imagine any reason why anyone would want her dead?" Ethel replied. "She's just an ordinary woman. I'm sure her children would all love some extra money, but beyond that, I can't think why anyone cares if she lives or dies."

"The neighbours all seem to have reasons for wanting rid of her," Bessie suggested.

Ethel shrugged. "I've never liked Percy. Brian and Jill don't strike me as being clever enough to consider murder as a solution to their problems."

"I did think that whoever is behind the incidents, if there truly is someone behind them, isn't actually trying to kill Lora. It seems more likely that he or she is simply trying to frighten or upset her."

"What sort of motive would anyone have for doing that?"

"Again, the neighbours come to mind. They all seem to have reasons for wanting Lora to move."

"I don't know, maybe," Ethel sounded doubtful. "Lora can be overly dramatic, but if she's right about everything that's happened, perhaps someone is trying to kill her. There seem to have been a lot of attempts in a very short space of time."

"Yes, that's what's worrying, and why the police are involved. Any one or two of the incidents could probably be dismissed as accidents, but so many so close together makes it seem more likely that someone is behind them."

"Did you want to discuss the suspects with me, then?" Ethel asked.

The waiter delivered their drinks, giving Bessie time to consider her reply. "Who do you think is the most likely suspect?" she asked Ethel as the man walked away.

"Percy," Ethel said. "Or maybe Zack. I just can't see him being clever enough to come up with so many different ideas."

Bessie chuckled. "There is that. Our perpetrator has been rather clever. Now that the police are involved, his or her luck may be running out, though. I understand the police are tracing the tablets that were substituted for Lora's in her prescription bottles."

"What if they can't trace them?" Ethel asked.

"They've been taking a lot of fingerprints off the bottles."

Ethel nodded. "No doubt including mine. I've handled all of them in the past, I'm sure."

"Have you? I don't remember you touching them when I was with you and Lora after the last gathering."

Ethel frowned. "It may have been before that, then," she shrugged. "Lora drops the box quite regularly, and then everyone has to help find the bottles."

"So your fingerprints will be on the older bottles, but not the one that Lora had just collected from the chemist the morning before she moved to the Seaview," Bessie said thoughtfully. She was making things up now. She just had to hope that Ethel didn't realise.

"Have the police found fingerprints on that bottle?" Ethel asked.

Was it just Bessie's imagination, or did Ethel look a bit worried? "I'm not supposed to know anything, but I was told that they've found prints on all of the bottles, and not just Lora's prints."

Ethel nodded. "I didn't realise she'd only just collected something new," she sighed.

"I'm sure the police will want to take your fingerprints to compare with the ones they're finding on the bottles. Unless they've done that already?"

"No, no one has asked, not yet, anyway. As I said, my prints should be on most of them."

"But not all of them. Inspector Rockwell is quite pleased that Lora needed a new prescription filled that morning."

"Yes, I'm sure he is," Ethel said softly.

"Can you think of any reason why any of Lora's family members might want to scare or upset her?" Bessie asked.

"You really don't think the incidents were murder attempts?"

"No, I don't."

Ethel sighed and sat back in her seat. "How long do you think Lora will be out at the Seaview?"

"I think she's going to stay out there until the police have worked out what's happening. She feels safer there."

"How long do the police need?"

"That depends on what they find during their investigation. They've been talking to the man who repaired Lora's gas fire and to the man who repaired her car. I don't know if they can fingerprint any of that, but they may well try."

"And you don't think Lora will move back home until the police have worked everything out?"

"I doubt it. I wouldn't, if I were her."

Ethel nodded. "Was it your idea, her moving to the Seaview?"

"Yes, it was. I was hoping it would keep her safe."

Frowning, Ethel shifted in her seat. "Life isn't fair," she said in a low voice.

"Here we are," the waiter said brightly. He set plates of steaming pasta and sauce in front of each of them. "Was there anything else right now?"

"No, thank you," Bessie said, eager to get rid of the man.

He nodded and then walked away.

"What do you mean by that?" Bessie asked Ethel.

Ethel took a bite of her lunch and chewed slowly. After she swallowed, she took a sip of water before she spoke. "Did you have any siblings?"

"I had a sister. She stayed in America when my parents and I moved back to the island."

"Which one of you was the favourite child?"

"I don't know that I can answer that. I always felt as if my father preferred my sister, but my mother and I were close, at least until they dragged me back here against my will."

"How lucky for you. My sister was the favourite. My parents didn't even try to hide it, and Lora took advantage of it at every opportunity."

"I'm sorry. That must have been difficult."

"I was an argumentative child. I know I wasn't easy to love, but my sister could have done more, she could have helped me."

"That was a long time ago, of course," Bessie suggested.

Ethel shrugged. "She was older, that was part of it. I don't think they wanted any more children after Lora, but things weren't as easy in those days. I always felt as if my mother resented me for being here."

Bessie took a sip of her drink. The woman clearly had a lot of issues dating back a long way. Were they enough to drive her to murder after all these years? "It sounds as if you had an unhappy childhood," she remarked.

"Made all the more unhappy by watching my sister, who had a wonderful childhood. She was smarter than I was, so she did well at school. I was the one always being asked why I couldn't be more like Lora. No one appreciated me for who I was."

"I'm sorry."

"I thought it would get better when we got older, but it didn't," Ethel continued. "Lora finished school and married Cecil. They were ridiculously happy, of course. Everyone loved Lora. She got pregnant right away, giving our parents their first grandchild. As if they didn't already love her the most."

"Still doing okay?" the waiter asked.

Bessie nodded and waved him away, not wanting to interrupt Ethel's story. "What happened next?" she asked after a long pause.

"Oh, I met Henry and married him so that I could get out of the house. We were never happy together, but people stayed married in those days, regardless. Then Lora had Doreen, so she'd given Mum and Dad both a grandson and a granddaughter. Any children I had were, well, superfluous, really."

"I'm sure your parents didn't feel that way."

"They appreciated Marie the most, because she was the youngest. They fussed over her in a way they'd never fussed over me. Then Lora went and had Martha, just so that she could have a child younger than mine. Of course our parents loved Baby Martha. Everyone loved Baby Martha," Ethel said bitterly.

Bessie wasn't sure what to say. "You and Lora seem so close," she said eventually.

"Appearances can be deceiving," Ethel told her. "Of course, since Lora's children were older, one of them gave our parents their first great-grandchild, too. She always has to beat me at everything."

"She didn't have any control over when her children would have children," Bessie protested.

"She was even clever enough to be widowed while our parents were still alive. My goodness, you wouldn't believe how much sympathy and attention that earned her. My Henry waited to die until after Mum and Dad were gone. Oh, Lora was very sympathetic for a day or two, but when Cecil died, she took to her bed for a week. Mum and Dad couldn't do enough for her."

"You aren't suggesting that she had anything to do with Cecil's death, are you?"

Ethel looked surprised and then laughed. "Oh, no, nothing like that. Lora was just born under a shining star that's guided her whole life, that's all. Nothing bad ever happens to her. Our parents loved her best, her husband stayed faithful, she got three children and three grandchildren. Everything has always gone her way."

"Until now, when someone is trying to kill her."

Ethel grinned. "It's about time something bad happened to her, don't you think?"

"I can see that you've built up a lot of resentment towards your sister over the years. Does causing little accidents to upset her make you feel better?"

"Nothing can make me feel better," Ethel replied.

"But you are behind the various incidents that have happened, aren't you?" Bessie pressed. "You aren't trying to kill your sister, of course. You just want to cause trouble to get your own back after all these years."

Ethel stared at Bessie for a minute and then began to laugh. "Get my own back?" she repeated. "I don't think you truly understand how much I've come to hate Lora over the years. Make no mistake about it, every single thing that I've done has been a deliberate attempt to kill my sister. I don't want her upset. I want her dead."

"Because she was your parents' favourite?" Bessie was aghast.

"Because I'm tired of her always having everything her way. I have untreatable cancer and only a month or so to live. It isn't fair that I'm going to die and she isn't, not after everything that's happened. She's two years older. I was looking forward to watching her die. I was going to truly enjoy my life once she was gone. It isn't fair."

"You've been behind everything that's happened to her?" Bessie asked.

"I spilled the oil in her bath. That was almost an accident, really. I knew Lora used that really expensive bath oil and I'd always wanted to try it myself. I put a drop on my hands and nearly dropped the bottle in the process. That got me thinking about how easily someone could drown in the bathtub. I loved spilling out half the bottle, too. I've never been able to afford anything that luxurious."

"And the knife in the kitchen?"

"It only took two seconds to arrange that little surprise for her. I had to stand in the kitchen and guard the cupboard after that so that no one else got hurt, but no one else had any reason to go into the cupboard, really."

"The gas fire, the railing, the petrol tank, the kettle, those were all you?"

"The gas fire was fun. I just pretended to be a little bird, building a nest. The railing took more work, but not much more. It was in terrible condition. Pulling the cord out of the kettle was probably the easiest thing I did. That kettle wasn't safe before I touched it."

"And the petrol tank?"

Ethel giggled. "You know what's funny? I didn't do anything to Lora's car. I don't know enough about cars to manage anything as complicated as putting a hole in a petrol tank. I don't even know where the petrol tank is on Lora's car. I suppose I could find it, but damaging it never occurred to me."

Bessie nodded slowly, trying to think. "Does Lora know that you're ill?"

"No one knows. There's no point in telling anyone. The doctors can't do anything, so why bother everyone else with my problems? The doctors reckon I should be relatively fine until one day when I won't be. Once I get to that point, I'll probably die within days."

"I'm sorry," Bessie said.

"Then you'll help me?"

"Help you?"

"I want to die happy. You can help me accomplish that."

"I'm not sure I understand."

"I want Lora to go first. It's only fair. She's older. Tell her that it's safe for her to move home. She'll listen to you. I've worked it all out. All I need to do is block up that vent again. This time, I'll take the batteries out of the carbon monoxide detector first, though. It's the perfect plan."

"It's horrible."

"I've read that it isn't a bad way to die," Ethel said. "She'll fall asleep and not wake up. That seems quite nice, really, as I'm being told that I'll suffer greatly before I go. I already am suffering, of course. My headaches just get worse and worse every day. The doctors have given me some very powerful pain tablets. I may just take them all once Lora is gone."

"I'm going to have to tell the police what you've told me."

"It will be your word against mine. Just tell Lora to move home. Do it today, so I can get rid of her tonight. After that, I'll tell the police everything myself. They won't put me in prison, not when I'm dying anyway."

"I'm not going to help you kill Lora."

Ethel frowned. "But it's only fair. She's always done everything first, and been congratulated and fussed over every time. Now she should die first. Everyone will be sad, of course, but no one will really mind. Her children will be happy to get some money and the neighbours will all be thrilled to see her gone. I don't know why I didn't do this years ago, really."

"Because it's wrong?" Bessie suggested. "You're talking about murder."

"I'm talking about making things more fair. Lora has always had everything her way. This time I'm getting what I want instead of her. It will be the first and last time that ever happens."

"Anyone want pudding?" the waiter asked.

Bessie stared at him for a minute, the words not quite making sense to her.

"We don't," Ethel said firmly. "We're done, thank you."

The waiter nodded and then collected their empty plates. He set the bill on the table and walked away.

"Let me pay," Ethel said, picking up the bill. "I'm enjoying spending my children's inheritance, especially since I know it won't be long before I go."

Bessie frowned. She didn't want to feel indebted to the woman, not after everything she'd just learned. "Let me," she offered.

Ethel shrugged. "It's probably your last chance to buy me lunch," she laughed.

Bessie found her wallet and counted out the money for the bill. She felt as if she were moving in slow motion or were somehow slightly detached from reality. Ethel had just confessed to making multiple attempts to kill her sister, and she'd even asked for Bessie's help to finish the job. It all felt unreal.

"I'm tired," Ethel said as they stood up together. "I'm afraid the doctors were correct. I'm starting to find everyday life much more difficult."

Bessie offered her arm and helped the woman out of the restaurant. They climbed the stairs together, with Ethel stopping several times to catch her breath. When they reached the street, she stopped again.

"Can you just walk me to my car?" she asked. "I'm sorry, but I'm exhausted."

"Of course," Bessie agreed.

They made their way to the nearby parking garage. Bessie helped Ethel behind the wheel of her car.

"Are you sure you're okay to drive?" she asked.

"Oh, yes, I'll be fine," Ethel assured her.

Bessie nodded and then shut the door. She took a few steps away from the car as Ethel started the engine. Turning, Bessie began to walk back through the garage, heading for the lift that would take her back down to the street outside.

The loud roar of an engine behind her made Bessie start. Spinning around, she saw that Ethel was reversing out of her space very quickly. Bessie quickened her pace, as Ethel stopped to change gears. After Bessie pressed the button to call the lift, she glanced backwards and realised that Ethel was heading straight for her.

CHAPTER 15

𝒜s the lift door opened, a hand grabbed Bessie's arm. Bessie found herself being pulled to the side as Ethel drove straight into the lift. The sounds of crumbling metal and shattering glass echoed through the garage.

"Are you okay?" Pete Corkill asked Bessie.

"No, but you'd better see to Ethel," Bessie told him. She took a few steps away, deliberately not looking backwards. Her arm hurt where Pete had pulled on it, but the sick feeling in her stomach was much worse. She stood staring at a row of parked cars as Pete rang several people, using his mobile phone. Within minutes she could hear sirens.

"It's bad, isn't it?" she asked Pete when he crossed to her a short time later.

"It's bad," he confirmed. "I'm not going to say any more than that."

Bessie nodded. She didn't need the details. A moment later the garage was full of uniformed constables, paramedics, firemen, and a dozen other people that Bessie assumed had reason to be there. Orders and instructions were shouted back and forth as Bessie continued to stand in place.

After a while, Pete touched Bessie's shoulder. "I'm going to get you out of here," he said. "Constable Smith is going to take you down to the station and tuck you up in one of the staff rooms. It won't be great, but the staff rooms are more comfortable than the interview rooms, at least."

Bessie nodded. "I don't mind, really," she said. She was feeling numb anyway. Comfort wasn't really an issue. What she really wanted now was to tell someone everything that Ethel had said so that she could go home and try to forget everything that had happened.

"Someone will take your statement soon," Pete told her. "I suspect it's going to be an interesting one."

Bessie shook her head and then followed the young constable out of the garage. They went down the stairs. Just outside the garage, it looked as if a dozen police cars were parked going every which way. The constable led Bessie to one and helped her into the back.

"I can't sit up front with you?" she asked.

"I'm sorry, but we aren't meant to let people ride in the front," he told her.

Bessie nodded and then sat back in her seat. She was aware that cameras were flashing somewhere. No doubt the photo of herself being loaded into the back of a police car would be on the front page of the *Isle of Man Times* in the morning. Dan Ross was probably thrilled by the idea that Bessie had been arrested.

The drive to the police station didn't take long. The constable parked as close to the door as he could and then escorted Bessie inside. They rode a lift up several floors and then walked down a short corridor. The door they stopped in front of said "Staff Only." Bessie hesitated when the constable opened the door and waved her inside.

"Inspector Corkill's orders," he reminded her. "You'll be more comfortable here."

Bessie didn't think she'd be comfortable anywhere, but she didn't argue. The small room had several mismatched chairs and a long, lumpy sofa. Bessie dropped into the first chair and sat back with her eyes closed. The constable took the seat next to her.

"Do you want coffee or tea?" he asked after several minutes.

"No, thank you," Bessie replied.

They sat in silence for what felt like many hours. Bessie was surprised to see that only thirty minutes had passed when the door opened and John Rockwell walked into the room.

He gave Bessie a tight hug. "Are you okay?"

"I don't know," was her honest reply.

"Let's get your formal statement out of the way," he suggested. "Then I'll take you home."

Bessie did her best to repeat everything that had been said over lunch. John didn't comment as he took notes. When she was done, he put his pen down and sighed.

"I suppose I should be grateful that we now know who was behind Lora's incidents," he said.

"Yes, but it's all terribly sad. I assume Ethel didn't survive the crash."

"No, she didn't. She hit the wall head-on. Half of the car ended up in the lift."

Bessie shuddered. "Was there anyone in the lift?"

"Thankfully, no," John told her.

"Even so, this is all going to be very difficult for Lora to hear."

"Yes, and for the whole family."

He drove Bessie home and then rang Doona, who came over to sit with Bessie.

"I'll stay tonight," Doona said when she arrived. "Just in case you have any trouble sleeping."

"I feel as if I'll never sleep again, but I'll be okay," Bessie said. "You know I don't want you fussing over me."

Doona didn't reply. She made Bessie a pot of tea and then sat with her, holding her hand. A few hours later, she made a light dinner for them both. After their meal, they took a walk on the beach together.

"It all feels unreal," Bessie said.

"I'm sorry," Doona told her.

Bessie's sleep was restless, and Doona was there to soothe her when she woke up in the middle of the night from a horrible nightmare. She was tired when her internal alarm woke her the next morning, but she got up anyway.

"I made coffee," Doona said when Bessie walked into the kitchen.

"I didn't think you'd be up yet."

"I set my alarm for half five in case you were up at six."

"Thank you."

"That's what friends are for."

The pair spent the day together, doing not very much. John brought Chinese food for dinner. Hugh was right behind him, carrying a large bakery box.

"I suppose you have news," Bessie said as John spread boxes of food across Bessie's counter.

"I do, but we can discuss it after we've eaten," he replied.

Doona and John worked hard to keep the conversation light over dinner. Hugh chimed in now and again, but Bessie could tell that his mind was elsewhere.

"What's wrong?" she finally asked Hugh.

"Nothing, really. The case was just really sad, that's all. I'm a little worried that if Grace and I have more than one child, I'll have a favourite. I don't want my kids to hate one another."

"I don't have a favourite," John interjected. "Thomas and I are a lot alike, which means we get along well, but that doesn't mean I love him more than I love Amy. Amy is a lot like her mother. Under the circumstances, that can be, well, difficult, but I still love her dearly."

Hugh nodded. "I wonder if Lora truly was the favourite child."

"According to Lora, her parents did tend to spoil her more. She was older, and Ethel was a difficult child, prone to tantrums and angry episodes. Apparently Ethel was nearly as difficult as an adult. Lora didn't feel that she was loved more, but she did think that her parents preferred her company to Ethel's. She was very upset to think that Ethel had been harbouring a grudge for all these years, though," John said.

"It's almost impossible to imagine," Bessie said.

"You'd think, once she'd found out that she was dying, that she might have tried to make amends with Lora," Doona said.

"There's no evidence that she was ever told that she was dying," John replied.

Bessie felt her jaw drop. "But she told me she only had weeks to live."

"And she may have believed that, but she was never officially diagnosed with anything," John said. "The autopsy revealed a large brain tumour. Her doctor speculated that it might have led to any number of mental health issues, including delusions and hallucinations."

"She wasn't sick?" Bessie asked.

"She was very sick. She probably only did have a few weeks to live, but she hadn't seen her doctor in years. The tumour would have been giving her headaches at the very least, probably increasingly terrible ones. It may have been affecting her thinking, movement, memory, just about everything, and left untreated, it would have killed her, probably before Christmas," John told her.

"So she wasn't really responsible for what she was doing," Doona suggested.

"That's what Lora and the rest of the family are choosing to believe, anyway," John replied. "Lora is moving back home tomorrow. She asked me to thank you for trying to help and to apologise on her behalf for her sister's behaviour," he told Bessie.

Bessie nodded. "I don't expect I'll ever hear from her again."

"I doubt you will. I believe Lora wants to put the whole thing behind her."

"I hope the rest of the family rally around and help her get through this. She must be devastated."

A week later, Bessie was reading a book when someone knocked on her door. She was surprised to find Linda Sanders on her doorstep.

"Linda? This is a surprise," she said.

The girl flushed. "Yeah, well, someone had to come and talk to you and I got the short straw."

"The short straw," Bessie echoed.

Linda shook her head. "Sorry, I shouldn't have put it quite that way. The thing is, well, Grandmum wanted someone to come and tell you that she's sorry that she dragged you into her problems. Ethel almost killed you and she feels as if it's her fault."

"I'm absolutely fine," Bessie assured her. "Please tell your grandmother not to give it another thought. I wish things had turned out better for everyone concerned."

"Yeah, we all do. It's weird not having Auntie Ethel around, and it's even weirder thinking that she was trying to kill Grandmum. I'm staying with her now, for a while, anyway. She doesn't like to be alone. Mum's with her at the moment, because I'm here. Anyway, we're doing our best to look after her, but she's still really upset. Her doctor says she's fine, but I feel as if she's given up on life somehow."

"I'm terribly sorry."

The girl shrugged. "I'm hoping to take her on holiday across in the new year. Maybe a change of scenery will be good for her. She's only ever been off the island a few times. I thought a week in York might cheer her up."

"York is a wonderful city."

"Yeah, so I hear. I've never been, but Mum is coming along, too. She's been lots of times and she says it's great."

"What about Zack?"

Linda blushed. "We aren't together anymore. When everything happened, I wanted to move in with Grandmum to help out, but that would have meant leaving Zack with my parents. No one was happy with that idea, so we decided it would be easier if we just went our separate ways."

"I'm glad you chose to help your grandmother over Zack," Bessie said.

Linda nodded. "Once we're back from our holiday in York, I'm going to try going back to school. I want to give nursing a go. I think I'd like to work with the elderly. Maybe if I'd had some training, I'd have noticed that Auntie Ethel wasn't acting normally. Maybe I could have saved everyone a lot of upset. I'd like to think I may be able to help other families in the future."

"Good luck with that," Bessie told her.

"Mum and Dad are going to help all they can. It may take me a long time to get through the course, because I'll only be able to afford a few classes each year, but I'm determined now."

"The college has a few scholarship programmes," Bessie told her. "Ask them about the Cubbon Fund. It may be able to help."

"The Cubbon Fund? I'll ask."

After the girl left, Bessie rang her advocate. "Duncan? I need to set up a scholarship for a young nursing student," she said.

GLOSSARY OF TERMS

Manx to English

- **moghrey mie** - good morning

House Names – Manx to English

- **Thie yn Traie** - Beach House
- **Treoghe Bwaane** - Widow's Cottage

English to American Terms

- **advocate** - Manx title for a lawyer (solicitor)
- **aye** - yes
- **bin** - garbage can
- **biscuits** - cookies
- **bonnet (car)** - hood
- **boot (car)** - trunk
- **car park** - parking lot
- **chemist** - pharmacist
- **chips** - french fries

- **cuddly toys** - stuffed animals
- **cuppa** - cup of tea (informally)
- **dear** - expensive
- **estate agent** - real estate agent (realtor)
- **fairy cakes** - cupcakes
- **fancy dress** - costume
- **fizzy drink** - soda (pop)
- **holiday** - vacation
- **jumper** - sweater
- **lie in** - sleep late
- **midday** - noon
- **pavement** - sidewalk
- **plait (hair)** - braid
- **primary school** - elementary school
- **pudding** - dessert
- **skeet** - gossip
- **skint** - broke (out of money)
- **skirting boards** - baseboards
- **starters** - appetizers
- **supply teacher** - substitute teacher
- **telly** - television
- **torch** - flashlight
- **trolley** - shopping cart
- **windscreen** - windshield

OTHER NOTES

The emergency number in the UK and the Isle of Man is 999, not 911.

CID is the Criminal Investigation Department of the Isle of Man Constabulary (Police Force).

When talking about time, the English say, for example, "half seven" to mean "seven-thirty."

With regard to Bessie's age: UK (and IOM) residents get a free bus pass at the age of 60. Bessie is somewhere between that age and the age at which she will get a birthday card from the Queen. British citizens used to receive telegrams from the ruling monarch on the occasion of their one-hundredth birthday. Cards replaced the telegrams in 1982, but the special greeting is still widely referred to as a telegram.

When island residents talk about someone being from "across," they mean that the person is from somewhere in the United Kingdom (across the water).

Bonfire Night is the 5th of November. It commemorates the attempt by Guy Fawkes to blow up the houses of Parliament in 1605. Bonfires and fireworks mark the occasion.

ACKNOWLEDGMENTS

Thanks to my editor, Denise, for her continued hard work.

Thanks to Kevin, who takes the wonderful photos on the covers of my books.

Thanks to my beta readers, who help polish every text.

And thank you to my readers, who are the reason why I keep doing this!

AUNT BESSIE UNDERSTANDS

RELEASE DATE: MAY 17, 2019

Aunt Bessie understands why Hugh is so worried about his wife, Grace.

She's about to have their first child, and Hugh doesn't want her left alone in case she goes into labour. Bessie is happy to agree to spend an afternoon with the woman.

Aunt Bessie understands when Hugh, exhausted from a long day that culminated in the arrival of his child, forgets to drop Bessie off at her cottage before driving back to his own home.

Knowing that he's not in any condition to drive anywhere, she insists that they walk to her cottage, Treoghe Bwaane.

Aunt Bessie understands that the holiday cottages they walk past are all unoccupied during the winter months.

With Christmas just a few weeks away, there shouldn't be lights on inside any of them. When she and Hugh stumble across a dead body in one of them, Bessie understands that she's right in the middle of yet another murder investigation.

ALSO BY DIANA XARISSA

Aunt Bessie Assumes

Aunt Bessie Believes

Aunt Bessie Considers

Aunt Bessie Decides

Aunt Bessie Enjoys

Aunt Bessie Finds

Aunt Bessie Goes

Aunt Bessie's Holiday

Aunt Bessie Invites

Aunt Bessie Joins

Aunt Bessie Knows

Aunt Bessie Likes

Aunt Bessie Meets

Aunt Bessie Needs

Aunt Bessie Observes

Aunt Bessie Provides

Aunt Bessie Questions

Aunt Bessie Remembers

Aunt Bessie Solves

Aunt Bessie Tries

Aunt Bessie Understands

Aunt Bessie Volunteers

Aunt Bessie Wonders

The Isle of Man Ghostly Cozy Mysteries

Arrivals and Arrests

The Quinton Case

The Rhodes Case

The Isle of Man Romance Series

Island Escape

Island Inheritance

Island Heritage

Island Christmas

ABOUT THE AUTHOR

Diana grew up in Northwestern Pennsylvania and moved to Washington, DC, after college. There she met a wonderful Englishman who was visiting the city. After a whirlwind romance, they got married and Diana moved to the Chesterfield area of Derbyshire to begin a new life with her husband. A short time later, they relocated to the Isle of Man.

After more than ten years on the island, it was time for a change. With their two children in tow, Diana and her husband moved to suburbs of Buffalo, New York. Diana now spends her days writing about the island she loves.

She also writes mystery/thrillers set in the not-too-distant future as Diana X. Dunn and middle grade and Young Adult books as D.X. Dunn.

Diana is always happy to hear from readers. You can write to her at:

Diana Xarissa Dunn
PO Box 72
Clarence, NY 14031.
Find Diana at: DianaXarissa.com
E-mail: Diana@dianaxarissa.com

Made in United States
North Haven, CT
06 November 2023

43689066R00130